RULE NUMBER TWO

RULE BREAKERS SERIES
BOOK 2

NICKY SHANKS

LIMITLESS PUBLISHING, LLC

Rule Number Two

First Print Edition: April 2018

Limitless Publishing, LLC

Kailua, HI 96734

www.limitlesspublishing.com

Formatting: Limitless Publishing

ISBN-13: 978-1-64034-344-3

ISBN-10: 1-64034-344-X

DEDICATION

This is dedicated to everyone who says you shouldn't or you can't do something. For the dreamers who don't listen to the negativity and find their own way to shine. Your light burns bright for those who seek you.

ONE
JULIE

IT'S A DREAM. A very, very *bad* dream.

But the echoes of our angry voices haunt me so badly that I can't sleep.

Do you want me to ask if it's mine?

It hurt my insides a little when Oliver jabbed that into my head. The only thing that would've made it worse is if he'd demanded to know whether it was possible the baby isn't his after all. At least he trusts me enough to know that I'm nothing like Heather—his cheating, manipulative ex.

For someone who has spent nearly three months chasing me, he doesn't exactly know the right things to say. I smile into the darkness around me, because I know that's one of the things I love about Oliver.

Oliver Jackson.

Broad shoulders and shaggy, dark chocolate hair.

Full lips that spread into wicked grins.

Deep, electrifying emerald eyes.

1

I lick my lips and wish that he were next to me.

Now that he knows the truth, will he come back to me? I recap the entire night like a movie on a loop in my mind. Sleep has betrayed me, so the silence claims me instead. It's driving me crazy, but I keep looking for something—*anything*—that will make me feel better about the entire thing.

I don't know what to say to you right now.

Then don't say anything.

My stomach twists when I hear his angry voice in my head. I can still see the heat flushing his cheeks and neck, warning me. Oliver hasn't spoken to me like that before—at least nothing with that much *distaste* behind it.

I think about how I ran from him when he parked the Jeep outside last night. I always seem to be running from him; the damage that's been caused is almost unbearable to think about. I ripped down the walls he built and burned him the first chance I got. I know this isn't only one-sided, but Oliver is right...what exactly *did* I want him to say?

I'm only a few days late—it could be nothing.

It could be everything.

My phone buzzes on the table beside me.

NORA

Hey, you up?

I stare into the darkness and try to decide if I want to answer her. Nora has had a pretty rough few days herself, and though I wouldn't admit it to Oliver, I still somewhat blame myself for her being in the hospital right now.

I'm not exactly in the mood to admit to *anyone* that I should've made a different choice the moment I learned Brandon was asking about me years ago in high school. If I'd been a different person—or in a different place in life—I would've walked away at the first sign of trouble. But I *wasn't* that person. I was the girl who saw light in everyone; I believed everyone could have a solid chance at happiness, even if they needed a little help.

Brandon needed my help.

My chest heaves rapidly, because there's dirty truth embedded in my brain.

Oliver needed my help too. He was lost and confused just like Brandon—we needed each other to feel normal.

That doesn't mean what I have with Oliver isn't different from what I had with Brandon. I've forgiven Brandon to the point that I can find peace with Oliver; I'm trying my hardest to focus on that instead of letting my thoughts snowball into worries and regrets.

Nora doesn't waste time before calling; I let it ring a few times before obligation washes over me.

"Hi." I put the phone up to my ear. The bright light from the screen makes me close my eyes. "I was about to text you back."

Nora scoffs. "Uh, no, you weren't."

"Okay, I wasn't." I blow out air. "Oliver and I had a fight."

I hear her gasp, no matter how hard she tries to hide it. I imagine what her facial expression looks like right now; her beige skin looked pale when I saw her last, and without her signature gold hoops, she looked like a whole new person.

I know Nora and Oliver aren't big fans of each other, but she knows how happy he makes me. I recall the look on his face when I quickly kissed his lips and left him standing outside, alone. He was horrified; all he wanted was one reassuring kiss to make him feel like we were okay.

I gave him a goodbye kiss masked by a goodnight kiss.

I didn't mean to. I know this is all my fault, and I don't know how to fix it. I want to hang up on Nora and call him, but I stay strong and listen to her talk my ear off about him.

"—I mean, right? Oliver loves you, Julie. I don't think I've ever seen anyone look at someone like he looks at you."

I sigh. "I told him that I'm late."

She sucks in air through her teeth. "Holy shit, are you okay?"

I want to cry but I choke it down. "I'm fine. I'm only a few days late."

"Yeah, but Julie…it only takes one time—"

"I know that," I snap at her. "I took sex ed too."

She snorts. "Well, it could be nothing. I bet it's nothing—women are late all the time for various reasons, right? Maybe you're too stressed…I bet that's it. You're too stressed."

The silence between us is awkward, and I'm glad we aren't in the same room having this conversation. Something has happened to me in the last few months; I'm a stronger person. I can literally feel it. If this were last year and it was Brandon instead…I would be a tangled mess of insecurities right now.

Not anymore.

Oliver taught me how to be strong again.

...*No.* He taught me that it's *okay* to be strong again.

"Julie?" Nora's voice breaks through my thoughts. "Are you sure you're okay?"

I really don't know how to answer her.

"Just call him, okay? I promise that he'll come running."

I mumble something about being tired and I hang up the phone. If she thinks I haven't punched his number seventeen times into the phone and erased it every single time, she's wrong. I wonder what he's doing...or if he'll even answer my phone call.

How did I get myself into this mess? We used protection and I'm on the pill.

"The bathtub," I whisper, and my eyes widen. "We didn't use anything."

I pick up my phone and dial Oliver's number—this time, I push the call button and wait for him to answer. It rings five times and goes to voicemail.

"Hey, it's Oliver." His deep voice greets me. My hands shake so badly it's hard to hold the phone to my ear. "Leave me a message and I'll talk to you soon."

I don't bother leaving a message. What am I going to say to him? He obviously doesn't want to talk to me, or he would've answered. I think about so much that's jammed inside my brain that I don't realize I've been lying here, fretting, for hours.

The sunlight starts to burn my eyes, making me close them. I don't want to open them again because I know that when I do, Oliver won't be here. He won't be

5

pressed behind me. His warm, hard chest won't be sending flicks of excitement down my spine. My need for him grows so much inside my chest that I can't take it anymore; I *have* to open my eyes.

I stare at the periwinkle walls of the pool house. The white, vaulted ceiling houses a skylight that hovers over me. I lose myself in the king-size bed, like it knows I'm alone and Oliver should be right here next to me.

Rain mists on the glass of the skylight as the sun recedes quickly, almost as if my bad mood chased it away. I can hear loud voices coming from the main house, but I try to drown them out as the rain pings harder on the windows. For a moment—a single, solitary moment—I'm able to let the quiet wash over me, and slivers of pain trickle away from my heart.

"You're going, and that's final!" Randy's voice booms. "You belong at Belmont, so get upstairs and pack!"

"I want to go to a normal school with normal kids my own age, Dad! You always treat me like someone I'm not!" Clyde cuts in.

"I know how much potential you have, all right? Just trust me on this, Clyde. You're going to Belmont tomorrow!"

"Where's Julie? She'll take my side on this!"

"It doesn't matter whose side she takes; her vote doesn't count!"

The rain isn't drowning them out anymore, so I slide out of bed and slip my feet into the light pink slippers waiting for me on the floor. I feel completely exhausted right down to my bones. I check my phone to make sure Oliver hasn't called, but there's nothing…from anyone.

I slowly make my way to the main house to see what they're yelling about. Even though Randy is right —my vote *doesn't* really count—it still makes Clyde feel better knowing that *someone* is on his side. When I enter the room, Clyde and Randy are staring at each other and waiting for round two. They hardly notice me as I grab a bowl from the cabinet.

"Clyde. Cereal." I snap my fingers and he looks at me, surprised. He scoots the box of Lucky Charms toward me, and now they're both staring at me. I'm so hungry that I don't even care. I start shoveling the cereal into my mouth like I can't get full fast enough.

"Julie," Randy says. He sits down across from me. "What's wrong?"

I shake my head. "I'm hungry." Clyde snickers until his father shoots him a look to be quiet. "My god, let the kid go to a normal school," I say. "What are you so afraid of? We went to public schools and look at us now."

Randy snorts. "That's what I'm afraid of." He throws me a look. "Why are you so hungry? Have you not been eating?"

Clyde groans. "God, Dad. Can we focus on *me* again?"

Randy narrows his eyes at him. We both know that Clyde gets whatever he wants…we were having this very conversation last year when he actually *begged* to go to Belmont. What Randy doesn't know is why he suddenly wants to stay in Rockford. Over the summer, a new family moved in across the street; it just so happens they have a girl his age and he's crushing on her.

Randy grits his teeth. "Fine. But straight A's. I'm talking *genius level*, Clyde."

The redheaded wild child jumps for joy and gives me a hug from the side. I don't bother hugging him back because I just want to eat. I pour more cereal into the bowl as Randy makes a disgusted face. "Okay, go up to your room and pull up the website. I'll be up to enroll you in a minute."

Clyde is a genius, but it doesn't take one to figure out that Randy wants to talk to me alone. My nephew gives me a sympathetic look before bolting from the room. Randy puts his hands on the breakfast bar and stares me down.

"What?" I snap around a mouthful of cereal.

"Look, I'm glad you're back home." His voice is dull. "You know you always have a home here, Julie."

"I know." I shove more into my mouth. "Oliver and I might've broke up anyway."

Randy doesn't look surprised. "I'm sorry to hear that."

Cereal falls from my mouth as I snort. It hits the rim of the bowl and bounces with a soft splash into the milk. "No, you're not. You hate him."

"I don't hate him."

I wave my fingers in the air toward him. "It doesn't matter—he's gone."

"Do you want to talk about it?" His eyebrows furrow. His forceful emotions are a little too chilling for me to feel comfortable talking about Oliver Jackson and his inability to act like a mature adult.

"Hardly." I snort again and finish the cereal before putting the bowl into the sink.

"You're acting very...*abrasive* this morning."

"I'm just tired, okay?" I snap. "Look, just let Clyde go to public school for a year. One year isn't going to hurt college applications. It might actually look good—make him look like he's trying new things."

Randy watches me scoot around him and head for the door. I'm ready to fall into my bed and try to get some sleep. "Clyde isn't afraid of trying new things... what about you, Julie?"

I turn to face him; the darkness of Randy's eyes irritates me. "For the last time, Oliver is gone. I tried to be with him—twice, actually. I screwed it up the first time, but this time it's...just different." I bite my bottom lip to fight the tears welling in my eyes.

"What exactly did he do?"

I don't have the energy to answer him. I don't want Randy knowing that I'm late, so I wave him off and head for the pool house. The truth is Oliver acted like a complete ass when I told him I was late. His frustration got the best of him again, and he said some things he can't take back. I know he spoke out of his frustration, but it's getting really old being at the end of those tantrums.

But I miss him.

And I love him.

Did we actually break up?

Oliver and I are always hurting each other.

I find my phone on the bedside table and stare at the screen.

Do I call him?

Maybe I should let him call me.

I wonder what he's doing.

Is he awake?

Is he thinking about me too?

A wave of fear creeps over me as I think about different horrible scenarios where he could be doing something with another girl right now. Picking up some random woman and taking her back to his place, in his bed.

Our bed.

Would he do that to me?

I find his number, and my fingers shake as I hit the call button. The voicemail box is full and the call ends, making me frown. I throw the phone down, annoyed. I crawl back onto the bed and groan—then a cold wave washes over me.

Oliver isn't speaking to me.

"*Good morning, sunshine.*" I hear his smooth voice and close my eyes.

I have to admit...I didn't think it would end this way. I didn't think Oliver would freak out about the fact that I'm late. I honestly thought he would be amazed and excited, not leave me alone to deal with this. I look at Colin's journals sitting on the bedside table and I smile—at least I have some small part of him with me.

I can't stand it; I have to pick up reading where I left off. There's too much about Oliver's life that I don't know about, and Colin helps me understand why his son is the way he is. I reach over and snag the book that I'm on, pulling it underneath the comforter as I snuggle in and prepare myself for what's to come.

I bookmarked my page with a napkin from the Lake

Reed Inn, and it makes me instantly close the book and squeeze my eyes shut. The last time I read this was with Oliver in his bed. I can almost smell the spice of his skin in the pages of the journal.

"Don't be a coward," I whisper and open the book again. "You can do this."

May 8th, 1992

Oliver was nearly born last night, but then he decided it wasn't his time yet. Veronica has been ordered to stay in bed until it's really time. My father pulled me aside and started talking about a custody battle and how Veronica doesn't stand a chance.

I just want to have them both, and he doesn't understand.

It's hard to find someone who knows you to your inner core—someone who takes you for who you are and sets your mind on fire. I'll never be able to stop loving Veronica, or get her out of my mind, as long as I'm alive.

Oliver will always be a constant reminder of what we had.

It's not his fault that his parents are who they are. It's not fair to him, either. If Veronica wants to go after Oliver is born...I'll have to let her go.

I wish for everything to go back to the way it was.

I wish Oliver was here so we can read the journals together—he likes doing that.

I wish for *a lot* of things right now.

TWO
JULIE

"JULIE." *Oliver's voice wafts through my head.* "Come on, baby, can you hear me?"

I open my eyes and he towers over me. His face is twisted with heavy sadness. The room around us isn't my bedroom—it's an enormous space with pale yellow walls. A huge bay window with a flower-printed window seat is behind Oliver as he walks over to join me on the bed. I swear that I feel his weight—like this isn't a dream and he's actually right here with me. The mattress sinks down at my hip, tricking my mind.

"Oliver." *I breathe his name with too much surprise.* "What are you doing here? I thought you might be ignoring me."

His warm syrupy laugh stuns me. "I could never ignore you, sunshine. I love you way too much to stay away from you too long."

I sit up and gaze into those deep emerald eyes of his. He brushes my hair behind my ear and smiles down at me. "I called you and you didn't answer; I want to talk about this." I *touch my stomach and Oliver's wicked smile paints his lips. "I want to talk about what we're going to do if it turns out we aren't only a twosome anymore."*

He shakes his head, his chocolate hair brushing the top of his ear. "What is there to talk about? Nothing has been normal for you and me this far..." I notice wetness form in the corners of his eyes. "But what's normal for us, really? Have you even taken a test to make sure?"

I want to scratch his eyes out.

Then...I think.

"No, I haven't." I smile. "I just assumed...and then, damn! I should have taken a test before telling you! I should've kept my big mouth shut."

He smiles and his cool laugh sends shivers down my spine. "It doesn't matter, baby. Either way, I'm yours. I belong to you, Julie. No matter what direction life takes us in."

He leans into me and I feel his warm lips sliding in between mine. The heat from his tongue inside my mouth ignites the fire inside my chest. With each second he touches me, the world around me goes up in flames. Oliver slides his warm, rough hand up my thigh and underneath my t-shirt; my body temperature rises instantly as his fingertips touch my bare skin.

I let myself relax as he tickles the small of my back, pushing me against him. He swiftly pulls me up into his lap, our lips only inches from each other. "You are absolutely everything to me." He breathes against my lips as he laces our fingers together and squeezes. "You have completely unraveled me and convinced me to break the first rule I made to protect myself."

I try and remember his rules.

Rule Number One: Don't let your guard down.

Rule Number Two: Don't take anything for granted.

Rule Number Three: Keep your secrets safe.

Rule Number Four: Don't destroy your own happiness.

To be honest, his rules don't even make sense. How can someone be so on guard about themselves, yet be able to make themselves truly *happy?*

I'll just have to re-write his rules for him—something more my style.

Rule Number One: Don't let love pass you by.

Rule Number Two: Be open to love, no matter the consequences.

Rule Number Three: Never lose sight of who you truly are.

Rule Number Four: If all else fails...hold on and never give up.

Something like that. Rules are meant to be broken—the past six months have taught me that—and if I want to live in a magical fantasy world...then that's my prerogative. Not that Oliver follows his own rules anymore, anyway.

I made him break his first rule. He fell in love with me.

"You've made me into a man I never dreamed I could be. How can I love you so much when you don't trust me?" His sadness drips into my mind. I search my thoughts quickly for something to make him feel better; when he hurts, I hurt.

"I trust you." The air in my lungs is spent. "I trust you, Oliver."

He shakes his floppy hair. "No, you don't. If you did, you wouldn't be worried that I would hate you for helping me create a fucking miracle, Julie." His arm slides around me and he rests his warm hand on my stomach. "That's what this is, a fucking miracle."

I laugh. "Such a charmer."

He isn't amused. I watch the shadows flitter around his eyes. "Hey, I don't want you to worry, okay? I love you, Julie. There isn't anything I won't do for you—I think I've proven that a few times over." Fear dances in waves in his electric green gaze; how can I be truthful when I'd give anything not to hurt him again?

"I know you love me." My voice is small. I try to comfort him by nuzzling into his chest, and he kisses the top of my head. He nestles his nose in my mess of blonde hair; the hard-on in his pants is poking my thighs. I think about staying silent for a few minutes until he realizes I'm aware of the hardness rubbing against my skin; when his eyes meet mine, he catches me thinking about it and I blush.

There's no harm in indulging in a fantasy, right?

Oliver cradles my ass with his rough hands. His full lips graze mine and send shockwaves through my entire body; I want him so freaking badly. He kisses the soft parts of my neck, and with each light stroke I become more and more his. He is so strong that it's overwhelming—but I want him to take me. I need to feel the anxiety in his touch.

The softness of the mattress feels so erotic as he sets me down on the bed in a sitting position. There isn't much for subtleties anymore; I find myself reaching for his jeans and quickly unzipping them, careful not to get his hardness caught in the crossfire. His leg muscles tense when my fingers grip the inside of his boxer briefs. Slowly, I push both the briefs and the jeans down his muscular thighs, and he moans so deep that it vibrates my body. His lips attach to mine before he gently pushes my back to the bed before he climbs on top of me, his weight comforting as it presses me into the mattress. He roughly kicks the jeans off from around his ankles and smiles down at me with fire in his eyes.

He tugs my pajama shorts and panties to the side, and his thick erection pushes into my flesh as both of our bodies sizzle with pleasure. I don't remember hearing him open any wrappers, but what's the use in worrying about that now? His breathing hitches as he pushes gently against me, suctioning his lips to my collarbone. His hands find the sides of my throat and rest there, careful not to squeeze unexpectedly.

"I fucking miss you," he breathes.

I let the warm air brush over my exposed ass as he keeps moving in and out slowly. Our lips meet and he crushes my body against his, pushing harder this time. I can't control any part of my body as he thrusts into me, moaning into my hair.

Sex with Oliver blows my freaking mind. He's so attentive to the little things: sensory things like touch and taste motivate him. The feel of my skin seems to turn him on in the most intense way. It's exciting to know that with one smile I can turn him on; it's hard to not love someone when all they think about is you.

"I love you," he whispers as our bodies tense and the walls melt around us. Explosions fill my head for a few seconds before I can catch my breath. He clutches onto my body as if he needs me to make him feel safe. "You drive me so damn crazy." He laughs and pushes sweaty, matted hair from his forehead.

I open my mouth to speak, but he picks me up and wraps his arms around me. I feel his hard stomach inches away from my touch. I hear his breathing even out and his broad smile widens as he looks at me. "Are you willing to follow the rules now?" he says, and I feel his thumb against the inside of my *thighs. He is dangerously close to slipping it inside of me, and I can't think straight. "Julie. Answer me."*

"I-I don't know," I stutter, and his silky laugh returns. "Maybe we can make a new set of rules, ones that don't contradict themselves and set us up for failure."

Did I really just say that?

Oliver lowers his head down to mine, and his lips press against the corner of my mouth. My body is in a frenzy—it's like I'm being pleasurably electrocuted. I can feel him getting hard again and it drives me crazy; I know he's not finished with me yet. It's hard reading him sometimes, but I know he hasn't had his fill. I get ready for him to enter his space again and prepare myself for the intensity that is coming now that he's gotten his sweetness out of the way.

I can't move.

I can't think.

I can't speak.

I can't even freaking blink.

"Four simple rules, huh? I think we can manage that." His voice gets rough as he positions himself to push inside of me again. My body bucks against his for more—I want more. He lays me on my side and wraps my legs around his from behind. The room vanishes and he pounds into my flesh with such force that it takes me to another place. I hear him whisper my name but he's far away—I'm in a land where nothing can ever go wrong.

"Fuck," he grunts, and a trillion colorful pieces of glass break in my mind, hovering over us like glittering shards of satisfaction. I force my eyes open and his gaze is locked onto mine, searching. "Are you okay?" He tries to catch his breath. "I'm sorry, that was too rough—"

I heave in deep breaths. "No. That was perfect."

Oliver snorts. "There you go again, using words I don't understand."

"You understand them." I turn to face him and press my legs together, because they're shaking uncontrollably. "I think you're just scared of the truth."

A loud beeping noise hurts my ears. Oliver glances around the room for the noise; he looks back at me and smiles. "Time to wake up." He smirks and reaches for my phone on the bedside table.

———

"OLIVER." I say his name into the air above me.

I'm in the freaking pool house.

I groan and sit up. *"Did you have a nice sex dream?"* I hear Oliver's voice from the first night we met. It startles me, but I know he's not here.

I was dreaming.

Of course I was. Oliver isn't here anymore.

However I choose to look at it, my face flushes even though I'm alone. Instantly, I get angry with myself; how can I be like this? I need to do something other than lie in bed all day sulking, waiting for him to call me back. Nora is in the hospital resting and I don't want to bother her with any drama unless absolutely necessary; she's had enough of her own to last a lifetime.

I pick up my phone and sift through the contacts. I have no one else to call—no one else that can help me escape from this. I see Staci's number come across the screen and instantly hit the call button. She answers on the second ring.

"Julie?" Her voice is bursting with surprise. "I'm so glad you called me! I haven't talked to you since Lake Reed. How are you? How's Oliver?"

I clear my throat. I don't know what to say, but I decide not to tell her about the fight or about the fact that I'm late. For once, I just want one conversation to not revolve around the things that are up in the air in my life.

"We're all fine," I lie. "I just thought I'd keep in touch."

"Did you want to get together?" she asks.

I nod like she can see me. "Are you free?"

"Yes!" she squeals. "I'm about to finish up here at work; a few of my clients canceled, but as soon as I get this perm set, I can meet in about an hour for a late lunch. At Berk's Café, okay? See you soon!"

She hangs up before I can talk myself out of this. I know I need the distraction, but Staci is a bit too much, too soon. Not to mention she tried sleeping with Oliver not long ago. To be fair, she stopped pursuing him after his feelings for me weren't a secret anymore.

I force myself to get up and shower. The hot water doesn't help wash away any of my bad thoughts or worries, but that's okay. I need them. I want them as a reminder that life is messy and unpredictable. I touch my stomach and groan. As if I really need a reminder of life's unpredictability, considering the one I might already have.

After a long fifteen minutes in the shower, I make myself get out because I know I can't hide in here forever. There's a real world out there waiting for me to take and make my own.

Unfortunately, my positive attitude fades as I stand in the doorway of my closet. With a towel wrapped around my body, I look into the full-length mirror behind the door to my left and frown.

I don't recognize myself.

Physically *or* mentally.

Even the jeans and pink blouse I pull on don't help me feel any different. I brush my thick, blonde hair and braid it down the side of my neck…and I think about Oliver. I've always known he likes when I wear my hair like this; he tugs on it too much for it to be a secret.

I sigh and take a look in the bathroom mirror as I rest my hands on the cold marble countertop.

I'm pale.

I brush my teeth and put some makeup on, then take another peek at my reflection.

I am really, really *pale.*

My stomach growls and I cross my arms over my torso.

And I'm seriously hungry.

I search for a pair of sneakers and finally find a matching pair, pushing my feet into them before leaving the pool house behind. I need to borrow a car, but I don't want Randy knowing where I'm headed. The spare keys to his BMW are hanging on the key rack in the kitchen, so I grab them before anyone catches me leaving. I can hear Clyde in his room talking on the phone, but I don't know where Randy is, so I try to sneak out the best I can after scribbling him a note so he won't worry about me—or his missing car.

The garage is cold from the nip of the late September air coming through the cracks of the door. I stare at the car for a few minutes, remembering what happened the last time I borrowed it. I ran it into a tree—on accident. This time, though, my mind is much clearer. I slide inside and buckle in, making sure I'm careful over my stomach.

There is so much I want to say to Oliver, and I don't even know how to say it.

One thing is for sure: I'm not going to be this mousey, soft-spoken girl anymore. I'm going to fight for what I want, and if that means giving Oliver an ultimatum…then so be it. The sour feeling in my stomach returns when I think this, because I don't want to be that kind of woman. I don't want to force him to do something he doesn't want to do.

But he can't have me unless he embraces what could be, either.

What if I am pregnant and Oliver never speaks to me again?

Can I do this on my own?

I pull out of the driveway and head to the Rockford Women's Clinic on my way to Berk's Café to meet Staci. I have to know—once and for all—if I'm late because of all the stress I've been under lately…

Or if I'm carrying Oliver Jackson's baby.

THREE
OLIVER

THESE DAMN RULES are supposed to be saving my life, yet I can't keep myself from getting in my own fucking way.

Lucy follows me up to my apartment and touches my shoulders; I don't fucking like it, and I pull away from her immediately. The only woman who should be touching me like that is Julie, not some random what's-her-name that has no business being here. But *I'm* the one who decided to go to The Tavern after me and Julie's fight, and *I'm* the one who decided to bring Lucy home with me even after Harley warned me not to go down this path.

What the hell is wrong with me?

Julie is going to *kill* me—how can I come back from this? I'd like to say that I hate myself for picking up random women in random places, but I never really thought twice about it before now. Whatever made me feel good in that moment, that's what I did. That's how

I got *in* this damn mess, after all—when I picked up *Julie* for the first time on our way to the cabin.

Lucy's silky, emerald-green dress brushes my skin, and it doesn't leave an exotic burn like Julie's touch always does. A hole forms in my mind that all of Julie's memories get crammed into. My body is in two halves, and they're fighting over what I'm going to do with Lucy.

Jesus, Oliver, you're in trouble.

I break free from her and rummage around the kitchen for more booze. I'm going to need to be plastered to do this; not that it's a valid excuse. When I find some tequila, I open the bottle and start drinking straight from it.

I really need to think about this…maybe Julie *isn't* running from me again and everything will actually be okay for once.

"Whoa, there." Lucy snickers. "Slow down a little. Life isn't that horrible to drown your sorrows like that."

Screw you, Lucy. You don't know what my life's like.

I was just like you once, Lucy: careless and slutty.

Then Julie crash landed into my lap.

Now, my insides are twisting and turning because I miss her so fucking much, but I'm here with Lucy… someone nowhere near what Julie is.

Before I realize it, I've damn near guzzled half of the bottle of tequila. The room spins so much that I collapse onto a kitchen bar stool and look at her. I don't bother looking into her eyes—I don't even care to remember what color they are. But I *notice* her.

Long, wild red hair.

Slender, pointy nose.

Thin, blood-red lips.

Easy. Ready. Willing.

"I'm in love with her," I mumble and take another swig from the bottle. I don't even feel the sting of the alcohol anymore. "I fucking love her, do you know that? And yet here I am—with you. What the hell is wrong with me, Lucy?"

Her gaze locks onto mine. "As far as I can see...nothing."

I scoff. "She's literally perfect in every single way. Every single fucking *way*, Lucy."

It doesn't even cross my mind that I'm being an asshole to her. Actually, it *does* cross my mind, but I really don't fucking care. I shake my head, trying to get the fuzz out.

"I mean...what the hell is *actually* wrong with me? I have Julie—*had* Julie—and now she's gone because I can't quit fucking things up."

At this point, I hardly remember Lucy is even in the room. I chug another mouthful of the nasty liquid and sniffle. The room grows intensely hot so I pull off my jacket, followed by my shirt, baring my chest. Nothing is clear inside my head anymore. Thoughts of Julie swirl in the space around me, but I swat the memories of her away. I want her to mean nothing to me. I can't afford to think about her this much when it's hurting me so damn bad.

And then there's Lucy.

She's waiting for me to get over my shit and sleep with her.

I take off my boots and socks and throw them to the side. I walk toward her and her face morphs into Julie's.

I can't shake her; the sunshine she fills my head with pierces my body as I look at her. My fingers reach out to touch her honey hair without hesitation.

"Julie." I nearly choke. I grip the hair at the back of her head and force her head to tilt up so our lips can meet, but something stops me. Lucy's face comes back into view. Her eyes are wild with fire as I hold her tightly, and her body trembles as I keep her in the unknown. "I'm in love with Julie," I say before releasing her.

"Then why are you here with me?"

I know I'm in trouble.

Serious fucking trouble.

Lucy's lips reach mine and she kisses me in a flash. It feels so…*wrong*. Her tall body presses against me and I don't even hold onto her. I regret how much tequila I forced into my body—now I'm barely able to stand up with a girl I shouldn't even have brought home.

Julie is going to fucking *hate* me.

"You have to go." I push her away. "Go home."

She pouts. "I thought you wanted to have a good time?"

I feel like picking her up and throwing her out, but my phone rings, distracting me. I can hear the faint ringing somewhere inside my jacket, and as I search for it, my eyes well with tears. Julie would know exactly where I stashed my phone—she *knows* me.

I find the phone after the ringing stops. "Shit." I see Julie's name across the screen. I can't talk to her when another woman is here; I have to get Lucy the hell out.

Harley was right; I'm going to mess everything up with just one stupid, meaningless night. I don't even know what's in Julie's head...or my own, for that matter.

"You have to leave." I shove the phone back into my jacket. I'm damn near naked; my jeans are even making me too hot. I don't dare take them off in front of her, though—I've done enough damage to myself for one night. "I don't want you here anymore."

She doesn't believe me. "You should relax. Maybe drink a little more?" She struts toward me on her long legs and I take a step backward. "Come on, Oliver, she left you. I'm right here. What's the problem? She obviously wasn't woman enough to handle someone like you. But lucky for you, I am *more* than enough."

The more she speaks, the more pissed I get. She doesn't even fucking know Julie—how dare she talk about her like that? It takes all I have left not to pick her ass up and drop her in the hallway so I can shut the door in her face full of smudged makeup. But that's not the kind of guy I am—drunk or not. I can't be the other type of guy, either: the guy who blames his infidelities and fuck-ups on being too drunk.

No. This is all me.

Oliver fucking Jackson: Grade-A asshole.

And deep down, I know insulting her isn't going to make the pain go away.

She reaches me, and her fake fingernails lightly scratch down my chest. I am so fucking desperate to be touched that I don't push her away this time. For a moment, I start to actually believe what she says. She may be a little right, though. Julie never *thought* she was good enough for me, and that put a strain on our relationship from the start. In reality, it's always been me that isn't good enough for her, and I'm starting to think that'll never change.

There's nothing I learn about Julie that isn't fucking perfect.

Don't give up on her, Oliver.

"Stop." I hold her hands in between us. "I can't do this."

She slumps forward and I take in a deep breath as I hear her knees hit the hardwood floor with a deafening *thump*.

This is happening. This really is fucking happening.

I can't make myself look down at her when I feel her fingers undo the button of my jeans. My dick isn't getting hard—which I'm thankful for. This validates the fact that I'm not into her, but I still don't make her stop quick enough for my own comfort.

The room spins out of control. I push her away and wobble to the sofa. I collapse and every ounce of energy I have left washes away. The amount of time I spend worrying about Julie is crazy, but she's more than worth it.

Lucy groans and plops down next to me. "You're *obviously* not into this."

For the first time since we've gotten into the apartment, I smile. She relaxes her thin body into the sofa next to me and we don't look at each other.

"I'm not a whore," Lucy says. "I mean...I'm not someone who just sleeps around all the time, just so you know."

I can't help but laugh. "Before I met Julie, I wouldn't have hesitated to sleep with you. It's just really complicated now. I lo—"

"I heard you. You *love* Julie."

The note of jealousy in her voice makes me uncomfortable. I still don't bother looking over at her; there's nothing for me there.

She isn't Julie.

She will never be Julie.

No one will.

I miss her so fucking much. It hasn't even been twenty-four hours and I can't even function without her. What the fuck has happened to me?

I broke my own stupid fucking rules. These are the consequences.

"Can I ask you something?" Her voice breaks through my thoughts. "What is it about her that makes her mean so much to you? It doesn't sound like you mean that much to her."

I scoff. "You don't even know her."

"Humor me."

Before I can answer her, a loud knock on the door vibrates the apartment walls. I panic; I hope to fucking god it isn't Julie. My life would be over. The knock booms through the apartment again and I leap up from the sofa, ready to punch someone's lights out. When I fling the door open, I nearly have a damn heart attack.

"Hey, boy," his gruff voice greets me. "Remember me?"

Mac. My mother's dealer. The man she disappeared with, leaving me behind.

My mouth doesn't move. I can't fucking believe this crackhead is standing in my doorway. His shiny bald head and sunken-in face make me relive memories I'd buried a long time ago. I wait for my mother to come around the corner and scream, "Boo!" but it's just him.

I find my voice. "What the hell do you want?"

Mac laughs and I want to vomit. I really, *really* need Julie right now. His solemn gaze focuses on a spot past me, into the apartment. "You ain't gonna invite me in, boy? I want to meet that little pretty blonde girl you've been following around."

All I can see is red.

Blinding fucking red.

"You leave her the fuck alone, you piece of shit." Even though I only have jeans on, my entire body flushes with heat and I realize that I'm still drunk. Mac isn't that much taller than me—the endless drugs that my mother and he pushed into their bodies has made him age a lot quicker than a healthy person in their forties would.

When my mother left us, she'd let Mac beat the shit out of me and leave me for dead…Okay, that's dramatic —I was able to crawl to the kitchen telephone and call for help. But I was only five, nowhere near mature enough to understand what was going on.

I just knew my mother didn't love me like I wanted her to.

"You shouldn't talk to me like that." He laughs and Lucy approaches from behind, her eyes widening at the dirty man in the doorway. "You never know what'll happen to you."

Lucy cowers a little. I know she isn't Julie, but I have to protect her from him just the same. I can feel her shaking next to me. My first instinct is to put my arm around her waist to let her know I won't let him hurt her.

But she's not Julie.

I brush my side against hers instead just to give her some sort of comfort; I'm still a little chivalrous no matter who the woman is.

"You better scram," I bark. The alcohol is flooding my veins more now. "Before I kick your ass and *make* you leave."

Mac snorts. "And who do we have here? Got yourself a new bitch, have you?"

I growl at him, but Lucy tugs on my belt loops, trying to keep me from killing him. I don't want to put her in harm's way, so I push her backward and start to shut the door in his face. His large boot stops the door from closing. "Nice place, kid." He snarls and pushes the door open, stepping a few feet into the apartment. "Guess that's what Grandpa's money will do for you though. Livin' the good life."

I'm too drunk to fight him and win, and Lucy seems to know it.

"Do you want me to call the cops?" she squeaks.

My heart nearly stops completely when I see a second person step into the doorway and enter the apartment. She looks *horrible*—her skin is gray and cold. She has the same green eyes as me, but they're lifeless and dull. Patches of her once-thick, chocolate-brown hair have fallen out and the dark bags underneath her eyes make her look dead.

"Hello, Ollie Bear." She smiles. "It's been a long time."

"Look, I don't know who you two are, but you need

to leave." Lucy crosses her arms over her chest. I silently applaud her for standing her ground, but she has no fucking clue what she's up against. When people have nothing to lose, they do crazy shit. "I'm going to call the cops in two seconds if you don't get out of here."

Mac laughs again and my mother gives him a look to shut the hell up.

"Mother," I choke. "What are you doing here?"

Her laugh is the same as I remember: scratchy and spine-tingling. I let Lucy clutch my arm as my mother takes a few more steps toward us. I position my body in front of Lucy's, just in case. Just because she's not Julie doesn't mean I'm going to be responsible for someone hurting her. "I'm here to see you, son, why else?"

"You need to leave," I growl. "I don't want you here."

She doesn't look hurt—she looks *annoyed*. "Give me the money I'm entitled to, and I will."

"What money?"

She cackles, and shivers run down my spine. "I know your grandfather left me money in his will; he told me so himself before he died. I want my money, Oliver, and I want it now."

The floor feels like quicksand beneath my feet. I don't have much left in me to listen to this shit now that the tequila has filled my veins and destroyed my ability to control myself. "The lawyers read the will. He left everything to me. You weren't even mentioned in it, so I guess you were misinformed."

"Then you better find a way to get me some money,

boy." Mac smirks. "Or your little girlfriend here will know what it's like to lose someone."

"Mac," my mother scolds him. "We're not here to threaten him. We're here to talk."

I don't know what the fuck to do.

"You talked," I spit. "I listened. I'm not giving you shit, and I don't want to see your faces anywhere near me or anyone I know, got it?" My defensive stance and bold voice is enough for the two of them to back down and step back out of the apartment.

I shut the door and Lucy is still gripping my arm so tight it hurts. We both stand in silence before we can even make eye contact.

I shrug off her hand and walk back to the kitchen to rummage around in the fridge for more to drink. I can't stuff anymore tequila in my body or I'll explode, so I settle for the case of beer that sits on the bottom shelf. One after another, I drown out the bullshit that just happened.

"Do I still have to leave?" Lucy squeaks from across the room. "What if they wait for me downstairs or something?"

"You can stay; I'll sleep out here." My words slur, and she knows it's time to leave me the fuck alone. "I don't give a shit."

All I can think about is my mother using Julie to get to me.

I have to keep Julie away from my mother.

I can't let my mother find her.

I have to keep her safe.

Because if my mother finds her...

I black out before I can even finish that thought.

FOUR
JULIE

THE COLD STEEL building towers over me. I read the sign out front over and over until it's seared into my brain.

The Rockford Women's Clinic.

It's just taunting me, waiting for me to step one foot inside of it so my life can be ruined more than it already is. Oliver isn't going to forgive me for coming here alone, but I couldn't bring myself to call him again just to be sent to voicemail. I think about Oliver's rules as I stare at the building. I made him break his first rule when he fell in love with me. I don't know how I did it. I don't know what I did to make him fall so hard. For me, it's like Oliver is something I've been searching for without realizing it. Brandon messed me up so bad that Oliver just got stuck with the dirty job of fixing my broken heart.

And then he kinda broke it again.

But he's breaking his second rule: Don't take anything for granted.

He's taking *me* for granted.

"Are you going in?" someone next to me says. "They're really nice inside."

When I turn my head to look at the girl, a small wave of panic washes over me. She's young and *very* pregnant. I see the twinkle in her eye when she rubs the bump on her stomach and smiles. "Just tell them you're friends with Quinn; they'll get you in faster." Her giggle is refreshing and light. Even though the dark bags beneath her eyes tell a different story, she's upbeat and positive. "I'm Quinn."

"Julie," I croak. "You're really young—"

She giggles again. "Very observant, Julie. I'm eighteen."

I almost pull her into a bear hug. She's just a kid… she had to grow up so fast. The world starts spinning so much that I need to sit down. I know I can't rely on Quinn to help me, but it doesn't matter—I fall to my knees.

"Eighteen? How can you be so…" I look up at her with wet eyes and so much fear that it's leaking onto her. "…*okay* with all of this?" My hands hover over her stomach. "I'm only twenty-two and I'm scared out of my mind."

Her giggle has changed to a thick and hearty chuckle. Her belly jiggles and she has to cross her legs while standing above me. "There's nothing to be *afraid* of, Julie. Things can always get better, right? I didn't have a job or a family when I got pregnant, and now I have both. I couldn't be happier. Are you still with the father?" Her eyes travel to my stomach as I stand and try to get my bearings back.

I think I'm going to vomit. "I'm not sure."

"Well, that's okay."

I clear my throat and try to save a little face. "I mean...I *think* we're still together; he just doesn't know I'm here. I'm not even sure I'm pregnant. That's why I came."

Quinn shakes her head. "Well, Julie, you have a friend in me." She squints her eyes and pats my hand. "Good luck in there." She smiles and gets into a waiting pickup truck. The guy in the front seat is smiling from ear to ear as she approaches; he gets out and helps her inside, looking back at me with the same determined look Quinn has. He nods, silently telling me that everything is going to be okay, and I believe him for a split second. It gives me enough courage to step inside the building and put my name on the sign-in sheet, at least.

When the nurse calls my name, I follow her down a long, white hallway and into a completely cold and sterile bathroom. She hands me a cup and tells me to pee in it before shutting the door. Everything just happens so fast that when it's all over and the doctor sits in front of me with no hope in her eyes, my freak out finally begins.

"This was a mistake," I say. "I don't even need to be here...what was I thinking?"

"Miss Remington, please sit down." Her voice isn't giving me much choice. She raises her penciled-in eyebrows, sending shivers down my arms. "You've come this far and now you don't want to know?"

I nod instantly. "That's right."

She sighs and takes a yellow envelope from the top

of her desk. "Tell you what. I'll give you the results and you can look at them when you're ready."

I snatch it from her hands and mutter a small "thank you" before rushing from the building. The clinic fades behind me as I make my way to the café where Staci is meeting me. The envelope in my bag holds my entire future inside, and it's weighing heavily on me. I want to open it in the privacy of the pool house, where I can be alone and cry if I need to. Every time I look over at my bag, I see the corner of the yellow envelope sticking out —taunting me.

I pull into the parking lot of the café and don't think about anything else but finding Staci. She jumps out of her seat when she sees me, and the envelope's still peeking out of my bag as I hug her and set it at my feet.

"I'm so glad you called me!" Staci's bubbly voice fills the air. "How are you?" Her question actually sounds sincere. Then again, Staci and Nora have always been the ones I'm able to relate to the most. "I already ordered mimosas and chicken and avocado salad—I hope you don't mind. I know you don't eat meat." Her lips purse like she has a joke on the tip of her tongue about the meat situation.

I think about Oliver.

"*How do you like your meat, Julie?*" I hear his voice in my mind.

I sigh. "I eat meat sometimes, just not all the time." I hold my stomach when it grumbles loudly, and it hurts from the lack of nutrients to digest. I suddenly find myself the hungriest I have ever been in my life—*again*. "I'm actually trying to stay away from alcohol." I eye the yellow envelope at my feet.

She snorts and sips the water in her hand. "Why? You're not pregnant, are you?"

I nearly throw up in front of her.

Her eyes widen when she sees my expression. "*Are* you?" Her gaze trails up and down my body several times. "Holy shit, you're pregnant."

I shush her so no one can hear. I don't know for sure and I don't want it spreading around town, just in case someone in here knows me or my brother. "I don't know yet. I have the results in my bag. I haven't read them yet."

The waitress brings the mimosas and Staci takes them both, gulping half of the first one down in a single tip of the flute. Her fingers tap on the glass and she snickers. "Well, I guess since you're eating for two now—"

"It's not funny, Staci," I scold her. "This is serious. The first reason being...it's why Oliver and I aren't speaking right now."

"You bet your sweet ass it's a big deal." I notice a small twinge in her voice as she finishes her mimosa and starts on mine. "You're having Oliver Jackson's baby!"

I look around nervously, and a few women at the table across from us start whispering when she says that. Oliver isn't exactly a celebrity, but around Rockford people *do* know him. "Not to mention, he's completely gorgeous and so totally in love with you," she continues.

I shake my head and dig into the salad. I eat like I've been starving for months—it's crazy how nothing satisfies me. This uncontrollable empty feeling in my stomach can't be normal with me only being a few weeks late. *Nothing* makes it go away. "He's probably not even in love with me anymore—you didn't see his face when I told him."

"What happened?"

I think about my answer. What do I tell her? I don't even know what happened, really. Everything is just a mess. No one understands Oliver like I do. I know what he wants before he does…I know he wants to be with me and anything that's a part of me too.

"He sort of…embraced it and then shut me out." She frowns, and I just shrug. "It was a weird situation anyway, but his reaction didn't make it any better."

As I tell her a play-by-play of the story, her eyes widen and my lips are so dry that licking them doesn't help. "I don't even know if he'll answer my calls. I tried, and he sent me to voicemail. He was pretty clear he had nothing left to say to me."

She laughs and blows a raspberry. "That boy is so in love with you that it kills me. It's been so obvious since you both walked into the cabin and started making googly eyes at each other. Trust me, your story has a happy ending if *I* have anything to say about it. Maybe he's just too busy preparing for an apology to talk."

Our eyes meet and we both erupt in laughter at the same time. "You are *such* a bad liar." I snort and it makes us laugh harder. "But I do appreciate you trying to make me feel better. I just can't imagine what's going through his head right now…when I don't even know what's going through mine."

She listens to me rant about Oliver for ten solid minutes without interruption. I can feel her genuine concern for me as I keep talking; that's something I never felt when I told Nora my problems.

My phone starts to ring, but I hardly hear it over our laughter. "You should get that…it's been ringing for like five minutes." Staci shoves salad into her mouth and smiles. When I bend over to search the bag for my phone, my stomach twists and I feel like I'm going to vomit again. I excuse myself to the bathroom and drink some cold water, trying to calm down. I look at my phone.

Oliver.

He left a voicemail.

I think about just deleting it, but I don't want to be that way with him. He deserves so much more from me than that. I close my eyes and push the button, ready to listen.

"Julie, it's Oliver. I'm sorry I didn't answer when you called—I was a little busy. I'm not in a good place right now…I just need a little time to think. Don't mistake this for something it's not, because I *do* love you, Julie. No matter what happens, remember that. I'll call you in a few days when I'm ready to talk. Again, I love you, sunshine."

My stomach drops to the floor and the room starts to spin. Somehow, I make my way back to the table and Staci eyeballs me with suspicion. "Are you okay?" She scoots closer so she can whisper. "Did you throw up?"

I chuckle and shake my head. "No, almost. Oliver just called."

"That was him calling? That's a good thing, right?"

"I don't know. He sounded sad. Like really, really sad. He said he needed time and then said he would call me in a few days." I hand her the phone and let her listen to the message. She replays it twice then hands it back to me, a crumpled look on her face.

"That could mean anything." She must see the reservation in my eyes. "Okay, here's what we're going to do. I'll pay for lunch, and you and I are going shopping to cheer ourselves up. Then later on, we'll open that envelope you've been guarding." Her gaze goes toward my feet. "I don't want to hear a word about it until then. You need to relax a bit. If you want to open it with Oliver, I understand."

I smile at her and she hops up to pay our bill. It's nice to have a friend who takes charge and knows what to do in a situation like this. I feel bad for Nora, still nursing a broken leg in the hospital, but Staci has turned out to be a pretty decent friend too. All I really know about Staci is that her mother was a famous model a few decades ago and her father is a film producer, but they've always kept her out of the celebrity limelight. Her gold credit card shimmers next to her manicured fingernails as she slips it back into her clutch.

"The rest of my day is free since my clients canceled. There's an outlet mall about twenty minutes from here. Let's go there first." She winks at me. "I never pay full price for designer anything, Julie. That's one of the many lessons I have to teach you today."

I laugh. I have nothing to lose. "Okay, let's do it."

Staci pulls me around to dozens of stores in the outlet mall; we shop and have dinner like old friends. It isn't until the ride home when I really start to appreciate her for who she is. I feel bad for always treating her like she's just another dumb Rockford socialite when she's clearly much more than that.

She doesn't ask why we're headed to the pool house when we park. We sneak around the house so Randy doesn't bombard us with questions. I turn on the lights in my little safe haven and Staci's eyes grow wide. "This is amazing! I wish I had a pool house." She sighs loudly. "It's like a huge, rich dorm room in the backyard of your hot brother's house."

I roll my eyes. "Growing up, all of my friends thought Randy was cute, but it's always grossed me out. It still does." I squint at her in warning.

She laughs. "I think he's absolutely adorable."

I don't want to fuel that fire anymore, so I lower my eyes to the floor, hoping she'll change the subject. "Do you miss Oliver?" she asks me. "He *will* come around, I promise."

"Why should I wait for him to come around?" The anger rises in my throat. "I shouldn't have to wait. We are together, or at least we were. This is too much drama."

My eyes fix on the damn yellow envelope.

"Call him and tell him you have the answers," she says.

I groan. "Fine." I take out my phone and dial Oliver's number before even thinking about it. Of course, he doesn't answer and I get his voicemail, but I don't leave one. Staci feels bad for me—I can see it in her eyes. She grabs the phone from me, finds his number, and sends a text message.

> Oliver, we need to talk.

He answers almost instantly.

OLIVER

I thought I said I would call you in a few days?

I want to cry.
Or throw up.
Or both.
Staci growls and smashes her fingers on the screen.

What is there to think about? Either you love me or you don't.

You know I love you, how can you question it?

You're going to have to wait for me. I love you.

Staci is pissed at his reply, so I take the phone and shove it into my pocket. She's done enough damage already...he doesn't need anything else to be angry about. But the more I think about it, the more I get furious that he's acting this way. I take my phone back out and look at it.

I think you're scared.

I'm not scared. Busy.

Staci sighs. "Too busy to talk to you?"

I miss you. Can you come over?

I miss you, too, sunshine. I can't see you right now, I have someone here.

My heart sinks and Staci growls louder. "Are you fucking kidding me?"

I shake my head. "I guess that's that, then."

"Julie—"

I want to cry. "I guess he doesn't care after all."

"Well I care," she snaps, snatching the envelope from my bag. She hands it to me and sits down next to me. "Let's just open it without him. You want to know and he doesn't. Don't torture yourself anymore, Julie."

She's right. I know she's right. "Okay." I don't waste any time ripping it open. I start reading the paper to her out loud, line after line until it's all gone. I can't read Staci's expression like I'd hoped; she sits back on the sofa while I fold the paper up and put it back where it belongs. I can hear her heavy breathing and it calms me a little.

"Are you going to tell him?"

I shrug. "He doesn't seem to care."

Her eyes dart from me to the envelope. "Are you okay with what it says?"

I don't know how to answer her. I don't even know if I wanted any of it to be real.

"I think you should get some rest," she says, standing up. "I have more errands to run anyway. I'll check on you later, okay?" She puts a blanket over me. I cuddle into it and close my eyes, listening to her leave the pool house. I know she just wants to give me space to deal with everything, but the silence quickly suffocates me. I want to read the results again—alone—so I can really let it sink in. I look around for the envelope, but it's not anywhere near me and I haven't knocked it down on the floor.

My eyes get wide.

Staci *took* it.

FIVE
OLIVER

THE SUNLIGHT IS SHINING through the curtains, but my head is still completely fuzzy from the tequila. I doze off on the sofa and dream about Julie. I dream about her soft, honey blonde hair next to me on the pillow. I dream of her puffy pink lips and how good they taste when she kisses me. I dream about her thighs, her curves...everything.

Dreaming about her doesn't help me not to miss her. I don't stay asleep for long; the same things I love about Julie haunt me in my dreams. I know she was texting me last night, but I'm too scared to look at whatever my drunk self said back to her. I flick my eyes open to stare at the ceiling, but my phone taunts me from the table in front of me. It's laughing at me because even *it* knows that I'm fucked.

When I hear shuffling in the bathroom, I frown.

Lucy.

Why the fuck is she still here?

I know I blacked out after my mother left.

She turns on the shower and I almost throw up. No woman should be showering in my apartment except for Julie. This is all my fault. "I have to fucking get her out of here," I whisper, but I can't move. The more I try and think about what happened last night, the less I remember. My mother showed up with her dealer—or boyfriend, whatever he is—but it's something I never thought would happen in my lifetime. I honestly thought she would be dead by now. I remember Mac saying something about a blonde girl and my heart burns with a thousand fires.

They know about Julie.

They've seen her. They know what she looks like.

"Fuck." I jump off the sofa. I smell like sweat and booze, so I let Lucy shower while I change my clothes. My bedroom is in disarray…she's been through my shit. I notice that the dresser drawers aren't closed completely. "She better not be wearing my clothes," I say like Lucy can hear me.

Before I can stop myself, I'm pounding on the bathroom door. The water turns off and it takes a few seconds for her to open the door; I hope to fucking hell she isn't naked. Lucy starts humming and the steam billows from the shower. A towel is wrapped around her tanned, naked body, and her fire-red hair is tied into a bun on top of her head. Her long legs walk toward me and she winks before disappearing into my bedroom behind a locked door.

I am going to lose Julie for sure now.

How could I do this to her?

I lower my head into my hands and quietly cry. Something is seriously wrong with the way I've been handling things...maybe Julie is right. I need to grow the fuck up.

When I hear the door unlock, I push through it, not really caring what the hell she's doing on the other side. Lucy's humming gets louder the farther I get into the room. It finally stops when she notices the strained look on my face. "Are you okay?" she asks, but I don't care enough to answer. All I can think about is Julie and how it should be her in my apartment right now. The more I think about it, the angrier I get. I face her and I almost rip the t-shirt right off her body.

That's Julie's shirt. And her jeans. And her shoes.

She's wearing Julie's things.

My head spins with so much angst that it's hard to keep my composure and not yell and scream at her. I wish Julie was here to see that I'm really trying to grow up a little.

"You need to fucking leave," I snarl. "And you need to take off Julie's clothes."

Her tongue finds the outside of her lips. "Oh, you want me to take off my clothes?"

I growl loudly. "Julie's clothes.... I want you to take off *Julie's* clothes. You don't fucking belong here. Why the fuck are you even still here?"

She snickers and plays with her phone. I can tell she's in another conversation entirely. Her long finger-nails tap on the screen for a few moments until she feels my annoyance. "Whoa, hey there," she says as I step closer, my eyes dark. I'm blinded by love for someone else. "What's the matter with you? You told me I could stay because I was too scared to leave after those crazy people showed up."

I look at her body and nothing inside me ignites.

Because she's not Julie.

"What happened after those people left?" I demand. "I don't remember shit after that…tell me what happened."

She giggles. "You blacked out for a few minutes, woke up, and drank the rest of that tequila, that's what."

I'm able to relax a little. "So, we didn't…"

Her dull eyes meet mine. "I'm not sure I'm following you." She snakes her long arms around my neck and giggles again. "If you're asking if we had sex…"

I push her off me and want to punch a damn hole in the wall. "Tell me we didn't. Tell me we didn't fuck…*please* tell me we didn't."

Lucy looks a little hurt. "You could at least *pretend* to remember."

I fall to my knees instantly. I am such a piece of shit —I can't fucking believe I did this. Julie deserves better than this…what am I going to do? The colors of the room blend around me until everything fades to black. The fire that burns inside of my body for Julie explodes with such force that I can't catch my breath. I don't know who I'm more pissed at: myself or my mother for showing up on my damn doorstep.

"Get the fuck out of here," I sob into my hands. "You can't tell anyone what we did, do you understand? I'm not going to lose Julie over some nobody I met in a bar."

Her eyes narrow. "Well, don't sugarcoat it or anything."

"Trust me," I scoff, "I won't. You don't compare to her, not by a mile."

Lucy scoffs and puts her hands on her hips as I stand up. She's wearing one of Julie's tight-fitted t-shirts that is crumpling at the sides, showing her bare skin. I glue my eyes to the wall opposite her. I don't even want to fucking *look* at her. I hear her pull her own emerald green dress back on—the zipper creaks and I frown. I can't think of anyone else but Julie and how she's going to hate me when she finds out.

But maybe she doesn't *have* to find out.

"Sure you don't want me to stay longer?" Lucy winks and throws Julie's clothes onto the bed.

This bitch cannot take a damn hint.

She licks her lips and runs a finger down my bare chest. I'm still half-naked, wearing nothing but jeans. "You were having so much fun last night…think about how much fun it could be sober and in the daylight."

I groan and push her off me again. "No offense, but I'm going to pretend like I don't know you. You literally mean nothing to me…it's amazing that I even remember your name. I don't know how much clearer I can be." I eyeball the front door. "Get. Out." She doesn't move, so I grab her arm and escort her to the front door. All I want to do is take a hot shower and wash this mess away. "So, yeah…thanks for stopping by."

There's hurt in her eyes. "Look, Oliver—"

I growl at her. "I don't want to fucking hear it."

Her lips press firmly together. "I have something to tell you. We didn't sleep together. I lied."

"Are you fucking kidding me?" I scream at her. "Are you trying to ruin my life?"

"You wouldn't even touch me, if that makes you feel any better."

I close my eyes and give myself a few seconds to think about this shit. "No, it really doesn't make me feel any better. What kind of person would do that to someone?"

Me. I'm no better than she is.

"I don't know what's wrong with me...I just wanted the attention," she murmurs. I know exactly what she means. I rub my chin as I walk to the sofa and sit down. "Oliver, please don't hate me—it really had nothing to do with you. It's all me."

I laugh loudly. "First of all, you don't know me, so don't use my name like you do. Second, it had nothing to do with me? You must be fucking kidding, right?"

Tears form in her eyes but she doesn't let them fall. "I'm so sorry...if Julie finds out—"

I nearly jump up and shake her. "You don't know her, either. Would you believe us if you were in her shoes?"

Now she's starting to sob louder. It's really hard for me to handle since I know this isn't Lucy's fault. It's *my* fault; Julie is going to hate me because of *my* screw-up. "I'm so sorry, I didn't mean to hurt you. I shouldn't have pulled you into my insecurities."

I hold my hand up for her to stop. "Does anyone else know you're here?"

"Just your friend from last night."

Oh, shit. Harley.

"I'll take care of him," I say. "Julie hardly knows Harley, and he's loyal to me. If he even says anything, we can act like we don't know each other, right?"

Lucy blinks a few times, processing what I'm saying. "Sure—"

I blow out hard. "Okay, so this could work. I'm not lying...we *don't* know each other." I feel bad because I know that if I have to make up a story, it's lying. "She doesn't need to know anything else. It would crush her, and I don't want that."

"It sounds like you do really love her." She sniffles. "It must be nice to have something like that in your life."

I clear the lump from my throat. "She's everything to me...everything good in my life."

She makes a swoony face and pouts. "That's so sweet."

Oh, fuck. That word. *Sweet.*

I growl. "Don't say that. I'm here with you...that's not so sweet."

"I can help you get her back, if you want."

I scoff. "No thank you."

Lucy laughs and it's kind of nice: light and airy like Julie's laugh. "I mean, give you some pointers to get her back. I watch a lot of rom-coms."

"What the hell are rom-coms?" I blurt, and we both laugh. "Like chick flicks?"

She nods. "Exactly. You can actually learn a lot from them."

This girl lives in a dream world. Out here in the adult world, we have rules. We have several, fucked-up rules that we put in place to protect ourselves even though we don't follow them. Life is messy—it's not dozens of roses and chasing the girl of your dreams and actually getting her...without obstacles getting in your way, anyway. Life knocks you down; life takes away the one person who kept you alive inside and gave you a new life. Life takes away your hope that someday you can change and be a better person.

Life hates you sometimes.

"Hey, you sure you don't want me to stay and talk?" Her phone beeps in her hands and I know she's distracted and wants to leave. "I'm supposed to meet up with someone, but if you want me to stay—"

I choke. "I'll be fine. You should go."

She doesn't press it further and stands up to leave. I make sure not to make eye contact with her so she lingers, and after a few minutes she takes the hint and heads for the front door. When she opens it, I hear her gasp and someone say, "Who the *hell* are you?"

I jump up so fast that my head spins. The voice is familiar, but it's not Julie. Lucy backs up into the apartment again and the girl steps toward her.

Tall and thin.

Long, sandy blonde hair.

Red lipstick on her wide lips, which contort in a snarl.

Staci.

She is *pissed.*

Her hands are on her hips and her heels click on the floor as she starts to approach me. Lucy looks pale, and I can tell she thinks it's Julie. I shake my head at her and she relaxes, but she's still on alert for a possible cat fight. Staci is steaming as she looks from Lucy to me. "Are you kidding me with this, Oliver?" She steps a few feet farther inside. "I consoled Julie all damn day today and defended you, and *this* is what you're doing? This is why you're too busy to talk to her? You're *cheating* on her?" Her gaze snaps to Lucy. "Did you know he has a girlfriend?"

Lucy nods. "I know."

"Oh, so you think it's okay to sleep with someone who's taken, then?"

I hold up my hand to stop her. "What are you doing here? How do you even know where I live? Where's Julie?"

Staci snorts. "Like you even care."

She rummages through a huge bag and walks past Lucy to slam a yellow envelope against my bare chest. It stings a little, but I match her glare like it doesn't affect me at all. "You don't know what you're talking about," I say.

"Julie tried to get you to come over so you could open this together." Her voice is like thick ice against my skin. "But you were too busy fucking someone else, probably getting her pregnant too."

I feel the blood rush to my face. "So, she *is* pregnant?"

Staci flips her long, sandy blonde hair over her shoulders. "Open it and see for yourself. Maybe you can pretend to love her enough to do what's right."

My jaw clenches. "Again, you don't know what the fuck you're talking about."

She rolls her eyes. After she glares at Lucy one more time, she turns and leaves without saying another word. I'm in shock for so long that I don't even notice Lucy leave too. I stand in the middle of the apartment with the envelope in my hands, alone—*again*.

I picture Julie dancing in the kitchen, making breakfast and swaying her curvy hips to music that isn't there. I want to cry when I think about opening the envelope because regardless of what it says…I won't ever stop loving her. No matter what this envelope says, she's always going to be the one for me. I can't explain it—she's asked me to many, many times—but there's just something so *cosmic* that happens inside of me when she smiles that makes me too weak to deny the magic.

Right now, I can't move.

I'm so frozen that it hurts.

Staci is going to tell her.

I have to get to Julie first.

I put the envelope down and rush to the bedroom, throwing on whatever clothes I can reach first. I find my phone and call Julie—it rings several times before going to her voicemail.

Staci already told her.

"Fuck this." I grab the envelope and my keys, taking the stairs to the garage where the Jeep is. I don't waste time waiting for the elevator—I have to get to Julie. At this point, I don't care about anything but her. I don't give a shit about rules or how to fight to keep myself from breaking them. Julie is all I have left that's keeping me tethered to a normal feeling in my life. I can't lose her to my own stupidity; I have to stop acting like every day is our last day and just open myself up to whatever comes our way.

Rain is pouring down as I pull the Jeep onto the streets and race through the sea of other drivers on the road. I don't pay attention to what I'm doing. All I can think about is how much I've fucked up and how I can fix it.

I won't be able to stand it if she hates me.

The rain makes the roads slippery, but I press on like nothing is in my way. The Jeep is having trouble staying straight, but I don't bother slowing down until I reach an intersection and I'm forced to. I breathe deeply to try and calm my nerves so I can make sure I get to her safely…but it's too late.

I don't see what pushes me from behind into the intersection.

I *do* see the man's face across the road as I slam into him—the look of pure fear, of thinking that his life is going to end and there's nothing he can do about it. As our cars collide, everything quakes around me.

I hear screams.

Then…nothing.

But I sure as hell *feel* everything before it all goes dark.

SIX
HEATHER

I RIP the note off the door of my hotel room when I get back from "visiting" Nora in the hospital. I scoff as my fingernails scrape against the paste-white surface. The money I managed to scrape together selling my things is running out; the wonderful people of this lavish hotel are kind enough to give me a few more days to get my remaining things and leave.

I let the heavy door slam behind me. I shove the air back down into my lungs, but it aches to be free. I won't give in; I won't let the frustration get the best of me. I honestly thought Ollie would let me back in the apartment by now.

My once shiny black hair is dull and lifeless, making me frown at my reflection. I need better hair product than this hotel provides. I need new clothes and necessities too. I need something more than I ever thought I would.

I need Ollie.

I also need to let that go.

I crumple up the notice and throw it in the trash. I've been thinking about how I'm going to get out of this for days—I know I can't ask Ollie for any more money. He's made it pretty clear that's over for me. I'll just have to take more extreme measures to keep living the way I was born to live: worry-free and with Oliver Jackson.

I already decided that karma is a bitch. No, she's a *heinous* bitch. Therefore, I'm cleansing myself of who I am and digging deep to find who I want to be. I want friends who don't follow me out of fear, and I want someone I love enough not to hurt. That's the only way I'm ever going to be truly happy.

I'm going to be an entirely new person.

I fluff up my chest and smile into the mirror. The white, sleeveless blouse washes out my tanned skin, but it doesn't matter. I'll *always* be the fairest one of all. I rummage through the rest of my clothing and find a pair of skinny jeans and flats.

Now I look like I did before I met Ollie…the real me.

Heather Michaels, small-town girl with small-town worries.

I was a naïve sophomore at NYU when I met him; his boyish charm and handsome face drew me in the instant he introduced himself. I'd scraped together money and took out loans for the rest just to *get* to New York in the first place, but he whisked me into a life of diamonds and pearls and even paid off my loans for me as a birthday gift the year we met. I felt wanted, and Ollie gave me something I never knew I needed more of.

Love.

My phone rings and I struggle to find it under the takeout containers littering the table. They were once full of fattening, carb-loaded food—not that I kept any of it down long. The nerve-wracking drama I've been through has turned my stomach against me. I wipe off the screen and Nora's name shows up.

"Thank you *so* much for forgiving me, Nora," I say when I answer the phone. I don't bother saying hello. People are drawn to me...they *want* to be my friend. I didn't make it that way—that sort of just happens on its own. "I shouldn't have lied to you; I just wanted Ollie back so bad."

Nora sighs. "Save it. I'm calling to tell you to stop calling me."

I want to laugh. I don't think that would make her believe me, though. I place my index finger—that's in horrible need of a manicure—to my lips. "No matter *why* you called—I'm glad you did," I say, forcing my voice into the unknown territory of remorse. "I really wanted to apologize—"

"Just leave me alone, okay?" Her voice is strained. "Julie and Oliver are my friends, something you know nothing about. Not to mention you slept with Casey."

Okay, I let a little laugh slip out. "There's nothing I can say about that, other than I'm sorry...again. I don't want to be that person anymore."

She hangs up on me.

I turn the phone over in my hands a few times. Where did I go wrong here? I didn't ask for Oliver to captivate me and bring me to Rockford—I was doing just fine where I was. Of course, staying at school would've meant I wouldn't have him or the money anyway, but right now…that actually seems nice and relaxing.

I dial Casey's number next.

"What?" he roars.

I frown. "Hey, you. Can we talk?"

"No," he spits.

"Look, Casey…" I'm lonely, and I think he knows it. "I just want someone to talk to."

I shouldn't have messed things up with Casey the way I did…he's always been fairly nice to me throughout my relationship with Oliver.

He growls. "Someone like *me*?"

Okay, now we're getting somewhere. "Exactly."

He laughs hysterically. "I'm good, thanks."

"Casey, please?" I turn on the waterworks and throw a little whine into my voice. "I have no one anymore. Nora won't talk to me and Ollie is gone. You're all I have left."

"You've never *had* me, Heather. You're nothing to me."

My stomach sinks. No one has ever said that to me before. Ollie didn't even talk to me like that when he found out about everything and kicked me out. He was stoic and sad; it probably didn't help that I never apologized. I just assumed he would come to his senses and call me, begging me to come back.

Then Julie happened.

"That's not true," I say. "You wouldn't have slept with me if I meant nothing to you."

His laughter fills the entire room and he's not even in it. "Trust me, me fucking you had nothing to do with me actually wanting you. That's something I'll never do again—you can count on that. You better fucking leave Julie and Oliver alone."

He hangs up and it sounds like a prison cell door slamming in my ear.

Okay. Now I'm getting worried. That's two people who want nothing to do with me. I'm not used to this; people don't just drop me like that. I mean, sure, I piss people off sometimes. Lately, though…they haven't been coming back.

I call Staci and she doesn't even answer the phone.

I run through the now short-list of people who might still be loyal to me. I have to talk to someone before my insides explode. If I'm going to try and let Oliver go, I'm going to have to start by finding myself again. I search through my online social media profile, looking at my friends list to find someone—anyone—to talk to.

I come across Lucy Peterson's name and freeze. This girl was basically my shadow in high school, and she's someone I could always count on. I wonder if she's still in Atlanta; I heard she moved there after high school. There's only one way to find out.

I look through her pictures and frown. She's almost as hot as me now. Her wavy, fire-engine red hair has been amplified, and the acne on her heart-shaped face has cleared up.

I write to her anyway.

> Hey, Lucy. I don't know if you remember me. I found you online and wanted to see how you've been since high school…what have you been up to?

I send the message and wait. I'm thinking about searching through the takeout containers to see if I can scrounge up something to fill my growling stomach when I hear the phone ding from Lucy's reply.

LUCY

It's so good to hear from you! I would love to catch up...I'm in Rockford right now. I'm getting ready to escape a one-night stand, actually.

I smirk at her aloofness. Being proud of a one-night stand is something the old me would have tackled her down for. I wonder what's brought her to Rockford?

Wow! That's awesome! Can you meet up?

Of course! The coffee shop on Eleventh? I could use a macchiato. I work just around the corner at Rita's Boutique, but my shift isn't for a few hours.

I agree to meet her at the coffee shop in an hour. Lucy is the ticket to helping me get back in touch with my former self. I'm sure that even if we can't pick right back up where we left off, there's enough friendship left there to satisfy me.

I don't bother changing my clothes; I'm not going there to impress her. I snatch the hotel keycard from the desk and move swiftly through the hallways, hoping no one notices me and tries to collect their money. I open my wallet and see a twenty-dollar bill. I hope that maybe Lucy will be so tickled to see me again that she'll treat me to whatever I want.

Alejandro, the concierge, is busy with some new guests, so I'm able to slink out of the lobby unseen. I escape onto the streets of Rockford unscathed by his demeaning looks. I feel the last of my jewelry flutter around in my pocket and frown. The pawn shop that I've been using for my things is on my way to the coffee shop; I decide to stop inside and pawn what's left of my life with Ollie just in case Lucy doesn't offer to pay for lunch.

I look at my flats and smile. I love these shoes. They're so…simple.

When I turn around a corner, I look up and see someone staring at me. He looks familiar, but I don't keep his gaze; he's probably just some random guy checking me out. I walk a little faster but he moves with me, his dark shadow bouncing behind him on the sidewalk. He tries his best to blend in, but his bad boy vibe oozes from him and saturates the ground he walks on. Suddenly I realize that I *do* know him.

"I thought you were leaving town?" I say as I draw closer. I snicker when he jumps and faces me—I half-expect him to frown, but instead, he flashes a toothy smile and his happiness at seeing me glows through his skin. "Nice to see you again…" I act like I'd forgotten his name.

"Brandon," he says, his voice ragged. "I turned myself in, but Nora didn't press charges. She doesn't remember if I pushed her or if I fell on accident." He winks at me and it excites me a little inside. I look behind him at the large clock on the side of Rockford Bank and Trust.

He turns to catch a glimpse of what I'm staring at, so I can get a better look of him without being caught. His six-foot-tall body is slender enough to wear tight navy-blue dress pants; the pale sky-blue dress shirt clings to his small chest as he turns back around. Even though it looks like he hasn't shaved in a few days, the dark, scratchy-looking patches of his facial hair are stomach-tingling.

Brandon's hazel eyes follow mine. "Looking for someone besides me?"

"Yeah, I thought I saw someone better. See ya." I glare at him with heavy suspicion that I'm not getting rid of him that easily.

I start to walk away but feel his strong grip tug at my arm, spinning me back around to face him. In that moment, I feel like Bambi, and he's the hunter trying so desperately to track me down and consume me.

Okay, it's not like me to panic, but this is—

"So, now that I'm a free man, we should get together again." He licks his thin lips and his gaze devours my thighs. "Nora told me something quite interesting when I visited her that night…before she fell."

I roll my eyes. "What's that?"

I'm scared.

…And excited.

He lets me go and my arm tingles where he grabbed me. He rubs his jawline and sits on a bench next to us, looking up at me with wide eyes. Even though I'm totally grossed out by public benches—and bathrooms—I make an exception and slowly lower myself next to him. "Are you going to tell me what Nora said?"

His nostrils flare as he thinks about it. "Julie Remington is my ex-girlfriend."

My eyes snap to his.

"And I know Oliver Jackson is your ex-boyfriend."

I scoff. "That's not a secret." I narrow my eyes. "Julie is your ex?"

He nods. "She was the love of my life until Oliver came along."

I start to laugh hysterically. Brandon looks annoyed and pinches my side gently. "I fully intend to get over her and maybe we can help each other out," he says. "Maybe we can have a little fun ourselves."

"What exactly do you have in mind?"

He puts his hand on my inner thigh and squeezes. "After I take care of a little business, you and I should go back to your place so I can tie you—"

"—I'm meeting someone," I flatly say. This is so not what I want my life to be anymore.

He leans closer to me; his breath smells like rum and cigarettes. "You and I *both* know that was some of the best sex we've ever had."

I stand up and fake a smile. "I have to go. Thanks to Ollie, I have to pawn the rest of my nice things so I'll have a place to live. Come by my room later and we can talk about—" I look around to make sure no one is watching us. "—*anything* else besides sex." I look down at him and take a minute to appreciate how different from Ollie he is. He's tall like Ollie, but lanky and silver-tongued—he knows what to say to make me squirm a little in my skin.

He stands up. "Do you need money?"

"I don't need money from *you*."

He growls. "So, his money is good enough for you, but mine isn't?"

People on the sidewalk start to stop and look at us. The fire in his warm eyes goes out and he shakes his head. "Heather, please." My eyebrows rise at the fact that he remembers my name. "I'm trying to be a better guy, okay? I've been a dick lately, and I'm trying to be better."

Well…me too.

I actually believe him. I can't find it in my new heart of hearts *not* to believe him. "I can't take money from you—I hardly know you."

He takes my hand, and for a split second, it feels like Ollie all over again. The swooning and the charm dripping from his body reels me in; I can't resist a man who wants to help me. "Just let me do this for you. If Oliver won't take care of you, let me do it."

The jewelry in my pocket is weighing me down. I shove my hand in and finger the dainty pieces. I have two things left: the first diamond necklace Ollie ever gave to me, and the pearl necklace Ollie's grandfather left me in his will.

"Look, you need a place to stay, right? Stay with me until you find something else. Save your money and save the rest of your nice things."

I'm not buying it. "I'm not looking to trade sex for rent."

He laughs and holds up his hands in defense. "I promise I won't make you do anything you don't want to do. We can sleep together if you want—I know *I* want to—but you can have your own room and your own space. Just consider this an act of good faith that I truly want to start being a better person than I've been."

I have to think about this...*right*?

"Can we talk about this later?" I check my phone to see if Lucy has messaged me about being late yet. I hardly want to face her when I'm feeling sorry for myself like this, but Brandon has made it crystal clear that he thinks I can't take care of myself.

I have no skills.

I have no job.

I have *nothing*.

"Of course," he says and hands me a business card with his cell phone number on it. He leans in and I think he's going to kiss me on the mouth, but he plants his cold lips on my cheek instead. "I'll come by your room in a few hours and we can talk then."

"Are you sure about this?" I blurt out. "I'm not exactly someone to take home to your mother."

His breath is on my ear as he leans in closer. "It's a good thing I'm not looking to take anyone home to her, then." He winks and walks away, leaving me in a puddled mess on the sidewalk. How can someone so elusive and self-aware make me want to rip his clothes off?

I look down at the card in my hands.

BRANDON WHITEHOUSE
LAW ASSISTANT OF ROBERT GALLOWAY
ATTORNEY AT LAW

The coffee shop is a few blocks away, but it takes me

forever to walk there. I shove the card into my pocket when I see Lucy sitting at a table. I instantly want to turn back around. She isn't the same as she was in high school, and her profile pictures didn't do her justice. The once wiry-haired, frumpy nobody is now the object of every man's attention as they walk by. The bold green dress she has on perfects everything it's supposed to, and I find myself green with envy over it.

"Heather!" she squeals and jumps up, entangling me in a bear hug.

"Wow, you look—"

She giggles. "I know. Crazy, right?"

I notice her expensive clothes and jewelry, and the twenty-dollar bill weighs heavily inside my bag. Now I'm kicking myself—I should've taken some cash from Brandon before coming here to be on the safe side. Lucy orders a bottle of strawberry champagne for us and throws a judgmental look my way.

That was *my* look.

The look I gave people when I felt sorry for them.

And now she's giving it to *me*.

I've hit rock bottom.

"I need your help, Lucy," I say. "I need someone to talk to, and you're the only person that won't turn me away."

She puts her hand on mine and gives me that look again. "Tell me all about it."

Pity.

She pities me.

That's okay, because right now I don't feel so hot about myself.

But I'm going to do everything I can to change that.

SEVEN
JULIE

I HEAR my phone ring as I'm putting away everything Staci insisted on buying for me on our shopping trip. The few journals of Colin's I managed to sneak home with me fit nicely in the slouch bag she forced me to buy. I shove them inside for safe keeping and look in the mirror—the entire pregnancy drama has taken a toll on my hair and skin. Oliver isn't speaking to me, so I don't rush to find the phone. It's probably Randy wondering where I'd been all day.

The lavender blouse that she picked out feels nice against my skin; I smooth out the fabric over my stomach and think about Oliver. I'm sure Staci mailed the envelope for me; I'd scratched his address on it when I debated on mailing it myself.

Can I forget about Oliver and move on?

No. I love him. He's been slowly fixing me, putting all of the broken pieces back together one by one.

There's a knock at my door and it opens before I can get to it. Clyde peeks his head in with his eyes squeezed closed so tightly that it's comical. I laugh as he enters, opens his eyes, and blushes. "Oh, hey Aunt Julie."

"Clyde, is everything okay?"

He looks sad. "You haven't been around much lately. You've been going on vacations with your new boyfriend."

I smile at him. "We didn't take a vacation. More like…a getaway."

He rolls his eyes. "Whatever. You're letting him take over your life just like Brandon did. At least that's what Dad says."

I sit across from him on the sofa. "Your dad shouldn't be discussing my relationships with you, Clyde. That's not something you need to worry about. I'll be fine."

He smiles and perks up. "Well, thanks for being there for me with the school thing. He said I still have to take smart classes, but at least it's a normal school." We hear sirens blaring somewhere in the neighborhood, and it distracts me for a minute.

The rain pounds against the roof with such force that it shakes the walls too. It's getting worse outside, and I can't help but feel like it's my fault. My bad mood has caused this thunderstorm somehow, and maybe that's dramatic but right now, I don't care.

My attention focuses back on Clyde when he snaps his fingers in front of me. "Did you hear me, Julie?"

I shake my head. "No, sorry."

"I asked if you'd take me to get some ice cream."

My stomach grumbles. "Yeah, that sounds good. Let's go." I smile and he jumps up, taking my hand and starting to pull me toward the door. The rain outside isn't letting up, so I grab a sweater before he manages to drag me into the main house.

"Come on, Dad, come with us," Clyde says. "Julie's taking me to get ice cream." My stomach hurts. I don't need to hear his criticism right now.

I raise my eyebrows at my brother. "We're going to Gerda's."

Gerda's Ice Cream Parlor has been around for as long as I can remember. Randy used to take me there when I was younger and would visit him for the summers, before I actually moved here. I think about Oliver and chocolate chip ice cream, frowning.

The sirens grow louder and it piques Randy's attention. "Okay, but I'm driving," he mutters, putting his newspaper down. He eyes me and puts his glasses in his shirt pocket. "If you think I'm getting into a car with *her* driving…you're not as smart as we all think."

Clyde laughs and looks at me. "Let's just go," I say, trying not to smile.

Clyde ushers us outside, and as we back out of the driveway, the sirens get louder. The rain starts to let up a little and we can see ahead of us now. A quarter mile away from the house, there's a long line of traffic at an intersection. We can see several police cars, fire trucks, and ambulances parked along the road. Broken car parts are scattered everywhere, and people are still screaming and crying, running around with no direction.

"Whoa, that must have been quite a mess," Randy says, nodding toward a police officer he apparently knows. "I hope everyone is okay."

I crane my neck to look closer as we inch toward the

accident. Shattered glass and debris come into view better with the car lights; people are standing around helping others while paramedics attend to the wounded. I swear that I see someone being rolled away beneath a white sheet before Randy blocks my view; he rolls down his window and waves the officer he knows down. The man walks toward the window with an intense look on his face. "Hey, Brad. What happened? Did everyone survive?" Randy asks.

Brad shakes his head in sadness. "Not everyone. The driver of one of the vehicles involved didn't make it. He was mangled up pretty bad. I think he died on impact." Brad looks in the backseat and notices Clyde.

My stomach starts to hurt so badly I nearly throw up. Clyde's hand lands on my shoulder. "How did it happen?" I force myself to ask.

Brad shrugs. "The roads are slick and the driver of the truck wasn't paying attention. It smashed into the back of the Jeep at a high speed and caused it to hit another car head-on. Then it hit two other cars in the intersection and flipped several times. Poor bastard." Brad looks at the traffic piling up behind us. "Well, better get you all on through. Stay safe out there, okay?"

Randy nods. "Let me know the drivers involved, okay?"

Jeep.

He said *Jeep*.

"Which driver didn't survive?" I ask in a panic, but Brad has already stepped away. We slowly make our way down the road, around the accident.

I see the truck that smashed into the Jeep.

I see the two cars that the Jeep hit.

Then, I see it.

The Jeep sits mangled on the side of the intersection, upside-down and almost unrecognizable to the point where I can't even tell what color it is. "Is there someone inside that Jeep?" I stretch my neck, then lean my body over closer to Randy to try and see better. "I don't see anyone…is there someone in there?"

He speeds the car up, forcing me to sit back down. I keep my eyes on the accident until I can't see it anymore. My stomach turns as I try and tell myself that isn't Oliver's Jeep on the side of that road mangled up. I have to make sure he's alive.

I take my phone from my pocket and dial Oliver's number.

What if he answers?

What do I say to him?

My heart skips several beats in a row.

I hang up and send him a text message instead.

> Please call me. I love you.

Now all I can do is wait as we pull up to Gerda's. Clyde hops out and sees some of his friends; he follows them inside. I can feel the tension between Randy and me; he doesn't make it worse because I think he can feel my fear.

"Did you get him?" he asks. His eyes are shaded and I get an odd feeling that he knows something. "I don't think it was his Jeep, Julie."

I suck in a deep breath. "I couldn't tell. I don't know why he would be in our area."

My heart freezes. The house he bought is near Randy's.

My body buzzes with fear and I shake so badly that Randy takes my hand into his to comfort me. "Let's just go in so Clyde doesn't freak out, okay? I'll make a few phone calls and see what I can find out."

I nod. That's all I can do—wait. He leaves me in the Jeep so I can have a few minutes of silence by myself. My phone rings and it startles me, making me nearly drop it on the floor of the car.

"Hello." My voice is dark and sad.

"Julie?" Staci says. "What's wrong? Did Oliver call you?"

"No, is he okay?"

"I don't know. I mean, he was when I dropped off your envelope. That was over an hour ago, though. I stole it from the table...I wanted you to know." I can hear her speaking, but I stop listening when she has nothing to say that I actually want to hear.

She doesn't have any good news about Oliver.

She doesn't have any bad news about Oliver, either.

I sigh. "Thanks for doing that. I'm actually with my family right now—"

"Say no more. Call me later, okay?"

I hang up the phone. I don't have time to think about fun when I don't know if Oliver is alive or not. I have to calm down; there are tons of people with Jeeps in Rockford.

RANDY

Are you coming in?

I look up and Randy is standing in the window, waving me inside. I step into the rain and hope my legs won't give out. All of the stress has flowed through my body, and the laughter inside the ice cream parlor doesn't make me forget about anything at all. I clutch my phone in my hand the entire time, hoping he'll just call and tell me he's okay.

The entire hour we're in the shop, it never goes off.

No call from Oliver.

No texts from Oliver.

My mind is spinning out of control.

On the way back home, the accident has been cleared and I can't see the Jeep anymore. I look around the intersection as if I'd be able to get any answers, but there's nothing.

"When was the last time you heard from him?" Randy asks me in the dark car as we park, careful not to wake Clyde from his sugar coma.

I don't want to answer him. He already hates Oliver as it is. "When he dropped me off last."

He scoffs. "You mean when you came stomping through the house all pissed off?"

I nod. "I guess."

"Why do you let people walk all over you? Why do you only stay with men who hurt you and make you feel this way?"

I slam my hands on the dashboard, waking Clyde up. "Clyde, go inside." The velocity of anger in my voice startles him, and he does what he's told without question. Randy looks a little taken aback by my boldness. He's never heard me stick up for myself before.

"Oliver and I love each other, okay? I love him and

he loves me." I glare at him in the moonlight. "People fight, relationships aren't perfect. I'm sorry you lost the most perfect woman in the world to you, but in the real world, people fight and sometimes make up. And another thing—" I whip my head to look at him directly. "—Oliver would *never* do something deliberately to hurt me like Brandon did. He takes care of me. He bought a *house* for me."

His eyebrows rise. "Oh, really? Where?"

"A few blocks from here, so it'll be closer to my classes."

Randy nods his head in approval. "I like that you've taken notice of my offer of paying for you to go to school. And I never said I didn't like Oliver...you know that, right? I just hate seeing you make the same mistake over again. The last one did you in pretty good."

Brandon. They have names.

I'm not sure he even cares.

"You are so judgmental that I don't want to tell you anything anymore, Randy. I had parents, remember? They mistreated me and I left them behind—don't make me do the same to you." I narrow my eyes at his look of surprise. "You *know* what I mean. I grew up without parental supervision, and I think I turned out okay. I just want you to be my brother, not my father."

He sighs and rubs his hands over his forehead. "Look, I'm flying blind here with Clyde and you both, okay? Marianna always took care of these things, and since she's been gone, it's been hard. I want to do right by both of you. Can we just leave it at that?"

I smile. "Fine, we can do that."

I think about our newfound respect for each other as I walk back to the pool house, but I still can't shake the awful feeling about Oliver. I haven't heard from him, and even though he's upset with me, he would at least contact me in some way.

Before I can take my sweater off in the pool house, there's a loud knock on the door. I sigh and don't bother turning around since it's probably Clyde again. "Come in," I say. Peeling the sweater off of my shoulders, I toss it into the laundry basket because it's wet and smells like rain. When I turn around to talk to Clyde, a weird feeling washes over me because it's not my nephew staring back at me from across the room.

It's Casey.

"H-Hey." His voice is weak. "Sorry to surprise you…I got your address from Oliver's apartment. I'm looking for him so we can talk."

I snort. "You and me, both." I wave my hands at him, gesturing him inside. "Come in and join the party; I haven't heard from him."

He smirks and sits down on the sofa, stretching his legs like he belongs there. I'll admit, Casey is a pretty easygoing person to be around. I know he's had his difficulties with Oliver, but that doesn't mean I can't be his friend. I need all the friends I can get these days since it's hard enough to trust one person.

"So, did you see that wreck down the street?" he asks, his eyebrows rising as I sit on the opposite end of the small sofa. It's still close enough to be a little uncomfortable. "I passed what was left on my way here —that must've been a damn mess."

I nod. "It was. I saw it when my nephew dragged my brother and I out for ice cream."

Casey's smile is warm and wide. "That's pretty cool. I don't have any real siblings...none that I can say I've *known* as a sibling, anyway." The flush in his cheeks lets me know that he's said too much. "I'm sorry; I'm not here to drag your mood down."

I still haven't heard from Oliver. That thought has to be pushed to the back of my mind or I'll explode.

"What *really* happened with you and Oliver?" I blurt.

Casey doesn't get angry or defensive; the sadness of the breath he exhales tickles my skin. It's hard not to like him and his all-American boy demeanor, but it's also hard to not respect Oliver enough to feel a bit uncomfortable about getting into his business like this. I know Casey had sex with Heather at least twice, including once while he was involved with Nora, but not much beyond that.

"I slept with Heather when they first started dating —I'm talking about within the first few weeks." His back straightens and he frowns. "That doesn't excuse it, but it happened. I didn't know he would keep her so long...they were so different that I thought he'd tire of her and he'd never find out."

I shake my head. "That's horrible. So, what? Oliver and I are different—are we not meant to be?"

"That's not the same. It's not that you and Oliver are different people...*you're* different from anyone he's ever been with. Maybe that's the key to his happiness."

I swallow the lump in my throat. "You're a good friend, Casey, even if you think otherwise. Oliver told me that you helped him look for me at Lake Reed when I ran off—only a good friend would set aside their own crap and help someone they care about."

He makes an agreeing noise and looks down at his hands. "Can I talk to you about something...more personal?"

I nod. "Of course you can. We're friends, right?"

A slight smile spreads across his face. When his chocolate brown eyes meet mine, a sense of security washes over me. The same safe feeling that Oliver gives me.

Oliver.

Where is he?

Casey clears his throat. "Well, you know that obviously Nora and I broke up." The sadness is placed perfectly in his voice. "I can't say that I blame her. So, I know where I fucked up, but why do you think I did it?"

Oh.

Well, how should I know?

For the sake of friendship and trying to ease his troubled mind—to take my mind off of my *own* troubles —I take his hand into mine and pat it like you would a crying child. It's weird, holding the hand of someone else, but Casey needs some sort of comfort and I need to take my mind off of where the hell Oliver is and what he's doing.

"I don't know, Casey. I don't know you that well. I mean, I guess I would say that maybe, deep down, you wanted something different but were afraid to end it with Nora? She liked you a lot—and I love Nora—but she's not exactly known to be...monogamous, either."

His eyebrows rise. "Oh? She didn't—"

I shake my head instantly. "No, she never cheated. Why people do that is beyond me. I've never been a person to have my cake and eat it too."

Casey's laugh is fresh. "You're pretty much a saint, Julie. Maybe someday I can find someone like you to tie me down." He winks, and it makes me let go of his hand. I don't want to even think about Casey flirting with me; this isn't an okay situation to put myself in.

"Sorry." He lowers his gaze to his lap. "I didn't mean to make it awkward."

Oh, this poor guy.

No...think about something else. He doesn't need you to save him.

"What do you want out of life, Casey?" I ask. "What do you really, *really* want?"

He doesn't waste time thinking about it. "I want what Oliver has."

Oh, crap.

"I want what you and Oliver have, let me be clear."

The sick feeling in my stomach fades. "Oliver and I aren't perfect, Casey. We have our faults and we drive each other crazy."

He scoffs. "No, you don't get it. You made him into a whole new person. Before you, he was...lost. He slept with a different woman every night." He notices the grimace on my face but keeps going. "And he literally didn't care about anything except working out and getting that next one-night stand. You changed him, Julie. That's what I want."

"You can change yourself," I say. "You don't need someone to do it for you."

"But Oliver did."

The unrestrained annoyance is seeping out into my voice. "Casey, your first problem is that you need to stop comparing yourself to Oliver. He isn't perfect. *I'm* not perfect, and you aren't, either. That's the beauty of things: you can be whoever you want to be. Don't strive to be someone you're not."

Before he can answer, my phone starts to ring in my hand. I look down and notice that it's not a number I recognize, but I want to get out of this conversation with Casey. I answer the call.

"Hello?"

"Is this Julie Remington?" a woman asks.

I take the phone away from my ear and check the number again. I figured it must be someone from the clinic following up with me.

"I looked at the results—everything is okay," I say.

I hear loud beeping and voices on her end. "I'm not sure what you mean. This is Nurse Mary Callahan at Rockford Memorial. Do you know an Oliver Jackson?"

The phone drops from my hand onto the floor. Casey looks at me, puzzled, then picks up the phone and greets the woman himself.

I'm going to throw up.

"I understand," I hear Casey say, and his hand is around mine again, squeezing and letting me know that he's here for me. I don't wrap my fingers around his, but I don't take my hand away, either. I need his comfort because something bad is about to happen...I can feel it. "Yes, we'll be right there." He hangs up the phone, shoving it into his jeans pocket.

He says my name, but it's like he's a million miles away.

"Hey..." The softness in his voice shines through. "Did you hear me? Oliver is in the hospital. We have to go."

I can't move.

"*Julie.*" Casey's voice sounds closer now. "Come on, we gotta go." I feel him pick me up and start to carry me outside. The rain is now a light mist, so the heat coming from his body is calming...and terrifying. I squirm in his grip, signaling for him to let me go, and he sets me down on the sidewalk in front of the house. His eyes are wet with tears.

"I can walk," I say, my voice raspy. "Can you drive?"

Casey nods. "I won't let you down."

Oliver, I'm coming. I need to see you.

Dead or alive.

EIGHT
HEATHER

THE REST of the lunch with Lucy grew awkward as time dragged on. I listened to Lucy talk about her job at the boutique for over an hour, and when the bill came, she happily tugged it from my limp grip and handed the waitress a gold card. For someone who lives in Boxwood, she dresses and spends money like a Rockford socialite. I should know.

"Drinks?" She smiles and slips her wallet into her handbag. I finish texting Brandon, telling him to meet me at the hotel, and look up at her amused face. "There's a rustic bar a few blocks away called The Tavern I've had some luck getting a few free drinks in. I went home with someone last night, but it...didn't work out."

I know that bar—Oliver loved it.

"No, I have someone waiting to hear from me." I sweetly smile. "But thanks for the offer. It was great catching up. I needed someone to talk to."

Even though she didn't let me get a word in edgewise.

The look on her face confirms that she can see right through me. "Well, anytime. I'll see you later, okay? I'm going to find me some trouble."

I let her walk the opposite way from me without a second thought. I don't know what I was thinking; Lucy isn't the same kind of person anymore. She isn't going to help me find myself again. The only thing she's going to do for me now is take all my free drinks from guys if we ever go out together.

The walk back to the hotel is peaceful, but I know what's waiting for me there, so the peace doesn't last long. Alejandro narrows his eyes at me when I walk into the lobby, but I don't care. There's not much more he can do to me now.

Brandon meets me at my door and smiles. "Took you long enough."

I snort. "Did you ever even leave the area?"

I turn the door handle but the keycard doesn't work; my face flushes with embarrassment. I start to panic when I can't get in a second time. "Everything I have left is in that room," I choke out. Tears sting the corners of my eyes. "I *have* to get in there."

He watches me with sad, deep hazel eyes. "I paid the outstanding balance on the room and bribed the concierge another hundred to let us get inside one more time." He holds out a new keycard and slides it between my fingers. I grip it tightly, not understanding anything I'm feeling right now.

The new card works and we open the door; my things have been untouched, and I breathe a sigh of relief. When he shuts the door, my phone dings in my pocket.

LUCY

Thanks for catching up! We'll do it again…soon.

I read the message and feel pain in my chest.

Jealousy.

Motivation.

Something like that.

Brandon sits on the white loveseat in my room as I pace back and forth in front of him. I still have the last two pieces of my life stashed in my pocket; I'm hoping that Brandon's offer is real and I won't have to sell them.

"Can you sit the hell down?" he says. "You're making me nervous." I instantly park myself in the matching armchair across from him. I cross my legs and his eyes are hungry as he watches my bare skin where my capris ride up. "So, what's your answer?" His voice is softer now, like someone is listening in on us. My mind races when his dark eyes meet mine and his lips turn up into a wicked smile.

"If you're sure it's okay…I'll take you up on your offer," I tell him. "But I'm not exchanging sex for a free room, if that's what you're thinking."

His laugh is smooth and intoxicating. I've never met anyone quite like Brandon before—his presence is just so demanding and controlling that it sets me on fire. Not to mention, he dresses like he owns a yacht or something. He crosses his long legs. "That thought never crossed my mind. I don't want sex in exchange for kindness. I can get sex anywhere I want."

I scoff. "Oh, really?"

He nods. "I can get people to move your stuff, if you don't want to do it."

"I'll *definitely* take you up on that."

Brandon snickers. "They aren't so much movers as eager law interns."

I blush in embarrassment. I don't have much left other than what's in my pocket and littered around the room. Brandon takes my hand, pulls me out of the room, and into the elevator; with his free hand, he's texting someone on his phone. Once his attention returns to me, he squeezes my hand like Ollie used to do when we first started dating.

At the beginning of our relationship, Ollie and I were so *vanilla* that people couldn't even stand to be near us when we were together. He gave me everything I ever wanted, and I basked in it until it became a game to me. Then suddenly, I found myself competing for his attention after his grandfather died—with all the business he had to finish up in New York, I wasn't number one anymore.

My sister, Kate, and her husband, Chris, came into town for some sort of convention and stayed with me while they visited. On the second day, Kate made plans to meet up with some of her new friends, leaving Chris to wander alone by himself in a city he didn't know.

We stayed in, downed an expensive bottle of scotch, and…well, one thing led to another. Oliver got home early, found us, and called my sister to come back to our apartment for a "surprise."

Days after he caught me in bed with Chris and I was packing my things to leave, I found the diamond engagement ring in Oliver's drawer, and the rest of my world crumbled. Not only had I hurt both Ollie and my sister, but I'd also lost my one chance at ever being his wife.

He'll never speak to me again, let alone ask me to marry him.

That's Julie's place now.

For a brief moment, I think of trying to be nice to Ollie. I think about calling Julie and trying to fix things with her, but honestly...I don't even have much good karma saved up yet. The more I look at Brandon and the darkness looming over him, the less I care about Ollie. I have a burning feeling that he needs me, somehow. He wants the same kind of love that I want.

Ever-lasting.

Like wildfire, spreading so quickly that it catches both people up in flames before they even know what's hit them. That kind of love.

Brandon seems just as messed up as I am, though. Would us as a couple just make things worse?

He notices me staring at him and corners me in the elevator, the wicked smile on his lips again. "You're gorgeous." His lips graze mine, and his mint toothpaste makes me dizzy. "I'll never let you forget that."

My legs are jelly as I try to resist him. I fake a snort and push him away, making sure I touch his chest and feel the warmth that I've missed having next to me. I bite my lower lip so he can see it. "I think you're just a little too wound up for me right now," I whisper, backing away a few steps. "Maybe I should just go back to my room."

I smile at my play in our little cat-and-mouse game. When the elevator opens, he grabs my hand again and drags me through the lobby and into the cold, late September air. My lungs expand a few times, trying to catch my breath from his brisk tug-a-long when he catches my eye. The smile he throws at me is gentle now, and I feel like it's just for me.

A flash of hope floods my veins.

I can forget everything and start anew with Brandon. I can be a better girlfriend, a better person.

"Get in," he says, opening the passenger door of his black Audi for me. "Let's get away from here." I do what he says and he shuts the door behind me, locking me inside. There's no going back from here as he jumps in next to me and speeds off before I even get my seatbelt on. The coldness in his eyes returns as he looks around the streets and weaves in and out of traffic.

He is *really* scary sometimes.

"So…" He clears his throat and looks over at me. "Are you planning on getting a job?"

I laugh. "I definitely need one, but I'm not sure what I'd be good at."

"You've never had a job, have you?"

"Yes, I worked when I lived with my parents in Georgia. I went to college for a few years, before Ollie—"

He growls. "Don't say his fucking name."

As we start to get into the higher-end section of Rockford with its townhouses and condos, the air thins in the car. He pulls into a driveway and turns the car off, looking over at me. "I don't like that asshole...just don't say his name around me." He clears his throat. "What did you go to college for?"

"I hadn't decided yet at the time."

He snorts. "Well, not much around Rockford except retail."

I wrinkle my nose. "I'm not a minimum wage type of person."

"You are if you don't have any wages at all, Princess."

He gets out of the car, walks around to pull me out, and drags me into his townhouse. He looks around. "This is it." He blushes. "Sorry for the mess. Your room is that one." He points to an open door to our right. "You can put your stuff down before the rest of the tour."

I hesitate but enter the doorway of the room. Brandon squeezes my ass as I pass him. I glare at him. "Unwanted contact."

He winks and shakes his head, his dark hair shimmering in the light. "Lies," he hisses, and it sends electric jolts through my body. I follow him through the house as he points out where things are, and when we return to my room, I really notice it.

Purple.

Everything is purple.

I *hate* purple.

"Uh, yeah sorry about the purple. I hope you like it —I didn't have much notice to change it, really." He blushes again. All I can do is stand in place and look around. I haven't felt anything like this lately—feeling so...*wanted*.

Oliver used to treat me this way in the beginning of our relationship too. He would make me feel like I was the only girl in the world. To him, I *was* the only girl in the world. I try and shake him from my head; he looks at Julie like that now.

Brandon's dark eyes are full of confusion as he watches me try and drain my sorrow. "Let me ask you something." His smoky voice closes in on me. "Do you think two people like us can ever find honest-to-god love?"

"I hope so." I sigh. "It seems like bad things we've done in the past always haunt us, huh?"

I step into my purple bedroom. The air around my body changes as he follows me; it becomes thicker with frustration and tugs at my skin. "We should talk about that sometime—" his breath is on my neck, "—the bad things we've done. Maybe we can find some common ground in each other." He presses himself against my ass for a few seconds. "Come and find me when you're ready for dinner—I'll order in. Get used to your room. The interns will be here any minute to drop off your stuff."

I snort. "You must be something special if you have those fancy suits and interns fawning at your feet."

He shrugs, trying to hide his blush. "I'm a low-man, trust me. I'm just an assistant to a *really* good lawyer, that's all. Don't get me wrong, though—I've worked hard for all of this." He gestures around the room with wide circles. "I make good mon—"

My lips move before I even think about it. "I don't care about that."

Did *I* really just say that?

I blush and try to change the subject. "Anyway, you didn't need to call in those guys, really. There wasn't much to pack."

He winks at me and taps the doorway. "It's time to change that."

I want to jump, scream, and cry all at once. Oliver wasn't my ticket out of that hotel after all—it's Brandon. His need to redeem himself with someone and my need to be wanted make us a perfect match. Maybe except for my smart mouth, which might get me in trouble. He has a severe need to be in control of someone other than himself. I don't mind it, as long as it means that I get to live without looking over my shoulder again.

The deep purple quilt on the bed is soft underneath me as I lie back and run my fingers over the silk sheets. I smile and take in a deep breath.

Then I think about Ollie. My smile fades and I frown. I have to make things right with him and Julie— I need that weight lifted off my shoulders.

Making amends is the first rule of changing yourself for the better, right?

Taking out my phone, I text Nora, asking for Julie's number. I add that I want to apologize and send a smiley face just in case she doesn't take me seriously. There's a huge chance that she won't even care to answer me, but the phone chimes and her name is there. She gives me the number alongside a middle finger emoji, and it makes me smile. At least she's answering my text messages. I dial Julie's number and it rings several times; on the fifth ring, she picks up.

"Hello?" Her voice shakes.

I should have rehearsed something nice.

"Don't hang up," I start pleading with her. "It's Heather."

"What the hell do you want?"

I want to bitch her out, but I'm hopefully going to undo some bad karma by talking to her so I decide against it. I bite my lip so hard I pierce the flesh. "I'm calling to talk to you about Oliver. Is this a good time?"

She starts to sob into the phone, barely catching her breath. "What did you *do* to him?" she screams into my ear. "Why can't you leave us alone, you crazy psycho?" Her cries deafen me, and I try to cut in between each sob.

"I have no clue what you're talking about," I say. "What is wrong with you?"

She hangs up on me.

"So much for that," I say. "I guess she hates me too."

"She doesn't hate you," Brandon says from the open doorway as young, nerdy guys bring in the boxes from my room. When they leave, his eyes find mine and his wicked smile returns. "She doesn't even hate me, and I cheated on her." His chin tilts toward the floor and his gaze drops. "And did other things I'm not fucking proud of. She's basically Mother Theresa. She sees good in anyone. She was the first person to believe in me when I needed it the most."

My jaw drops. "Have you been in contact with her?"

He shakes his head. "She won't answer my calls."

"Sounds like she hates you, then."

He laughs and crosses his arms over his chest. "She's busy fucking your ex. She doesn't hate me." He saunters toward me. I want to pull him against me and let him hold me, but I doubt he would even try to comfort me. "Unpack your things and I'll order Chinese takeout." He shuffles from the room with a sour look on his face.

After the last box is empty, Brandon returns and takes the stack of cardboard to the front door. "Come and eat with me," he demands. "Please."

For a long few minutes, we fill our plates with the food and I stare down at it with distaste. I hate eating things that burn if they come back up; that's something I can't let Brandon see or hear, either. I have this weird quirk when I get too nervous—I can't manage to keep anything down. I sip on a small bowl of hot and sour soup while his gaze wanders over my body. "So now that you're unpacked, what do you need?"

I lick the soup from my lips and his wicked smile brightens. "A laptop, probably a new phone, some clothes and makeup—"

He holds up his hand. "Just write it down and I'll make sure you get them."

He doesn't say another word to me through the entire meal. Earlier I'd had the feeling that things were all going to be okay for once…and now he showers me with silence.

I excuse myself and sneak into the bathroom to shower quickly before Brandon can just burst in uninvited. I curse myself for not bringing clothes, so after I finish I wrap myself in a towel and run across the hall into my room. I find some pajama pants and a tank top, not bothering with a bra, before climbing into the soft bed. Something eats at my insides as I lie in the dimly lit room.

I let my mind wander.

When Oliver and I first met.

Our first date.

First kiss.

First...*everything*.

I hear Brandon walking around in the hallway and he opens my door to peek his head inside. "Everything okay in here?" he whispers, and I blink into the rapidly darkening room. I wait a few seconds and hold my breath. "Heather?"

"Can you sleep next to me?" I blurt. "It would make me feel better if you did."

He rubs his chin and thinks for a few seconds. "Are you sure that's a good idea?" He walks toward the bed and sits down next to me. His eyes are concerned and brighter than usual. He folds the quilt back and slides in next to me, letting his body relax next to mine. "Is this okay?" His breathing is rough; his nervousness bleeds into the air.

I smile and inch closer to him. "Yes, much better. Thank you."

He's changed into a t-shirt and sweatpants. The soft, worn fabric feels nice between my fingers.

I know it won't be the same as it was with Oliver... but it can be better if I play it right. I'm not the same person I was years ago—I've changed so much that I don't even remember that girl.

I don't *want* to remember that girl.

My mind wanders back to Oliver and I try to pinpoint when his feelings for me changed. He treated me like arm candy when we met, glitzing me up and showing me off to anyone that would indulge him. He made me break out of my Southern belle shell and I became what I thought he wanted me to be.

And look at me now.

It's me that's changed—I can't deny that. I *allowed* myself to become someone else. It's not Oliver's fault anymore, and I know it deep down inside.

It's going to take a long time to get over Ollie completely—I know that too.

But you know what they say: The best way to get over someone…

…is get under someone else.

NINE
OLIVER

RAIN.

I feel it soaking my hair…at least I think it's the rain that's matted it to my forehead. My clothes are soaked through to my skin; the fabric of my jeans and t-shirt is ripped and my skin burns from the water on my open wounds.

I smell the gasoline pooling around me.

I'm hanging upside down—being held in by only my seatbelt.

The groan that escapes me is horrible; I see a pair of legs run up to the window and kneel on the pavement so the person can get a better look at the tangled mess inside. "Hold on there, man…we called for help!" a man screams at me. "You're lucky to be alive right now…that other guy—"

Julie.

I think about her soft, honey blonde hair.

She smells like strawberries and everything I could ever want from love.

She's all I think about. Now I might not be able to ever see her again.

Or feel her warm skin against mine.

Listen to her laugh.

See her big, blue eyes burn into mine.

My limbs are betraying me—they got disconnected from my mind during the crash. I'm so tired that I close my eyes and drift off, unaware of the tragic scene outside the Jeep. The broken pieces of the other people involved and the cries of their families.

I have no one here.

Am I dead?

————

I CAN HEAR Julie humming and sunlight seeps through my eyelids. When I open my eyes, the sunlight is pouring into the open windows of our new house. I smell her strawberry shampoo and smile. Her naked body stretches next to mine and she moans and opens her eyes to look at me.

I pull her closer against my own naked body and she smiles.

"Good morning, sunshine," I whisper to her.

She lifts her body up a little to find my lips and graze hers against them.

I want to fucking cry.

Is this the way it's going to be now?

I can't die. I have to go to her.

I need more time.

————

Rain.

I force my eyes open and see the blood.

My blood.

It's everywhere; I don't know what parts of me it's coming from, but it surrounds me, pooling in thick, red puddles.

"I have more people hurt over here!" someone screams.

"Please, *please* help us!"

"I didn't see him—I *swear* I didn't see him until it was too late. You gotta believe me. I wasn't trying to run off, man!"

"Just fucking *call* someone!"

I can't focus. I can tell that I'm upside-down still, and there are pieces of the Jeep lying around the pavement outside. People are still screaming and I hear sirens getting closer, but I just want them to take me to Julie—load me up in the back of an ambulance and take me to her before I die.

I'm fading. I can *feel* it.

"Hey, stay with me." I hear Julie's voice. I move my neck as much as I can to try and see her, but she isn't there. I know she isn't there. *"I love you,"* I hear her whisper, and the world gets black again for a few seconds.

I wake up to the sound of a machine cutting the door of the Jeep off. Several hands reach in to pull me out, but they all fail. "He's strapped in!" someone yells, and he kneels down to look at me. It's a different man than before.

He looks worried. "Hey, man...can you hear me?

The car is overturned. You've been in an accident. What's your name?"

My mouth doesn't work.

My eyes barely work.

My heart doesn't even feel like it's working.

The man nods as if I'm actually answering him; he's trying to get me to focus on him rather than what he's doing to me. I can feel him cutting through the seatbelt and he places an arm around my torso so I won't fall and crack my head open more than it already is.

Pain.

I scream so loud that it hurts my own ears.

"I'm sorry, I'm sorry...look," the man says and holds up his hands. "I have to finish cutting off the seatbelt to get you free."

I grunt in approval.

Just get me out of here and take me to Julie.

He cuts through the seatbelt and my body falls. I hit my head against the hard surface despite his valiant effort to soften the blow.

Darkness.

———

"HEY, COME HERE," Julie says as she pops back into my head. I run to her and scoop her up into my arms; I can literally feel her warm, soft skin on mine. I squeeze her with no intentions of ever letting her go. "Come on, it'll be okay." She coos and strokes my head. "You just have to wake up."

I make a promise to myself right then. If I somehow make it out of this alive...I'm going to start following the rules again. It doesn't matter how many rules I've broken; this rule can't be shattered like the first.

I can't take life for granted anymore now that I'm fighting for my own.

I can't take Julie for granted anymore, because now look at me: I may never see her again.

I can't take myself for granted anymore; I have to be a better person than I have been.

When I wake up, I'm grabbing Julie and never letting her go. We'll live a long life full of excitement and fun—no more arguing and pissing each other off out of spite. We know we will run back to each other. It's an unspoken agreement between us.

Does she know what happened? I think about her alone in the darkness, crying when she finds out I died and she didn't get to say goodbye.

Or, "I love you."

She is going to kill me herself if she can't say goodbye.

I think about who will comfort her.

Harley.

Casey.

Brandon.

Each person I think about pisses me off more.

I have to stay alive.

———

"WE HAVE to get him outta there!" a man screams, and the loud machine takes off the other door at my feet. "Get the damn crowd back! Is he alive?" He screams louder and several people are crying outside of the Jeep. I wonder if Julie is out there, waiting to see my mangled body for confirmation that it's all over. "I said, get that crowd back!"

Fire.

I smell fire.

"Shit, the hood's smoking! Put that fucking fire out!"

"Get him out of there...*now*!"

"Grab his shoulders and pull his ass out! I don't care if you have to force him! It's about to go up in flames!"

"Hey, buddy, can you hear me?"

My eyes flutter and open enough for me to see him. I feel a rush of adrenaline from something that's injected into my leg, and suddenly I'm alert and aware.

"Julie," I croak out. My mouth is dry. "I need Julie."

My body *hurts*.

My heart feels like a thousand needles are being jabbed into it.

I can't even feel my legs.

I definitely know several bones in my body are broken.

The man tugs me harder and I feel myself slide against some broken glass on the pavement, slicing through what's left of my skin. The engine of the Jeep is on fire and several firefighters are putting it out. I manage to pry my eyes open a little wider to watch two paramedics scramble toward me and start working on my wounds. One of them holds a flashlight to my eyes, making me shut them tightly so I can just listen.

"He's about to go into cardiac arrest. Where's his wallet?"

"I'll look for ID. Was there anyone else in the car?"

"No, just him. He's lost a lot of blood."

"Here, I found his wallet."

"Good, that's more than we usually find."

"He can't breathe—lift him up!"

"Get him, get him! We're losing him!"

———

Strawberries.

We sit on the golden chaise in her library at the cabin, in front of the huge window that looks across the lake. It's springtime because the lake is calm and no one is buzzing around on speed boats or jet skis. Julie brushes her hair from her face and her big eyes capture me. I kiss her nose to make her smile.

I love her fucking smile.

"I want to stay here forever." I pull her as close to me as I possibly can without suffocating her. "I never want you away from me again. I can't take it when you're upset with me, and now look—I could die and you'll have to live with the memory of me forever."

Julie giggles and her sunshine fills my head. "If we stay here forever, you'll get tired of the same things every day, over and over."

"It's not possible to get tired of you...I'm addicted to you in every way imaginable. You were made for me, Julie. I loved you before I even met you, and there's nothing you can do to make me not love you."

"I will love you forever," she whispers, but I can't see her anymore.

———

Slam.

The paramedics toss me into the back of their bus with only a little bit of care. I feel it start zooming through the still slippery streets; they're working on my body as much as they can, assessing the injuries out loud.

"Jesus, there's so much fucking blood."

"Here, get this IV in him. He'll need an infusion, I'm sure."

They stick a needle into my arm, but I can barely feel anything at this point, so it only stings a little.

"Shit, he's messed up. Just from what I can see…he's got a broken leg, some broken fingers, several deep contusions to his legs and middle torso and cuts on his face…"

"There's no telling what damage has been done on the inside."

"Right…I can see he's got a few broken ribs, but I don't want to press down in case of any internal bleeding."

"That seatbelt saved him from being thrown out of the front window for sure."

I feel the drugs kick in from the IV. Everything goes numb.

"Don't worry, we're almost to the hospital. You have a fighting chance."

Liars.

I feel like death.

"You got his ID, right?"

"Yeah, here. Oliver Jackson, twenty-five. Got his phone for next of kin too."

Next of kin.

My heart races and I panic. They only want your

next of kin when they know something they aren't telling you. They know I'm not going to make it. My heart starts burning like a flame has been shoved into my chest. I scream loud in pain as one of them holds me down; I hear a monitor beeping quickly and then slowing way down.

"His heart's failing!"

"Get the paddles!"

They shock me four times and the monitor's beeps stabilize. I can't scream anymore, but I really fucking want to. Someone gets on the radio, their voice frantic as my body burns and I'm trapped inside my own head.

"Bus three to base—we're in route to Rockford Memorial with a twenty-five-year-old male, victim of a motor vehicle collision. Multiple contusions, broken bones, and possible internal injuries."

I hear static. "Base to bus three, we're ready for you."

"Okay, buddy, hang in there. We're three minutes away."

"I love you, Julie." I feel my lips move, but I don't know if my words come out. Hot patches of tears form in the corners of my eyes; I can't fucking believe this is happening.

The rules.

The fucking rules.

They didn't save me from getting my heart broken.

They sure as hell didn't keep me alive, either.

I try to call out for her, but there's so much dirt and glass in my mouth that my tongue feels like sandpaper. I can't breathe; I don't even want to try. I shut my eyes tight and wait for the bus to stop. Fresh air breezes over my body, but I'm so numb that I can't move anything. A woman's voice cuts into the conversation around me, asking the paramedics questions and trying to talk to me loudly.

"Mr. Jackson? Can you hear me?" I hear electronic doors open. "My name is Dr. Johnson, you've been in an accident…can you hear me, sir?"

She reminds me of someone…I can't quite place her soothing tone of voice. I'm too out of my mind to place her in my past.

I open my eyes a little and force them to stay open so I can see what's happening.

Dr. Johnson is tall, thin, and in her forties, her white-blonde hair pulled back into a ponytail. Her smile is inviting like Julie's, and I feel like I'm going to be okay.

"Good boy, there you go." She walks closer to me. "I'm going to take good care of you, but I need your help, okay?"

How the hell can I help you? I can't even move my fucking legs.

"Julie," I groan. "I need her."

The doctor smiles. "Is she your wife?"

No, but I want her to be.

I start to cough up blood and she wipes my mouth. "My wife…Julie…" I croak.

She looks up and motions to someone outside of the room. I hear the door open and someone walks inside— a woman who talks to Dr. Johnson. I hear Julie's name being discussed. The second woman walks back out of the room and I frown.

I want to get up and walk out of here; I want to get

back into my Jeep and drive to Julie's like nothing ever happened. If I had only left a few minutes earlier, I wouldn't even be in this situation. But no...I was with another woman.

Lucy.

The monitors they're hooking up to me start rapidly beeping.

"We're losing him again!"

———

I'm asleep.

At least, I think I am.

"Oliver," Julie whispers.

Where is she? It's pitch black; I can't see her.

But I can hear her worrying.

I can smell her sweetness.

I can feel her love for me radiating through the darkness.

"You're in bad shape," she says closer to my ear. Her sadness makes it hard to concentrate. "I don't know if they're going to be able to fix you. There's more wrong with you than they are telling you about."

My stomach twists and I wince in pain. "I'll be fine. I don't want to leave you. I can't be without you—I don't want to be. Please don't leave me alone in here."

"If you don't leave me here, you will *leave me out there." I can hear her pain. "Try and fight, Oliver. You have to stay alive to see me again."*

———

I WAKE MYSELF UP, screaming in pain. I howl into the air above with fear and angst; there's someone digging around in my insides.

"He has three broken ribs and one has punctured his kidney. Did his chest get crushed?" Dr. Johnson is hovering over me again, worry in her eyes. "Let's get him to X-ray, but there's a rip in the lining of his right lung and his heart rate isn't stable. He's been into cardiac arrest twice in the field."

I wonder where Julie really is. I wonder if she knows I'm lying here—*dying*. I wonder if she will cry for me; if she'll get depressed and mourn me until she meets me wherever I end up. I can't stop thinking about what I said to her as they stick tubes down my throat and I gag. Someone lifts me off the bed a few inches so I can vomit in something; when I'm done, they act like it's nothing and continue working on me. I can feel the rest of my clothes being cut off and someone washes the blood off my skin the best they can.

Needles get poked into my veins to let magical liquid inside fill my body, and instead of wanting to thrash around, I'm now getting really fucking tired.

I think about the yellow envelope.

I wonder if the test was positive; I wonder if it'll be a boy or a girl.

Colin. I remember my dream about the small boy that looked like me.

How can you miss someone you've never met?

I want to cry, but I can't.

I should have opened that envelope. Now it's probably lost in the debris of the accident and I'll never know the results. My child—if there is one—will never know me.

I think about my father.

I'm going to die the same way he did.

My child will grow up without me.

Learn to walk without me.

Talk without me.

Laugh without me.

Learn to *love* without me.

My chest tingles and I can feel my eyelids closing on their own.

"Get some paddles—he's going into cardiac arrest again!"

"Shit, we're losing him!"

"Doctor, he's flatlining!"

"Get those damn paddles on him!"

"He's not going to make it!"

Then…nothing.

No screams.

No doctors.

No nurses.

No cabin.

No Julie.

No life.

Nothing.

Darkness.

TEN
JULIE

MY PHONE RINGS immediately after Casey puts me onto the pavement. He takes it from his pocket and hands it to me. I don't check the number—I automatically answer it. My hands are shaking so badly that I nearly drop it on the ground before I hit the answer button.

"Hello?" My voice shakes uncontrollably. I can feel the fear bubbling up in my throat.

The person on the other end hesitates, their shallow breathing floating into my ears. "Don't hang up," a woman says. "It's Heather."

"What the hell do you want?"

"I'm calling to talk to you about Oliver. Is this a good time?"

Dozens of things are swirling through my mind right now. I can't just chalk it up to coincidence that Heather would call two seconds after the nurse. I can't help myself; I lose control and start to sob into the phone. "What did you *do* to him?" My body shakes and

I raise my voice into a frantic scream. "Why can't you leave us alone, you crazy psycho?" I cry louder and she tries to talk to me through my tears.

"I have no clue what you're talking about. What is wrong with you?"

I hang up on her. I don't have time for her games. I stand still and close my eyes, hoping that it's all just a bad dream and when I open them, everything will be normal.

Casey puts his hand on my shoulder, and it pulls me back to where I need to be. I pretend that Heather didn't just call me; the more I put that out of my mind, the more I'll believe that it didn't even happen. I don't allow myself to feel bad about being mean to her.

"Julie," Casey says. "We need to go."

I have to lick my lips several times; the moisture in the air is making my mouth sticky. Or it's my anxiety. Either way, I'm glad Casey is here with me. It's nice having someone to trust when you're going through a tough time.

I rush back into the pool house and grab my new bag and tuck my wallet inside. When I meet Casey back outside, he's puzzled by how calm I seem to be.

"Okay." I breathe in slowly. "I'm ready. Let's go."

He leads me away from the pool house and to his parked car on the street. Randy runs outside to see what's going on, and Casey couldn't care less about his presence looming over us.

"Who the hell are you?" Randy demands. "Another jerk-off wanting to destroy her?"

"Calm down, man. I'm taking her to the hospital."

Randy looks me up and down. "What's wrong with you?"

There's something in his tone of voice that startles me. "Not me. O-Oliver is there."

"So, they called you." He shakes his head. "I told them not to."

The rain has stopped, and I freeze in place.

"What do you mean?" I snap at my brother, whose jaw is clenched in anguish. "What aren't you telling me?"

"I got a call back from earlier...I guess Oliver *was* mixed up in that accident."

I jump toward him, ready to start bashing in his face. Casey holds me back with all the force he can without hurting me. "What the fuck is *wrong* with you, man?" he yells at Randy as he forces me back against his body and holds me there. "That's her boyfriend! That's fucked up."

Randy's eyes catch fire. "I'm trying to protect her from assholes like you!" He lowers his voice and looks around to make sure no nosy neighbors are looking out their windows. "I've already dealt with enough drama because of morons like you. I had to peel her off a telephone pole the last time her heart got broken. Remember *that*, Julie? And now what? I saw you coming from the clinic. I know one of these idiots got you pregnant..." His voice trails off and he looks at Casey, then back at me. "Which one was it?" He points at Casey. "*You?*"

Casey's grip tightens on me. "You're *pregnant*?" he hisses in my ear. I can only see red as I turn my body and push Casey to his car; I'm furious that Randy has now become almost as bad as my parents were when it comes to loving me. Casey tucks me into the front seat and keeps an eye on Randy as he jogs over to his side of the car and gets in.

"Run away like you always do, Julie!" Randy yells as we pull away from the house.

When I can't see him anymore, I let out a long, deep breath. Casey hardly has the balls to look over at me, let alone say a single word to me right now. My anger steams the windows, so I push air in and out of my lungs as carefully as possible to calm down.

Oliver.

Is he dead or alive?

"So, your brother is pretty...fucked up." Casey clears his throat and sweetly smiles at me. He's trying to ease the tension, and I know it's not his fault that I'm angry. I'm actually glad Casey showed up when he did—I was ready to curl into a ball and let myself get lost in my own mind. He tries to speed to the hospital, but the streets are still slick; Casey is careful not to lose control of the steering. "Julie, can you talk to me?"

"I just want to get there." My voice is monotone. "I just need to see if he's alive. That's all I care about right now, Casey."

He nods and bites the inside of his cheek. "So...are you?"

My eyes find his in the darkness. "Am I, what?"

"Pregnant."

Oliver should be the first one to know that answer.

I think about the possibility of having to identify his body...I'm all the family he has left.

"Pull over," I croak. My mouth is so dry it hurts to talk. "I'm going to be sick—you have to pull over."

Casey immediately pulls the car to the side of the road and watches me leap from the already open passenger door. I stop near a dark patch of shrubs and greenery, letting out all of my anxiety at my feet. I'm so weak that I can feel my knees wobble, and then Casey's arms are behind me again, lifting me into the air and carrying me back to the car. I don't thrash around in protest—I let him buckle me back into the passenger seat and start driving again without saying a word.

"I'm here for you, Julie. I love Oliver too. He's like a brother to me. You're not alone." He runs his fingers through his sandy blond hair. "He's my best friend."

I nod. No matter what Casey says, nothing is going to make me feel better until I see life in Oliver's emerald eyes. The sadness that Casey has is wrapping around my body, squeezing and making it hard to breathe. I find his hand in the darkness and grab it, like friends are supposed to do. I want him to know that I'm here for him too.

Casey is the first to speak when he parks the car at the ER entrance. "How did our lives come to this? I mean…life gets so fucking twisted sometimes that it's hard not to fail."

I shake my head. "Honestly? I come from a messed-up family, and I thought I changed things around for myself. We keep taking things for granted because we get comfortable, but every rule is meant to be broken at some point. Plus…I just keep letting myself get into these situations that are just—"

"—Impossible," we both say at the same time.

Casey's eyes meet mine in the moonlit car and our gazes lock for a few more seconds than they should.

He laughs nervously. "I think we should go inside."

"Are you sure you're okay to go in with me?" I ask him, noticing his reservation.

He swallows hard and nods. "I'm not too sure he'll be happy to see me, especially if he wakes up to me standing next to you. You know how he can get jealous over nothing, and I've already done something to him. Maybe I should stay out here and wait."

"We'll cross that bridge when we get there. I don't want to go in alone." I sigh and open the car door, letting the millions of emotions pour into the ground beneath me. They dance around my feet as if competing for who I will play with next.

The walk to the revolving ER doors seems like it takes an eternity. Each step I manage to take is like walking through quicksand; they take me further into dark thoughts the closer we get to the bright light of the waiting room. It isn't until we reach the desk that everything comes rushing back to me and I nearly lose my balance again; Casey's arm is already around my waist to hold me up.

"Can I help you?" a tired-looking nurse asks us.

I'm so numb that I can't speak.

She nods at me but speaks to Casey. "Is she okay? What does she need to be seen for?"

Casey shakes his head. Even though he's right next to me, he sounds like a million miles away. "No, we're looking for someone. She got a phone call from a nurse...Mary Callahan?" I'm surprised at how calm he is considering that his best friend could be dying in the next room. I lick my lips and prepare to speak before the nurse types on her computer and her face drains of all its color.

"Let me get in touch with Nurse Callahan. Have a seat."

"Is he dead?" I say a little too loudly before she sneaks off. "Oliver Jackson…is he dead?"

She shakes her head. "I don't know, honey. Have a seat and I'll call her to come speak to you in private."

"I don't want to have a fucking seat!" I scream.

She isn't amused. "You either have a seat or I can have someone escort you off the property. Then you'll never know your answer, will you?"

I'm about to start cussing her out when Casey laughs nervously and holds his hands up to her in defeat. He pulls me away, pushes me down in a chair, puts his arm over me like a lap bar on a rollercoaster, and glares at me. "You're going to make this shit worse if you don't calm down," he growls.

I tap my fingers on the side of the chair. "She's going to tell me that he's dead." I bite my bottom lip and look around the room, which is littered with sad people waiting for news too. "Right here in front of all of these people who don't even know him."

Casey looks sick. "I'm right here, Julie." He snakes his arm around mine and intertwines our fingers, squeezing. "You aren't alone—I told you that. I won't leave you, no matter what happens next."

Tears stream down my face as I look at him. I know his intentions aren't as pure as he's trying to make them seem. He saddens when he sees me cry, and he reaches out to wipe my tears away, but I turn away. I sob into my hands and he rubs my back in small circles, letting me know that I'm not alone. I keep my hand in his because regardless of what his intentions are, I need just about anyone within a five-foot radius to comfort me right now.

"He has no family left," I whisper to Casey. "I'm the only person he has besides you."

He smiles at me warmly. "It's a good thing we're here for him, then." I feel his warm gesture in my chest and it helps me calm down.

"You're good in a crisis." My voice is more of a whisper. "You're a really good friend…to both of us."

I see him cringe. "Let's just see how this goes and we can talk about whatever you want later, okay? I just want you to focus on Oliver."

A woman in her late-forties with short, chestnut-colored hair smiles at us and leans over from her chair a few feet away. Her smile fades when our eyes meet, but she looks over at Casey with stars in her eyes. "You are very sweet to your girlfriend," she says. Casey blushes and doesn't bother correcting her. She nods at me. "You are lucky to have such a sweet man in your life."

I let go of Casey's hand instantly. "He's just my friend."

The woman gasps. "Oh, I just assumed by the way you held his hand—"

Casey exhales loudly. "Thanks for the compliment, ma'am. Please excuse Julie—she's a little distraught right now. We're waiting to see if her actual boyfriend is alive."

The woman frowns. "I see. Well, good luck." She stands up to go sit as far away from us as she can.

Casey snickers, and it makes me a little uneasy. I appreciate what he just did, but what the hell was *that* about? I don't like random strangers knowing my business.

A hot flash of fire zips through my body.

We both look in the direction of a set of double doors opening; a woman emerges exhausted and covered in blood. My heart races when she talks to the nurse at the desk, who nods toward us. My entire body buzzes as she walks over. Her face doesn't have the glow of good news.

I don't get the glow.

I get sadness.

A face full of regret.

When she closes in on us and reaches out her hand for me to shake, Casey intercepts her and takes her hand instead. I tell myself that I'll thank him later for doing that. Oliver will be pleased with him for taking care of me when he couldn't—I'm sure of it. They'll be back to being best friends in no time. I look at the white-tiled floor and close my eyes, waiting.

"You two are here to see Mr. Jackson?" I hear her say, but I don't look at her.

"Yes," Casey answers for me. "She's his—"

"—Wife, yes." The nurse exhales deeply. Casey swallows hard, but neither of us correct her mistake about me being Oliver's wife. "I was the one who called you…I'm sorry I had to hang up. We had an emergency and I had to help."

"Okay," I mutter and keep my eyes closed.

I don't bother looking at her—I know what she's come to tell me.

"Do you want to see him?" she asks, annoyance in her voice.

My eyes open and I make myself look at her this time. "In the morgue?"

She isn't impressed with my attitude. "I think you'd better come with me." She leads us back toward the doors she'd just emerged from. Casey pinches me to stand up and tugs me along behind him. The steel doors echo as they shut behind us.

That door.

That door is shutting me out from my old life, and my new reality is in front of me.

And I'm stuck in between.

ELEVEN
HEATHER

THIS ROOM IS SO VERY...*PURPLE.*

I like purple to an extent...but I'm going to have to change things around a little here. The bed is soft, and as I look at Brandon's long, dark eyelashes while he sleeps, I frown. All we did last night was sleep. He held me a little and pushed me away once his brain took control and remembered that I'm not the one he really wants.

While I'm in the bathroom, he gets up and disappears into the house somewhere. I hear his voice as I try to eavesdrop around the corner of the living room.

"Yeah, she's here," he says. "She didn't really put up too much of a fight. She just wants someone to take care of her like he did."

I raise my eyebrows.

"Yeah, she's coming around. I mean...she isn't Julie."

I scoff. "Really?" I whisper, hearing him shuffle his feet around like he's headed toward me. I tuck myself into a closet by the staircase and wait. When he passes me, his shadow moves through the light underneath the door and he turns on the TV in the living room.

"Hey, I'd better go. I have a feeling she's going to wake up soon."

The TV's noise grows louder and I open the closet door slowly, hoping he isn't aware that I was listening in on him. His head is turned toward the TV as he lounges on the sofa, so I smooth out my tank top and shorts and perk up my chest. I tuck my hair behind my ears and tiptoe into the living room.

"Hey, you." I draw out my words so they sound sexier. His eyes widen as I come into his view; he opens his arms to greet me and pull me into his lap. It feels nice—no matter how fake it is—to have someone treat me like this again. After Ollie kicked me out, I felt so unwanted that I actually convinced myself I didn't cheat because our relationship was basically already over.

Okay, I can finally admit it: I treated him like shit. I took him for granted.

"I woke up and you weren't there." I pout and his lips curl into a smile.

"I had every intention of making breakfast, but I had a phone call." His eyes fix onto mine and it makes me nervous; I think he knows I was listening.

I have to save myself. "I can make you breakfast, don't worry." I start to move to stand, but he clutches onto me with gentle force.

"You're not my slave," he snaps. "You don't have to take care of me."

My stomach grumbles. "I'm hungry," I say. "Don't read too much into it."

His laugh pierces my stomach more. "Sit down for a minute." He laughs more when my eyes squint in annoyance at him. "Please?"

I cross my arms and sit down next to him. "What? I really *am* hungry."

"You can make breakfast in a minute. I want you to understand something before we go any further with… whatever it is we're doing here."

I nod. "Agreed…"

"So, Julie and I met in high school when we were freshmen. We didn't start dating until our senior year… she saved me from a bad, bad life. My parents were drug addicts—" His mouth tenses for a few seconds as he remembers his past. "—and just not very good people. Julie's parents weren't good people either, so we bonded over that. She helped me in so many ways… I would be lying if I told you I never loved her."

I click my tongue. "Why are you telling me this? I don't want to hear about her, just like you don't want to hear about Oliver."

His lips thin. "You need to hear this. Julie was everything to me, and it consumed me so much that I kept her hidden. I wanted her to belong to me and no one else. I didn't let her have many friends…I stopped taking her out in public."

He looks at me like he can tell I'm thinking something petty, but he continues. "There will never be a day where I won't be in love with Julie, just know that. She saved my life and I destroyed hers in return. I'll never forgive myself for that, but I can change myself. I can start something new with someone and be a better person. I'd like that person to be you."

My eyes lock onto his. "*Me*?"

"You."

I inch away from him on the sofa. "You don't even know me."

"Let's change that." He turns to face me and scoots forward, forcing our legs to touch and making me weak. "Let's be honest with each other. What were things like between you and Oliver?"

I shake my head. "I'm not talking about that. Just because you're honest and open doesn't mean I want to be."

He holds up his hands in defeat. "Okay, I won't push you. But if you want a relationship with me, you're going to tell me sometime. It's what normal people do—they share things with each other."

I groan. "*Fine.* Ollie and I met when I was a sophomore in college and he was a senior. I grew up poor and it was like a fairy tale. My rich prince had swept me off my feet, and before I knew it, I'd dropped out of school and canceled my scholarships to move here with him after he graduated."

"So, he was able to graduate and you weren't? That's pretty shitty."

My gaze falls to my lap. "Yeah, but I made the choice to drop out. I could have stayed at NYU if I wanted to."

"He should've stayed with you. That's what I would've done."

I can feel the flush in my cheeks. "Things were different back then. I was a different person. But, I *do* like the idea of us being better people. I'm actually on a good karma quest right now…I need all of it I can get."

"Same here." He smirks. "Then I guess it's you and me, beautiful."

I feel uncomfortable talking about myself; no one has asked me any real questions about my life for years. No one ever seemed to care what I thought—they just wanted my attention. Ollie especially liked showing me off to his friends and didn't mind footing the bill for manicures and clothes. "I could look at some classes at the community college and try some new things out." I can't believe what I'm saying, but it piques his interest.

"I can help you with whatever you decide."

I have to swallow the lump in my throat before I choke. Without saying anything, I stand up and rush to the kitchen, ready to make something to eat. Thank god I find some bacon in his fridge, because I haven't had any for days. I don't know how to make anything else, so I open a few cups of yogurt and spread the food out on the table. When Brandon comes in to check on my progress, his eyes twinkle with amusement but he doesn't dare laugh out loud.

I blush and look at the food. "I don't eat much."

He grunts. "I guess maybe I need to do some shopping if *this* is what you came up with."

After a few seconds of awkward silence, he sits at the table and we eat the bacon and yogurt without speaking. His lips turn into a grin and he licks the bacon grease from them, smiling at me wider. I giggle and hand him a napkin, but instead he tugs me off my chair and into his lap.

"Let me down, let me down!" I squeak and playfully

smack his arms. He lets me go and places me back in my own chair, laughing. I haven't been flirted with in so long that I nearly missed the cues he was giving me. The wide-eyed, cheerful look on his face makes me smile the most genuine smile I've had in months. We continue to eat in happy silence, every few minutes grinning at each other around our full mouths.

He collects our dishes and puts them in the sink, then downs a glass of orange juice. He looks like his movements are thought-out and pre-planned, like he has to tell himself who he is before doing anything. He isn't muscular like Ollie, but he's not so bad. His dark hair is shining with pomade and he's just ruggedly manicured enough it can't be natural. While Ollie's lips are full, Brandon's are thinner and more serious-looking —except when he uses his wicked smile.

"I have to run out for a while…will you be okay here alone?"

I scoff. "I'll be fine. I'm a big girl."

He smiles and rubs his chin. "Not really—you could stand to eat a few cheeseburgers and not throw them back up." He notices the horrified look on my face and shakes his head. "I heard you when we first met, in the hotel room. Don't let me hear it again." His eyes are shadowed now…and scary.

I open my mouth but don't say anything. I don't want to argue with him, so I let him feel superior for a few minutes as he pulls out his keys and leaves without so much as a goodbye. It's not like he'd believe me about my nervous stomach even if I told him. I rush to the living room window and watch him leave, not really caring that he's left me here alone.

I want to snoop anyways.

His bedroom is the farthest room away from mine, and I want to start there. There's nothing out of the ordinary; his bed sits in the middle, a desk and chair pushed against one wall and a long dresser against another. The door leading to the master bathroom is open, so I peek inside and find nothing of interest in there, either.

There's no evidence of Julie anywhere.

"Well, he must have gotten rid of all things Julie," I tell myself out loud. When I see the closed door across the hall, I walk over and turn the doorknob, but it's locked. I remember seeing a few small keys on his dresser, so I grab them and try them out. The third one opens the door, and I get an eerie feeling in my stomach because I know I shouldn't be in here. I turn on the light anyway and see dozens of brown moving boxes lined up in rows around the room.

This is his life with Julie.

A whole life packed away in dozens of boxes.

I tear open the first box I reach and sift through its contents. I pull out pictures of various trips and outings —most with Julie and Brandon from years ago. I hear a noise downstairs, so I snatch a stack of photos and pocket them, close the door, and lock it back up. I almost forget to put the keys back on his dresser and race downstairs to find out that Brandon isn't home after all.

I take the pictures from my pocket and sit on my bed. In each picture, they're really close and almost always kissing. He smiled during their kisses, though… that was captured on film and guys don't just do that with someone they aren't in love with. As I get deeper in the stack, the pictures turn to Julie doing mundane things like laughing or washing the dishes. The last picture is Julie smiling and flipping the bird to the camera, and it makes me laugh a little.

I could probably like Julie if I hadn't already burnt that bridge. She made that pretty clear when she hung up on me.

I stash the pictures in my underwear drawer and sit back down on the bed, looking around the room once more. I really hope all of this purple doesn't make me vomit.

The pictures of Brandon *kissing her* make me want to vomit.

I have to make him forget about her.

This isn't about getting Ollie back anymore—this is about getting the life that was meant for me to begin with. Brandon is messed up, sure, but I'm messed up too. We've never followed the rules and look where it's gotten us. Although, following the rules never appealed much to me anyway.

My phone buzzes.

LUCY

Hey! The Tavern tonight? Are you sure you don't want to come?

I smile at her offer.

No, thanks. I'm rearranging a hideous room. Have a good time and talk to a hottie for me!

I send her a smiley face and put the phone down. It

actually turns out not to be such a bad idea to move some things around and do a little online shopping from my phone. I save several items to my cart; I'll wait to pay for them until Brandon comes back.

Lucy doesn't bother answering my text, and I don't blame her. We just aren't compatible as friends anymore.

I'm changing—things for me are changing. I just need to keep doing good things to keep up the good luck. I'm tired of messing things up for myself, and since I have no friends—or family—left to help me with my down-and-out luck...

...Brandon is my new best friend, boyfriend, and family wrapped up in one tight pair of black dress slacks.

TWELVE
OLIVER

BEEP.

Beep.

Beep.

Am I dead?

I'm not fucking sure.

Are my eyes open?

I can't see anything.

But...I can *hear* everything around me.

"Did you contact his wife?" I hear Dr. Johnson ask someone. I command my brain to tell my fingers to move...but nothing happens.

"Yes, but then Mr. Akers coded so I had to hang up with her. I told her who I was and where I was calling from, so I'm sure she'll be here soon."

"Make sure you follow up on that—he will need her here."

This is it?

I think of all the shit I've been through in my life: my drug-addicted mother, my father dying when I was a teenager, my grandfather dying a few years later. Heather—the worst thing that ever happened to me—and Julie...the best thing that's ever happened to me. Someone's playing a sick joke on me, letting me find her and then ripping her away from me like this.

"Well, he's stable enough for now, but she better get here soon. He might not make it through the night. The damage to his lung isn't operable...at least not by anyone qualified enough here."

Dammit fingers, move!

Julie will tell them to get someone to help me.

The voices are gone. I'm alone and I don't fucking like it. I can feel the cold but nothing else; the air just feels so...*sterile*. This isn't supposed to happen to me. I'm supposed to live a long and happy life and now that I have Julie...things were supposed to start getting even better.

The baby.

I'll never know if there's a baby now.

I want to thrash around in the bed; I want to cry and scream, but—

Am I even in a bed?

It feels like days since someone has been here with me; the voices were the only things letting me know for sure that I'm not dead. I wish I could've felt whatever they were doing to me when they spoke about it, putting tubes and needles in places every few minutes.

Beep.

Beep.

Beep.

I hear her voice again, the second familiar one.

"Now, we have him stable enough, but he isn't responsive."

I can feel her.

I can feel you, Julie!

I feel her rush to my side and whisper into my ear, "I thought you were dead."

I'm not dead, I'm just not exactly alive.

Are you pregnant?

I love you.

Don't forget me.

Nothing comes out.

I can't even open my eyes to see her.

"What are his injuries?"

Wait. Who is that? Is that Casey?

My mind races and I start to get angry because they've come together.

What are they fucking doing together?

"And who are you?"

He clears his throat to answer, but Julie gets there first. "He's with me."

Beep. Beep. Beep. Beep. Beep.

"Okay, I think you two better step outside."

Not her! She stays!

"I'm not going anywhere. Casey, can you step out?"

My entire body blazes with fire. I want to fucking feel her touch. I swear that if I ever wake up, I will never take her for granted again. I'll follow the fucking rules—I'll be the perfect picture of a man she deserves.

"So, how bad is he?" Julie asks the second voice.

"Broken ribs, right leg is broken, but the biggest issues are the rips to his lungs and kidneys."

"Is he going to be okay?"

Second voice doesn't answer her.

Answer her, dammit!

"It's too early to tell, but we can't find anyone qualified enough to repair his lung. It takes a special surgeon—"

"Do it. Find them." Julie's voice is dark and strained.

I fucking love you, Julie.

You are everything I ever want in life.

"That could take some time," second voice huffs.

Julie sighs and her voice gets angry. "You said yourself that he doesn't have a lot of time. So maybe go find that surgeon and get him here instead of arguing with me? I will pay whatever it takes."

"Miss, with all due respect—"

I hear the growl in Julie's voice. "*Now.*"

I love you so, so fucking much right now.

The second voice leaves the room and I hear the door close behind her. Julie is inches from me and I scream inside my head just to wake up and see her.

"Can you hear me?" Her voice is now soft and scared. She cries but I can't do anything to comfort her and it makes me angrier. "Oliver, can you hear me? If you can hear me, squeeze my hand, okay?"

I want to squeeze her damn hand so badly it kills me inside.

She sobs a little harder and I can't do anything.

Oh, Julie.

My Julie.

"You have to wake up," she says in between sobs. "You have to wake up so we can put all this bad stuff behind us and live our lives. I can't even breathe without you—"

I want to smile.

The second voice returns. "Mrs. Jackson?"

It takes Julie a minute to remember who she said she was. "Yes?" I can feel her sunshine rush through my body and I welcome the warmth. "Is there something wrong?"

"No, we've found a doctor in Virginia that can repair his lung. He can fly out in a few hours and do surgery first thing in the morning."

Julie's breath quickens. "Will he make it through the night?"

"That's the best we can do. Should I have him catch a flight?"

"Yes, get him here," Julie demands. She doesn't hesitate or ask how much money it will be. I love her more in this moment than I ever have before. She isn't the quiet, docile Julie I met months ago anymore...she's changed.

She's my perfect match.

I can't leave her now...I just can't.

———

A MOVIE PLAYS *in my head as I feel cold again.*

I see my mother and Mac screwing on my parents' bed, and Mac chasing me down the hall when I catch them. I see him beating the shit out of me—a scared little five-year-old boy.

"You've fucked things up for me for the last time, you little shit!" my mother screams.

The front door slams as they leave. I hear a car engine start and they peel out of the driveway before I even feel safe enough to pull myself out of the fetal position and creep to the window.

They are actually gone.

Not standing outside, smoking.

Gone.

I hold my sides and cry. I hurt all over from where Mac kicked me. The walk into the kitchen seems longer than it should; I reach for the telephone on the wall and look at it with sadness. At five years old, I'm fragile and small...and now alone.

I dial the number that Daddy had given me for emergencies.

A woman answers. "Hello?" Her voice is raspy and low.

I don't know what to say. "I'm calling because my daddy said to."

The woman chuckles. "Is this Oliver?"

"Yes, this is Oliver," I say, but I have to sit down on the cold, brown-tiled kitchen floor because my sides hurt so bad that I can't breathe. "I need help."

"I'll send help to you. What happened?"

I cry out in pain as the woman yells for me on the other end. "My sides hurt; the man that was here with my mommy kicked me."

She gasps. "Are they still there?"

"No," I say, and the world gets fuzzy around me. "I don't feel very good."

The world goes dark.

I think I must be dead.

I wake up to a middle-aged woman hovering over me. She sees my eyes open and kneels down to cradle me as if she brought me back to life herself. She makes a shushing sound and holds me close, patting my head. "It will be okay. There's a doctor on his way and your dad is on his way home, okay?"

I look up at her; she comforts me. "When will he be here?"

"Soon—he's on his way." She brushes my hair back. "My name is Mrs. Atchley, and I'll be taking care of you when your Dad's away from now on...would that be okay?"

I don't remember what I tell her before passing out again.

———

"Is he alive? What just happened?" Julie's frantic voice comes into my mind. Now there are too many voices around me to tell who they are. Through the others, her voice fades away and I can't even open my eyes to see her one last time. I'm so pissed that I want to kill every single voice in that room so I can hear hers. As they all shout around me, Julie's warmth fades and the chill of death attacks me again.

"Get those chest paddles, he's—"

"Ma'am, you need to leave the room!"

"What the hell is happening? Casey, *don't*! I want to be here!"

"You gotta leave, Julie..."

"Get her out of here!"

"No, *no*! Don't touch me, Casey!"

———

The sunlight hits my skin and I feel peace for the first time in a long time. I'm stupid enough to think that if I open my eyes, I won't be dead.

I am so fucking dead.

134

"Hey kid, open your eyes."

Dad?

"Hey, back up, son. I can't throw you the ball when you're five feet from me, can I?" His laugh makes all the air leave my lungs. As I stand in front of him, it's like looking into a mirror. There's no fucking way he isn't my father. His dark, shaggy hair falls in his eyes as he looks down at me; I hold out my hands and I have kid-sized arms and hands.

"Oliver, go long!" He laughs again and starts slowly backing down the plush, green lawn of the house we moved to after my mother left. He moved us to a gated suburb outside of Rockford so she couldn't find us. I know the real reason he stays so close: He will always love her.

I skip the opposite way from him and see someone's reflection in the kitchen windows who's trying to stay hidden. When I lock eyes with her…she vanishes.

My father says my name and I turn around, catching the ball. "Good job, Oliver!" He jumps and throws his hands into the air. "You did it!"

He's proud of me.

I smile.

Who was that woman? I don't remember seeing her before.

———

Beep.

Beep.

Beep.

"Hey, are you still with me?" Julie says, and I feel nothing. I don't know if she's taken my hand into hers, if she's kissed my cheek, or if she's even close enough to touch me. I can't feel anything except the annoying chill surrounding my body. "Is he stable now?"

The second voice returns. "For now."

Julie sighs. "Can Casey come back in now?"

"Of course, shall I get him?"

"No, I'll do it." I hear her stand up. Her voice gets closer to my ear. "I'll be right back; don't you go anywhere."

I beg my mind to let me reach out for her.

I was in perfect physical health until I broke the rules and love cracked my heart open, letting bad things inside. The monitors around me beep slowly, sometimes in sync like a song. The beeps are getting slower and slower with each minute that passes.

I'm dying a slow death.

———

"I HAVE to go out of town next week; Mrs. Atchley is going to watch you."

Dad.

I feel myself shake my head, shaggy dark hair in my eyes. "I'm almost fifteen—can't I just watch myself?" I watch him seriously think about it for a few minutes. "I mean, come on, Dad. I know how to take care of myself. When are you going to start letting me?"

He shakes his head in exhaustion and rubs the bridge of his nose. "Ollie, please. You know I can't let a fourteen-year-old run around without any adult supervision. You can stay home alone when you're seventeen."

"Seventeen?" I yell at him. "That's so fucking unfair!"

"Oliver Frankford Jackson, language!"

I feel the anger filling my chest. "Fine. When is she coming?"

"Any time now."

I throw my arms up in frustration. "Of course! Wait until the last minute to tell me like always!"

I remember this fight. This is the last time I would ever see my father alive.

I want to fucking wake up.

Right. Now.

"Okay, she's pulling up. I have to go…please mind her, okay?" His eyes meet mine and they are serious. "Need I remind you the list of things not *to do to Mrs. Atchley?"*

A laugh escapes me. "No, I still have the list you made me on my desk."

My father smiles, hiding his laughter as Mrs. Atchley comes in through the front door. She notices our exchanged smirks and frowns. "Oh Jesus, what did I walk into?"

"Okay, Ollie. I will see you in a week. Mrs. Atchley, thank you once again." He kisses her cheek and she swats him away. I want to reach out to him and beg him not to go. If I only knew I would never see him again—I would've grabbed him and made him stay.

Mrs. Atchley closes the door behind him, the heavy rain dripping from her graying hair. Loud thunder kept me up that night…I remember I wasn't able to sleep enough and fell asleep in study hall the next day.

I didn't know my father was dead until the next morning.

And it was too late to say goodbye.

———

Rain.

The face of the man I hit first is seared into my brain. I tried to pump the brakes so hard that my foot got stuck beneath the pedal after the wreck. I think hard about what happened as I hear Julie's faint breathing next to me.

Was the man alone?

I really fucking hope I didn't kill him.

I didn't see the truck push me into the intersection; I didn't see him panic and try to flee the scene, either. The machines around me beep a little faster, but I think I'm the only one who notices.

The man's face comes back into my mind.

The horror in his eyes haunts me.

Beep. Beep. Beep. Beep.

The chill has returned.

"Do you want some coffee?" I hear the second woman say. "My shift ends in a few minutes and I can get you some."

Julie sniffles close to me. "Coffee would be wonderful, thank you. It's cold in here, right?" she asks someone.

I hear someone walk away from my other side. "Let me turn up the heat for you. Is that better?"

I hear Julie move closer to my ear. "Much better, thanks."

No.

It's still freezing fucking cold.

That's my death you feel in the room, girls.

THIRTEEN
CASEY

THE WAITING room outside Oliver's room is small, but the sofa I manage to stretch out on is comfortable enough to make me try and forget why I'm here in the first place. I don't want to think about my best friend—my brother—lying in a hospital bed, dying. I think about Julie and hope she isn't hovering over him, crying her eyes out.

All I want is for someone to love me like Julie loves Oliver.

He's going to kill me when he wakes up. I know he'll be pissed about me going to her house; he's going to read too much into it and blow his top. Ever since she invited me to stay for dinner the other night, I know he's seen the envious way I've been looking at her.

I think about Julie and how suffocating it must feel to see someone you love, but not be able to talk to them. I know we had a moment in the car, but I can't allow myself to think about that right now. I've been like this forever; I always want what Oliver has.

Money.

Girls.

Popularity.

Charm.

Good looks.

Heather jumped at the chance to betray her new boyfriend.

Julie isn't like that.

I'm able to snuggle into the sofa and a tall, tired-looking nurse brings me a pillow and a blanket. I smile at her and she lets me doze off for a few minutes. I don't sleep long until I hear the nurse come back and shake a bag of chocolate chip cookies and a small can of lemon-lime soda at me. "You remind me of my son. Are you waiting for someone?"

I tear into the cookies. "My friend is in that room." I point to Oliver's door. The woman's eyes light up in intrigue and her familiar-looking green eyes peer into mine.

"Oh, Oliver Jackson." Her voice is like razors on my skin. "That poor boy. It's a shame what happened to him, isn't it?"

I open my mouth to speak, but she shoves more snacks and soda into my lap. "You might be here a while." She flutters her faint eyelashes at me. "Don't mention where you got those, okay?" I'm trying to place her in my mind; she doesn't look like a normal nurse. Her skin looks rubbery and cold; the bags under her eyes are a different shade than if they were just dark from exhaustion. She smells like cigarettes and alcohol so much it makes me gag.

I know her from somewhere.

I try harder to think about where I know her from, but she walks away, her pale-yellow nurse scrubs disappearing behind a blue door. I stash the snacks, but I hear someone with a familiar voice enter the room, distracting me.

"Is he going to be okay?" Nora asks me, her gaze fixed on Oliver's door.

She can't even look at me.

I look at her, sadness between our bodies. "I don't know. Julie is still in there."

Nora's glowing brown skin looks so delicious that I forget she isn't mine anymore. The way she found out I cheated on her plays in my mind as she sits across from me...as far away from me as she can get. She puts her crutches next to her and sighs. A burning ball of fear sticks in my throat and I watch her try not to look over to talk to me.

"Nora—"

She shakes her head and her gold hoops jingle. "Don't you dare."

I close my mouth. I just watched whatever feelings she had left for me float into the air and vanish. We wait in silence together for over an hour before her leg starts to hurt and she texts someone and looks at the wall next to my head. She doesn't even bother saying goodbye before she leaves. I put my head back down on the pillow and try to force myself to sleep.

My life is a train wreck.

"Hey, are you awake?" I hear a soft, sweet voice gently graze my ear. It makes me feel warm inside and I snuggle into the blanket, smiling. "Casey? Hey, can you wake up?" A small body scoots mine over a little and sits next to me. Her ice-cold hand touches the bare flesh of my arm, but I don't shiver or shake her off. I welcome the cool touch on my skin and wake up with a wide smile on my face. "Casey?" Julie's voice changes and she releases me instantly.

"Oh, shit," I whisper, looking at her. "I'm sorry…I was dreaming about someone."

She blushes and lowers her blue-eyed gaze.

Oh, no.

I'm starting to like her.

This is *so* fucked up.

She brushes her hair behind her ears and the pit of my stomach tickles. Someone as gorgeous as she is shouldn't be doing that herself.

Well…she *has* someone to do it for her: Oliver.

She clears her throat and tries to lock her eyes with mine again. "Do you want to come into the room and see him?"

"Of course I do—is he okay?"

She doesn't nod or smile. "The hospital found a special surgeon to fix the tears in his lung and kidney… he'll be here in the morning." I see the sob she's trying to hide, and I want to pull her against my chest and hold her there.

What is it about this girl that makes people fall for her?

She lurches toward me and falls against my chest. All I can do is rub her back and comfort her. Her sobs turn violent and louder, but she clutches onto me like she belongs there. "T-They aren't s-s-sure if he'll make it through the night," she says in between sniffles and coughs.

A hole burns straight into my chest when she says this to me. I don't know what else I can do for her, but I know what I *want* to do.

I lower my head on her shoulder and start to cry. The small grip she has on the back of my shirt excites me as it tightens and she cries harder. "He's going to die," I hear her whisper into my chest.

I pull her in front of me and look down into her eyes; I hope she can find comfort in the fact that I'm hurting too. I want to be here for her. "He isn't going to die, I promise." I move my hands up and down her shoulders in another attempt to comfort her. "Listen, I know we hardly know each other, but we both know he's stronger than this, right? It's okay to be scared."

Her eyes flicker and a small ember of blue light appears. Something clicks in her mind and she knows I'm right. Her sniffles stop and she contains herself, pushing away from me and clearing her throat. "I know, you're right. I *am* scared. I don't know what else to do but sit here and wait."

"Waiting sucks." I smile and watch her mouth form a faint one in return.

"Can you do something for me while we wait for him to wake up?" Sadness catches my breath and I hold it, hoping this conversation ends. "Something special." She blushes, careful not to catch my eye.

She knows I'm jealous.

I clear my throat. "Like what?"

Julie moves her tongue around in her mouth and I have to back away from her a little. It's hard to breathe when I can't calm down; I can't take my eyes off of her lips. They're small and...*juicy.*

"Well, the Jeep is totaled." I have to get away from her. "We'll need a car when we're ready to leave here." I don't have the heart to argue with her that she's counting her blessings before they're given. "I *need* you, Casey."

Whoosh.

The air freezes and I snap my eyes closed.

Magic. Words.

Breathe—they're just words.

"Casey?" She knows how desperate I am, regardless of who she belongs to. "Can you help me?"

I don't think. "Of course I will."

Her smile is full and relaxed. I could reach out and—

"Any ideas?"

"Where is the Jeep now?" I ask her, but I don't dare let my eyes leave hers. The ocean blue has been replaced with a steel gray, and I like it...it electrifies me inside. "I mean, where did the cops take it? Maybe—" I clear my throat and let my thoughts catch up with me. "—Maybe I can get the Jeep towed to Harley's shop if it's salvageable."

Her mouth twitches into a slight smile. "It's not, I've already checked. But I'm sure you'll think of something. Thank you, Casey. I knew I could count on you." Her lips meet my forehead, then she stands up and holds out her hand for me to take. "Let's go back in and see him."

I take her hand.

I can't *not* take her hand.

Julie Remington *is* addicting. Ollie's right.

I follow her into the room and it's so cold that I

shiver. "Here's the detective on the case—the nurse gave me his card. He would know any details about the wreck that I haven't been told." She hands me a small, slick business card. I take it from her and my eyes lock on Oliver's lifeless body in front of us. Julie makes a small humming noise. "Actually, would you mind running back to Oliver's apartment and grabbing some things? He'll want clean clothes when he wakes up, and maybe grab me one of his sweaters?"

I nod my head. "I'll bring some things. Call me if anything happens, okay?" I take her phone when she holds it out and put my number inside. I take another look at her before escaping the chill of death.

It isn't until I lock myself in my car in the parking lot when I fully realize what has happened in the past few hours.

Oliver might die.

Julie might like me.

No, that's wrong.

But I *definitely* like Julie.

"Dammit," I whisper, starting the car. "I'm such a fucking loser."

It's a little too late to be waking a police detective, so I drive toward Oliver's apartment so I can get the things Julie asked for. The misty rain covers the windshield before I click the wipers on; the streets are still slick from the rainfall before. The quickest way to his place is through a rougher part of Rockford, but I don't mind. I doubt anyone will be messing with me the way I'm feeling right now.

I pull up to a stoplight and look around. The reflection of the neon lights on The Tavern shine into my car's window. There's a woman walking in a very, very short skirt with her wild red hair matted around her body from the rain. She doesn't look like a normal hooker around these parts, but she's headed into a full circle of trouble as a half-dozen rough-looking guys eye her from the end of the block. Within seconds, they swarm her like scorpions on the prowl. I roll down my window and hear one of them say to her, "Hey, pretty girl. This is awfully far from where you should be, don't ya think?"

A second guy walks around the first and his smile even creeps *me* out. "I bet she's lost. Are you lost, little bird?"

Before I can stop myself, I'm opening the car door and stepping out into the dimly lit street. "Hey, there you are." My voice stumbles from my throat. "I've been looking for you—are you ready to go?" I hear the fear in my voice and I hope she realizes that I'm trying to help her. Her eyes meet mine and I can see her lips quiver in shame that she has to be rescued at all. She drifts past the men—careful not to touch any of them— walks to the passenger side of the car and gets in quickly.

The group of men start walking toward me, so I wink and say, "Thanks for finding her for me, guys." I lock myself in the car and speed through the intersection before they can gang up on me and kick my ass.

"Thanks." Her voice reaches me once the fear is gone. "I'm Lucy. What's your name?"

I don't answer her as I lurch the car toward Oliver's apartment, not even thinking about what just happened or what I'm going to do with her. I look over at her tall, shivering body and my defenses fall.

Here's another beautiful woman I'll mess things up with.

"Are you cold?" I ask her. "Not that someone should be dressed like *that* in rain like *this*...but everyone has their reasons, I guess." I smile at her and turn on the heat so she can get warm. "Do you want to tell me why you're walking down that road at night dressed like that?"

She bites the inside of her cheek. "I'm not a prostitute, if that's what you think."

I scoff. "I never said you were."

"What? Is that a bad part of town?"

I laugh and turn the heat back down. "You must be new around here. It's pretty sketchy around that area."

"I *am* new here; I moved a few weeks ago, but I work at Rita's Boutique, a few blocks that way." She wiggles her toes underneath the floorboard heater and points out her window. I know she wants me to strike up a conversation with her and flirt a little, but I make it a point to keep my thoughts to myself.

I already want someone I can't have; I have no business starting something with someone I don't know.

"Where do you live? I can take you home," I say, keeping my eyes on the road.

She hesitates. "I live in Boxwood." She looks sick to her stomach, like she's embarrassed to tell me where she lives. "I just moved here...it was the best thing I could afford."

I hold up my hands. "I'm not judging you; I have friends in Boxwood." I turn the car toward the small town outside of Rockford. It's a community of old Army duplexes that were converted into civilian spaces long ago.

"I'm 304, over there." She points to a house with a warm and inviting orange light in the window. "Just under those trees." I bring the car to a stop, making sure I illuminate her front door with the headlights. "Well, thanks for the ride." She stalls for a few minutes, but I don't know what to say to her.

I just want to please Julie and make her happy right now—she deserves that little speck of hope in the dark corner she's been forced into. I look at the girl across from me. Her eyes are trying to catch mine, and all I can think about is someone else's girl.

"Do you want to come in?"

I feel the hope return to my chest and the cobwebs start to melt inside of me. Lucy is igniting something that Julie started the day before: a flame that I don't want to put out. "I'll have to pass, but I'll wait for you to get inside, okay?"

She snickers. "Thanks for the ride—again." She gets out of the car, making sure I can see her perfectly shaped ass when she does. Her long fingers push the window down before closing the door, and she leans her face back through the opening to smile at me. "I'm Lucy."

I laugh. "You said that already. I'm Casey."

She winks, picks up my phone from the center console, and punches in her number. I hear a faint buzzing from her purse. She called herself from my phone. "There…now I have your number and you have mine. Use it sometime, okay?" Her smile is broad as she pushes herself from the car and makes her way into her house. I don't waste any time pulling back onto the road. I'm getting tired, and Oliver's is only ten minutes back into Rockford.

Except that when I get there and lie on the sofa, I can't fall asleep.

I think about Julie. Her hair looks like sunflowers.

I think about Lucy. Her skin looks tantalizing when wet.

I think about Heather...then Julie.

I think about Nora and her full lips and smooth, tan skin.

I think about Lucy...then Julie.

I can't stop thinking about Julie.

I don't *want* to stop thinking about her.

I have to do something; I pick up my phone from the table next to me and find the number that Lucy had dialed.

> Hey, sorry I just burnt out like that.

LUCY

No worries. Miss me already?

I scoff; she's almost as cocky as Heather. She isn't my normal type, either. I like modest women who don't walk around shady parts of town at night half-naked. I message her back anyway—anything is better than knowing I want someone I can't have.

> I just wanted to apologize for acting rude.

Apology accepted.

I frown at the keyboard in the dark.

Okay, I'll let you sleep. Have a good night.

Then, she calls me.

"Phone calls are much more personal." I can hear her smile through the phone. "You're my knight in shining armor, after all."

I blush, thankful she can't see me. I don't know what happens to me when women compliment me; I lose myself and do stupid things.

"I'm no knight." I laugh. "I'm just me."

She sucks in air and I stop thinking about Julie for a few minutes. "So, what's your deal?"

"No deal, I'm pretty boring."

Her laugh is amazing; it's real and full. "You were going to let me go to sleep when clearly you want to ask me out."

"Is that so?"

She giggles. "Unless I got the wrong impression…"

"No, you didn't," I blurt. "It's just…my friend is in the hospital right now…that's where I was coming from when I saw you. He's pretty bad and messed up, so I need to be there for him and his girlfriend right now."

Lucy gasps. "His girlfriend?"

"She's my friend too. She's pretty upset. He might not make it."

Lucy thinks for a few seconds in silence before saying anything. "I think that's nice of you, Casey.

There needs to be more compassionate men in the world like you. Is there anything I can do to help you?"

Yeah—you can help me take my mind off Julie.

Because I want her so bad right now it's killing me.

LUCY

THERE'S NO GREATER feeling than knowing you've made several wrong choices in a row.

Going home with Oliver.

Going *back* to The Tavern to try to find someone else to ease my woes.

Getting into the car with Casey…No, getting into the car with him was a good choice…at least it's better than the one that had been waiting for me back on that street. I really want to thank him for helping me, but he's right. I shouldn't be inviting him in.

When I jump out of the car and give him a show of what he's missing, it doesn't bother me that he's not reaching out for me and grabbing my ass.

I turn and wink at him, grab his phone from the center console, and put in my phone number before calling myself. "There…now I have your number and you have mine. Use it sometime, okay?" I have to make myself leave the open window and race into my apartment before anyone else shady catches me outside. I click the three deadbolts behind me and turn on the lights, scanning the room before stepping any farther.

I'm alone.

Alone and soaking wet.

I strip my wet clothes off and turn on the shower in the small bathroom. It's cold in the apartment, mainly because I haven't turned on the heat yet to save a little money. The water is hot when I step into the small shower, hitting my elbows as I turn my body around to put my forehead against the wall and think.

Casey.

He's pretty handsome.

And chivalrous.

I smile when I think about him not taking me up on my offer to come inside. Most men would want you to repay them for their kindness...but not Casey. To tell the truth, Oliver's rejection is still swirling inside my brain, and I would have slept with Casey just to make it even in my own mind.

The water only washes away so much guilt before I step out and dress myself. I wonder what Heather is doing—if she's having money problems or she just gave up on designer handbags. I look at my vanity full of body sprays and makeup from the drugstore and I sigh. This wasn't supposed to happen to me. I was supposed to come out on top. I think about all the surgeries and money spent on making my body into something I desperately wanted. I was supposed to live a lavish and free life.

All it's gotten me so far is nearly assaulted and rejected by two men.

For once, my neighbors aren't arguing or watching loud porn. The dogs at the back of the property aren't growling at each other or howling at the moon, either. The beats of loud stereo systems aren't shaking the walls, but I don't dare focus on all of that much so my peace isn't jinxed.

My phone dings and I find it on my bed where I dropped it after stripping my clothes off.

CASEY

Hey, sorry I just burnt out like that.

My heart jumps and I want to freak out.

No worries. Miss me already?

I just wanted to apologize for acting rude.

Apology accepted.

I put the phone down next to me and figure out my plan. He's playing me hot and cold, like he's scared to let me in. I think about sending him dirty pictures, but he gets to me first.

Okay, I'll let you sleep. Have a good night.

I'm not sure what to do, so I call him. I don't let him say hello before my mouth starts moving and words fall out. "Phone calls are much more personal." I smile and hope he can tell. "You're my knight in shining armor, after all."

"I'm no knight." He laughs. "I'm just me."

"So, what's your deal?" I twist my wet hair around my fingers.

"No deal, I'm pretty boring."

I laugh because most guys say this sort of thing because they don't like talking about themselves...or their feelings. "You were going to let me go to sleep when clearly you want to ask me out."

"Is that so?"

I giggle and flip my hair, even though he can't see me. "Unless I got the wrong impression..." I feel embarrassed but I know he can't see me blush. It doesn't stop me from getting nervous and looking around with the feeling that someone's watching me.

"No, you didn't. It's just...my friend is in the hospital right now. That's where I was coming from when I saw you. He's pretty bad and messed up, so I need to be there for him and his girlfriend right now."

I gasp. "His girlfriend?"

"She's my friend too. She's pretty upset. He might not make it."

I tap my chin and wonder how someone this great could have been thrown at me like he was. "I think that's nice of you, Casey. There needs to be more compassionate men in the world like you. Is there anything I can do to help you?"

His breathing thickens. "No, but can I call you later? I do want to take you out...maybe after this whole mess is straightened out."

I want to jump for joy and do a dance, but I keep my composure. "Of course. Just let me know if I can help you, okay?"

He agrees and we hang up the phone.

Casey is a mystery.

And I like mysteries.

FOURTEEN
BRANDON

I WATCH Julie leave with some guy from the other side of the street. Oliver isn't here—or at least he's not walking outside with her. I can't imagine he'd be letting Julie waltz around with another man either. I'm sitting in my car—in the shadows—and I hope her psycho brother doesn't catch me out here.

Shit. There's her brother.

He runs out of the house, waving his fist in the air. The guy that Julie is with protects her by putting his arm in front of her as a shield. As they have words on the front lawn, I swear I think her brother sees me lurking, but he doesn't do anything about it. When Julie's heard enough, she speeds off with the mystery guy—and even though it's not the great and powerful Oliver Jackson, I get pissed off. By the time I drive back home, I'm fuming with anger and frustration. I heard everything they fucking said, and I don't like anything I just learned.

None of the lights inside are on, but I don't care. I'm

so pissed that I make it a point to create as much noise as I can opening the front door, because I want Heather to wake up and fight with me. I need to let everything out on someone.

I make louder noises in the kitchen and I notice her bedroom light come on. I want to fight with her—I need somewhere to put my anger besides inside of me. Heather doesn't deserve that, but she knew what she signed up for.

When she opens the door, the light billows into the dark hallway, and I smile because I know I'm about to get the satisfaction I'm looking for.

Here it comes.

I grab a beer from the fridge and open it. The liquid is so cold on my lips that it actually chills my anger for a few seconds. I sip it and try to come to a truthful realization about my relationship with Julie: I don't have one anymore.

I hear Heather's small feet walk slowly toward the kitchen and stop. She tries to hold her breath in hopes that I won't hear her, but I know she's there. "Come in here," I demand, seeing her faint shadow jump a little. She peeks her head in through the doorway; her shiny, dark hair falls around her neck like silk strands of black licorice. "I *said* come in here." My voice is heavy with frustration.

"Are you okay?" she snaps at me. "It's pretty late to be making all this noise."

I scoff. "It's like ten."

She crosses her arms and bites her bottom lip, examining the way I'm chugging beer down one by one and throwing the bottles away. She isn't impressed by how many I can throw back, but I don't care about anything except my release right now.

"Are you drunk?" she whispers, like drinking is a sin.

I guzzle the rest of the third one, throw it away, and grab another one. "Are you my mother?" I growl, opening the bottle.

Horror paints her face and I feel bad; I want to make her pain go away because *I'm* the one who caused it. I can see the hurt in her eyes—the same hurt I would see in Julie's eyes for years whenever I put her down. Julie was always good to me, and Heather hasn't done anything wrong. I guess I'm just hardwired to be an asshole, and there's not much I can do to stop it besides try to suppress it.

"I'm going back to bed." She shakes her head and turns to leave. For a second, I think I'm going to let myself watch her walk away. The deeper I think about it, the more I want control over her. I throw the bottle away and breathe in deep, making sure she hasn't left yet. I grab her arm and pull her around to face me. Her eyes are scared, so I let her go, but she doesn't run from me or try to push me away.

She *likes* it.

She loves the thrill; she'll like fighting just as much as I do, and this is going to end up in much bigger fireworks than the ones I had with Julie.

Maybe I've met my match, then.

"You shouldn't grab people like that. You could seriously hurt someone with that grip you have, Incredible Hulk." She rubs her arm and glares at me with disgust.

"You could have hurt me, and then I'd have to kick your ass."

The fragility in her voice amuses me; I can see her fear dripping from her tongue as she squares her shoulders when I laugh. "*You*—kick *my* ass? I don't think so, Paris Hilton."

She scoffs and puts her hands on her hips, pretending to be offended. But I can see the sparkle in her eyes. "Well, I would try."

Heather's freshness makes me smile. I broke Julie down so much that she eventually stopped fighting back, but not Heather. She looks like she thrives on a challenge. This might eventually be a problem for us since I like to fight too. Two volcanos don't make a rainbow—that's just common sense.

"Speaking of sleeping with me—"

She laughs. "I never said I was sleeping with you."

I grin and slip my hands around her small waist, making her drop her arms to her sides. "Well, let's stop talking and make that happen. It's been a long and frustrating night. I could use a release."

She makes a disgusted noise. "I told you no sex and I mean no sex."

"I didn't think you were serious." I try to smile but end up frowning instead. "What's your problem?"

"*My* problem? Are you serious right now? What happened to that sweet guy from the past few days? I mean, you leave for half a day and when you come back, you're all pissed off and taking it out on me."

Smart girl.

"Just *stop!*" I yell at her. "I think you have me mixed up with Saint Oliver. I never said I was sweet and I never said I would treat you kindly. If anything, you should be thankful that I picked your sorry ass up from that hotel and gave you a real home." I'm growling at her and I want to rip her clothes off. "What part of that don't you understand?"

Her eyes get glassy. *Oh, please don't cry.*

"I think I better leave." She sniffles and runs from me, shutting her bedroom door behind her. I hear her sobbing from where I stand, frozen in place. What the hell is wrong with me? I know I can have her if I really want her—what's holding me back?

She's not Julie.

I don't bother knocking because I don't care if she wants to cry in private. I know it's my fault she's in hysterics, and I actually feel bad about it. I try and find a little softness in myself as I stand in the open doorway and she refuses to look at me.

"Hey, I'm sorry. I shouldn't have taken things out on you. I'm just...angry." I watch the light return to her eyes as she wipes them; all she wanted was an apology.

I have to do better. I have to stop thinking about Julie and start thinking about Heather. I have to stop wanting Julie if I'm ever going to have a normal life again.

Heather leans toward me and it makes me nervous. All she wants is someone to validate her and make her feel special again—make her feel worthy of spending the time making herself look the way she does. I can't hide the fact that I want her; the soft bounces of her small, perky tits taunt me as I walk to her and take her hand in mine. "Forgive me?"

She clutches my hand tighter. "I forgive you. I know

what it's like to be in love with someone you can't have."

My eyes widen because she called me out. That's not how I thought this would turn out, but I find myself not wanting to fight anymore. I think about her feelings—which is odd for me to even admit to myself. My fingers find her tears and I wipe them away. I know she can see right through me. "I'm still in love with Julie," I say to her. "But that doesn't mean I can't love you too."

"I found her things upstairs."

I want to yell at her. "Okay, and what do you think about that?"

She shrugs. "I can handle it."

I laugh then snap my mouth shut. "You seem like a woman who doesn't like to share."

She turns toward me and I let her crawl into my lap. Her legs are bony and jab into my thighs, but I try to think of something else. Once she nestles in and finds warmth, I hear her soft breathing and it slows the world down around me.

"I *don't* like to share," she says. "I probably will get tired of it eventually. You'll have to choose at some point. You'll have to answer to yourself if you want to keep chasing a ghost."

"Julie isn't a ghost."

"Your relationship is. You have to know how in love Oliver and Julie are, right? She isn't going to leave him, no matter what you have up your sleeve." There's thick sadness in her voice and I know she's still pining over Oliver just as much as I am for Julie. All I can do right now is mend this present moment with her and hold her for as long as she wants me to.

I just want to feel normal again.

I smile.

Normal.

My life *was* normal.

Now, my life is…a *disaster.*

"I can't be Julie for you just like you can't be Oliver for me." I cringe when she says his name. I overheard Randy and Julie yelling in their front yard before I left, and I debate on whether to tell Heather about his accident. I don't want her to run to him too.

I rub my chin and her eyes lock on mine. "I have something to tell you about where I was tonight."

Should I tell her everything? Even the parts before Oliver's crash?

No, stick to the basics.

"I was at Julie's." I watch her face, but she doesn't cry. "I went over there to see her, but she was with some other guy and found out something bad about Oliver." I think about the entire scene again, leaving out some parts so she won't be as pissed. "Did you know that Julie is pregnant? Or she might be…I'm not exactly sure."

Her jaw drops. "No, I didn't know that." The color drains from her face as she processes the information.

"Then I guess something else happened." I wait for her to climb out of my lap, but she snuggles in deeper. "He was in a car accident and he's in the hospital."

There.

Now, what are you going to do?

Are you going to leave me, or are you going to stay?

Your move.

FIFTEEN
HEATHER

FOR SOME REASON, when Brandon tells me about Oliver's accident...I don't panic.

"I'm sorry to hear that." I frown. "I hope he's going to be okay."

Brandon's eyes twinkle and he devours my lips before I even know what's happening. I missed someone kissing me like he does—like he wants me so bad that it overwhelms both of us when we touch. Oliver and I were like that once.

I can't think about Oliver right now.

The more Oliver slips away from me, the more Brandon seems within my reach.

The gold flecks in his brown eyes captivate me when he lets go. My legs are drawn to him; my body aches at the thought of his lips on my skin. I turn in his lap and face him, pressing my body against him. My hips move in circles against his pelvis and his rough hands grab my ass and squeeze hard. He pulls me closer and buries his face in my hair, pressing his hard-on into me and groaning softly.

"Are you sure you want this?" His breath is ragged. "I mean, you really want *me*?"

"I want you," I breathe into his ear.

Before I can change my mind, he grabs me and stands up, wrapping my legs around his waist. I feel drunk and the room spins with my excitement, but all I can focus on is how incredible it feels to have him throw me down onto the bed and rip off my pajamas. The chill of the room tickles my naked body as he tears off his own clothes and looks down at me. The adrenaline inside my veins is taking over every inch of me as he examines what I look like completely naked—he hasn't seen me this way since we hooked up in the hotel. Except then it wasn't anything more than a one-night stand.

Now all I ever need is going to be found in him.

"Wait." I catch my breath and try to swallow the air caught in my throat. "I don't want to end up pregnant like Julie."

He chuckles and I hear him open something. The sound of rubber squeaks between his fingers. He doesn't say a word as he forces my legs open and looks into my eyes once more for confirmation, just to be sure.

"I want you, Brandon." I lower my voice. "It's okay…you don't have to be scared."

He growls. "I'm not fucking scared."

His hard flesh pushes into me and I clutch onto his bare back for stability as our bodies buck on the purple bed. His thrusts get deeper and harder with each passing minute; the more he thinks about what he's doing, the harder he pushes. I rake my nails across his flesh and he growls loudly, pushing me harder into the bed and moaning.

I let him turn me over without pulling out of me, and he gathers my hair into his hands, pulling the tangled mess backward until he's satisfied with the level of pain he's giving me. It doesn't hurt...not in a bad way, that is. Something shifts between us as he lets my hair free and grips my sides, pushing into me with more longing than frustration.

I slide onto him and meet his every thrust until he turns me back around to face him. His eyes capture mine and he looks sad. My fingers reach up and touch his cheek; his eyes widen with surprise and a smile grows on his lips. "I want to do this right."

I giggle. "You're doing it right."

"No." His hair is matted to his forehead with sweat. "I want to do everything with *you* right. This isn't right...not like this. I didn't do things right before; I broke all the rules."

Rules.

I frown. "I don't live life by rules. This is what it is."

His lips lower onto my neck and he sucks it. "And what is this?"

"I don't know."

His breath is hot on my skin and I want more; I can't handle the games he's playing right now...and screw whatever rules he wants me to follow. He slides back into me and I wrap my legs tightly around him so he can't escape again. His body crumples into mine. He holds me as our bodies slide together, and when the room explodes...it *explodes*. The purple mess comes back into my view and the room is darkened by the night sky outside the open curtains.

Once he catches his breath and notices that I'm smiling like a damn idiot, he rolls off me and kisses my shoulder. "You confuse the hell out of me." His voice is barely above a whisper, but I can hear the smile on his own face.

"How so?" I prop myself up on my elbow.

"You tell me one thing and then do another—it's very confusing. You say you don't want to have sex, yet…" He sees the anger building in my eyes and kisses my lips. "Don't get me wrong. That was…pretty damn good…but what if we're both too messed up to make this work?"

I snuggle into his body and sigh. "I've never been the girl who lets someone in all the way. Oliver and I never connected like you and I have without even trying. I think we both owe it to ourselves to try and make it work."

He yawns and grabs the purple comforter from the bottom of the bed, draping it over our naked bodies. "Let's talk about this tomorrow, okay? I have to go to work early, but maybe we can have dinner after I get home."

He's already asleep before I can muster up the courage to say anything else. He wants to talk tomorrow, and that's all I can really hope for.

I can't expect him to be perfect when I'm nowhere near it either.

I remember how my mother was when I was growing up: She slept around and the whole town talked about her like she was a piece of trash. My friends' parents wouldn't let me hang out with them anymore and all I had left were guys to keep me company.

Just like her.

I haven't seen my mother since I left for New York; the last things she said to me never sat well with me, so I haven't made the effort to reach out.

"You go off and try and live a better life while I stay here and rot." Her snarl echoes in my head. *"You'll be back— you'll come crawling back, and then I'll get to tell you I told you so."*

I'm going to do everything I can not to have to return to her. I want to wake Brandon up and tell him all of my dirty, dark, and embarrassing secrets, but I know there's a time and a place for that. This isn't it. I like watching him sleep, though. He's peaceful and sort of…beautiful.

Not that any man likes to be called beautiful.

In the early pictures of him with Julie, he'd looked like he'd stepped out of a Marilyn Manson concert or something; his overgrown, somewhat greasy black hair was the first indication that I'd never be caught dead talking to him if I'd met him sooner. I wonder what changed for him—when he started to take better care of himself and see his reflection in the mirror as something more valuable.

We all have our demons—it's how we choose to live with them that makes us who we are.

Julie looked like a typical blonde and bubbly cheer-leader, someone I would actually have been friends with in another life. Talking to Brandon about her and judging by the way Oliver fawns over her…I'm starting to feel a pull toward her too. There's something about her that makes it damn near impossible to fully hate her guts, and that's different for me. I know I want to hate her for snatching Oliver up and leaving Brandon, but in all reality, she's a victim here too.

Maybe we can all be friends someday.

I smile. I know it's a pipe dream, but when I'm finished soaking up all the good karma I can get… maybe I'll work on being her friend next. A chill runs down my spine. I'll have to be able to stand to look at her first, but I'm trying.

I'm *really* trying.

So, Brandon has rules of his own.

I want to make this work.

I have to live by his rules.

Whatever they are.

SIXTEEN
JULIE

"DO YOU WANT SOME COFFEE?" the nurse asks me. I barely hear her; I'm thinking about something totally different and far away. "My shift ends in a few minutes and I can get you some."

I sniffle and look at her. She's exhausted; her tired eyes are shaded and low. "Coffee would be wonderful, thank you." I shiver in my seat and look at Oliver's face. "It's cold in here, right?"

The nurse checks some machines next to him before walking to the thermostat on the wall. "Let me turn up the heat for you. Is that better?"

I force a smile. "Much better, thanks."

The sound of her voice doesn't compare to the silent echo that radiates from Oliver's lifeless body in front of me. The fact that there's absolutely nothing I can do for him makes me sick to my stomach. I wonder if Oliver can feel the warmth now spreading across the room, or even my hand that's locked with his.

The nurse smiles at me and leaves the room. I'm

alone with him, and the silence is so chilling that I wish so hard that he'll just pop his eyes open and come back to me. I don't take a good look at his face or body in fear that I might hyperventilate at how mangled he really is. I force myself to push back his gown a little, but quickly put it back when I chicken out.

I wrap my hand around his lifeless and cold fingers. I look at him and want to talk to him; I want him to tell me everything is going to be okay. I see him in my mind sitting across from me in the sunlight, a smirk on his face because I've done something to amuse him once again.

"Well…" I choke and talk to him like he can hear me. "I'm here. It's crazy you had to do something like this to get my attention."

Great, give him a guilt trip.

I feel bad and squeeze his hand, hoping he squeezes back.

He doesn't.

I close my eyes and listen to the silence.

I don't notice the door open and the nurse walk back in until she holds out the cup of coffee in front of me. "Here you go." I nearly jump out of my skin. "Whoa there, I didn't mean to startle you." Her tired eyes look down on me and I fake a smile. I take the coffee from her hands and put it on a small table next to me so it can cool off first. I notice her looking at Oliver's body, trying to be nonchalant so I don't see her.

"Well, have a good night, okay? Mr. Jackson is in good hands, it seems. Dr. Osmond will be here in the morning—he's the surgeon you requested—and he can begin trying to repair the tear in your husband's lung."

She speaks of him like she knows him.

The ventilator that's helping him breathe makes a whooshing sound, making it hard to concentrate on my own thoughts. For a split second, I want to run. I'm only twenty-two—I'm not mature enough to be called someone's wife, and I'm sure not mature enough to make life-or-death decisions for someone I only met a few months ago.

Someone that I'm crazy in love with.

Someone that's crazy in love with me too.

The nurse turns to me before leaving the room and makes it a point to smile at me. She's so good at her job that she doesn't have to search for things to say to someone like me—someone who's literally hovering over her dying lover's body.

"Hey, just be with him, okay? He can hear you. You know how I can tell?" I follow her gaze to a small machine that isn't making any sound, but an electric orange line steadies as we watch it. "Say something and keep your eye on that screen, okay?"

I glue my eyes to the orange line on the screen. "What should I say?" I whisper, feeling the hot tears fall down my cheeks. The orange line jumps toward the top of the screen.

I look over to her as she smirks. "He can hear you; he's responding to your voice."

"My voice? Like he knows I'm here?" I don't take my eyes off the screen as the orange line jumps toward the top again. My heart skips a few beats with excitement. I know she's just telling me what I want to hear—this machine isn't really a connection from him to me. "That's him responding to my voice? That's crazy…it's like he's here talking to us. I bet when the line goes up quicker, it's one of his smart-ass remarks."

She nods and pats my shoulder. "Just hang in there. I'll be back in the morning, and hopefully his surgery will be over by then and he'll be in recovery." She starts to leave, but she stops when her mind apparently gets the best of her. "I know what it's like to lose someone you care about." Her eyes darken but she doesn't look at me. "All I can say to you is…hang in there."

"You said that already."

She smiles and leaves without another word. My gaze locks onto the screen, watching the orange line like an addict. My eyes burn from watching it so hard. I never thought I'd love hearing the sound of my own voice so much.

If he can hear me, could he hear Casey before?

Does he know he's only half-alive?

I grip his hand harder and lower my head, resting it on his lap. I could fall asleep here with him if I wasn't under so much stress. I quietly sob into the blanket over his thighs and silently pray that he'll just move his arm up and comfort me…*something*. For a second, I think I feel his warm hand on my back and I jump, but he's still lifeless beneath me.

———

"I'M HERE," I hear Oliver's voice whisper, and I jump again. The room is dark and I can barely see my own fingers let alone whoever is standing behind me. "How are you feeling, baby?" His voice is deep and sexy—I want to turn around,

but I'm afraid that he won't actually be there. "Julie? Hey, can you sit up and look at me?"

Before thinking, I open my eyes and see sunlight pouring into the room. We're in our bedroom at the cabin and I'm sitting on the floor; I turn my body and see a worried look on Oliver's face, but something isn't right. His face is...different. Older.

His smile still jolts my heart into a frenzy. "I know you've been dizzy a lot lately...did you faint?" The amount of concern that drips from his tongue shakes me to my core. I don't know what he's talking about, but he isn't cold and life-less before me, so I'll try to be positive. His lips thin into a small frown and his fear nearly burns my skin as he stares at me, waiting for answers.

I look at my hands and try to lift myself up from the ground, but I'm weak.

Very *weak.*

"I do need help." My voice is raspy and dry. "And water, please."

First, he takes me by the waist and lifts me into the air with almost no effort—his muscles are straining at the seams of his dress shirt. Even in his forties—I assume—working out still seems like a big deal for Oliver Jackson. He settles me into a chair and leaves me alone so he can fetch my water. I'm not sure what's wrong with me, but I know that I don't feel anywhere close to being right. I'm so weak and tired that it hurts.

"Here you go, baby." Oliver returns and his voice soothes my insides like magic. I feel painless and at peace. I nod and he smiles—there's nothing that can ever make me not love this man. He kisses the top of my head, and when I finish my

172

drink, he takes my glass back into the bathroom, where he stays for a few minutes in silence.

His face is pale when he reemerges. He kneels in front of me, brushing hair from my eyes. Our gazes lock, twin sadness in our eyes, but his is just too overwhelming to ignore. I reach out and gently pull him close to me, but I feel his hesitation when he puts his arms around my body, like he thinks he'll break me. After a few moments of trying to be stoic, he presses our bodies flush together and his woodsy scent fills my head.

I am free.

I am home.

"Just who the hell do you think you are?"

I hear a woman's rough voice cut through my dream. "Hey, wake up, you little street rat!" She nudges me with her foot. I flick open my eyes, ready to tear into the person who took me away from Oliver in my head. I realize where I am and frantically look at the machines around Oliver, just to make sure they're all still on and working. I watch his broad chest heave up and down with deep breaths thanks to the ventilator, and it comforts me.

Good. I didn't sleep through his death.

"*Hello*…still here." The woman snaps her fingers next to my face and I almost reach up to grab them so I can break them myself. I'm too tired to even try and catch them, though, as they wag in front of my fuzzy vision. "Care to explain what the hell you're doing here? Did you come to rob him or have your way with him while he's asleep?"

I look up at her and blink a few times. The woman standing over me looks rough and defeated. Her bleached hair is fried at the ends; her roots are chestnut brown, but the bleached part is so white that I can hear it crunch without touching it. There's so much caked, night-before eyeliner around her eyes that it's hard to see what color they are, but then I notice it.

They're the same emerald green as Oliver's.

She glares down at me while smacking on a piece of bubblegum, and I want to slap her across her gray, sunken-in cheeks. *Who the hell does she think she is?* She must have the wrong room. I sweetly smile and look around to make sure we're alone before I speak to her.

"I think you have the wrong room. I don't know you, and you can leave the same way you entered, lady," I snarl, but the smile stays on my lips.

She doesn't return my smile. "I don't think so, little girl. The mistake is yours. He is *my* son." Her bony fingers point to Oliver and she growls back at me, "So now *you* can leave."

Rage builds inside of me; this is the most pissed off I've been in a long time. The woman's oversized black dress doesn't quite touch the floor and I can see her muddy, tattered sneakers peeking out from beneath the hem as she continues to smack her lips in annoyance.

"I think you need a reality check," I snap. "His mother is long gone."

The more I study her eyes, the more I see Oliver in them. I stand up and push the emergency button. Nurse Mary comes in with a doctor in tow.

"Remove this woman from the room, please," I say to Mary. "I don't know her and I don't think my husband does either." It feels weird calling Oliver that; I know the lie that comes from my mouth is so transparent that no one will believe me.

The woman laughs. "*Husband*? She's a damn liar… remove *her* from the room! He's my son!" I notice the screen with the orange line is going out of control. I know that Nurse Mary was lying to me and that machine doesn't really mean what she says it does, but pretending that Oliver is right next to me in this conversation makes it easier.

The doctor touches the woman's arm to ask her to leave, and she snarls before lunging toward me. He catches her and drags her from the room—I can hear her screams until the elevator doors close.

Nurse Mary frowns. "All that family drama…I've seen it before many times."

I say nothing. She doesn't get to talk about things like that. She notices my reservation about joining her in conversation. When she leaves, the room is quiet again.

Cold.

I wish Oliver would just wake up; he's the one who deals with things like this the best.

A security guard nods at me through the window of the door, letting me know he'll stand watch just in case the woman comes back. I place my head back down on Oliver's chest, hoping I can hear something other than his slow, weak heartbeat.

Nothing.

He doesn't come up behind me this time.

No dream.

Just silence for three straight hours.

I can't really sleep, so I pull one of the journals from my bag. Thankfully I placed them inside and grabbed this bag before we left. I need the distraction right now.

May 15th, 1992

I have a son.

A living, breathing baby boy.

The amount of poison Veronica put into her body shows as my small infant wriggles with withdrawal symptoms before my very eyes. It's the worst feeling I've ever felt—watching my own flesh and blood writhe in terror only hours into this world.

But, he is beautiful and looks exactly like Veronica; he has her eyes and her smile. I see myself in him too, but the resemblance he has toward her is amazing. When the nurse handed him to me, I cried so hard that it was difficult to look straight at him.

Loving someone before meeting them is very possible.

Loving someone more than your own life is, too.

He's only a day old and already I find myself

forgetting my old self to be a better man for my son...and Veronica. I see the strain in her eyes—she wants to escape me again. Only this time, there's so much more at stake here. I can't let her take my son if she vanishes again...I have to keep him from whatever fate she has in her mind for him.

For now, she sleeps with him by her side, and they both smile. He's finally calmed down enough that we are certain he'll pull through. His head is covered with muddy brown hair that matches hers, and their eyes are the same exact color of green.

Oliver Frankford Jackson.

The boy who changed it all.

The boy who will never know his mother, at least not like a child should. I fear that she's going to strip him of a normal childhood. It's my job to make sure to counteract that the best I can and shower him with love.

A father's love.

There's absolutely nothing like it.

The bookmark I've been using, a napkin from the Lake Reed Inn, folds nicely behind the journal entry I just read. I close the book and sit in silence with Oliver for over half an hour.

I stare at the orange line the entire time; before I know it, the door opens quickly and people start pouring into the room. Doctors and nurses are chatting around us, looking down at me. One of them touches my shoulder for me to stand up, and they start pushing me from the room.

"Hey, wait," I say in a sleepy voice as they pass me toward the door. "Wait!"

"Dr. Osmond is here to do the surgery," a male nurse tells me. "We need you to leave."

I rip my arm from his grip and scream at the top of my lungs. "Everyone get the hell out of here so I can have a minute alone with him!"

A tall, tan man holds up his index finger to me. "He needs to get into surgery right *now*—I need to see what I'm working with."

I growl at him. "Give me sixty seconds."

Dr. Osmond nods and the room empties again as I rub the sleep from my eyes. I look over Oliver's lifeless body and take a mental note of exactly how he looks for what might be the last time. I quickly wonder if I should take a picture of him with my phone…just in case. Deciding against it, I kiss his forehead and push his hair back a little to somehow comfort myself in thinking he's here with me.

"I'll be waiting for you right here," I whisper in his ear. "You better not go anywhere, because I'm not going anywhere, do you hear me? I love you, Oliver Jackson."

The door opens and Dr. Osmond nods at me, letting me have space to leave before everyone filters back inside. Within minutes, they roll Oliver out of the room and I desperately watch them until they're out of my eyesight. I collapse onto the sofa where Casey was before.

Nurse Mary finds me, covering me with a soft blanket. "I'll wake you when he's out of surgery."

I shake my head. "I can't sleep when he's dying on a table."

She smiles; it makes me feel better. "I *promise* I'll wake you if anything happens."

I don't argue. I close my eyes and let the fatigue consume my body.

Damn you, Oliver Jackson.

Damn you.

SEVENTEEN
OLIVER

I FEEL Julie's sadness fade and her strawberry scent leaves my airways. I fucking hate when this happens; the sweetness of her skin keeps me grounded. Instead, it's replaced with an awful sulfur smell, making me want to gag. The room is still freezing cold wherever they take me. Most of the voices that have surrounded me are now leaving, and only a few remain.

"Doctor, are you scrubbed in?"

"I'm ready…check his vitals before we begin."

I hear shades open and the chatter of people across the room.

Are they teaching a class? Am I on display?

What the hell do they think they're doing?

"Okay, he's as good as he's going to get, I'm afraid. Let's begin."

It's silent for a long time while I hear shuffles and feel nothing. The doctor calls out several different names of tools he needs, followed by a second voice repeating them as they hand them over.

"There, now let's make the incisions."

The machines hooked up to my body beep steadily, but inside I'm screaming in fear and agony. The medicine running through my IV makes me drowsy, and I drift into a deep sleep.

Oliver, wake the hell up!

———

"WAKE UP, YOU LITTLE SHIT." I hear her raspy smoker's voice in my ear. "Wake up—let's get the hell out of here."

I see darkness when I open my eyes, but there aren't doctors around me. I'm in my small bedroom in Mrs. Atchley's quaint apartment, where she lets me stay when Dad is out of town. I look at the digital clock on my bedside table; it's just after three a.m. and the sky is so dark that nothing is visible inside of my room except for my mother's scowling face inches from me.

"Come on!" She tugs me so hard that I fall out of the bed and land with a hard thud on the floor. I purposely make more noise as I stand back up.

"Shut the fuck up!" a man says from across the room, near the window. "Do you want us to get caught? Get your little bitch boy and let's get outta here!" I look up and see his grim face outside the open window. He gives me a matching grim smile.

"I'm not supposed to leave." I act like it's no big deal and brush off my pajamas. "Dad said I have to stay here when he's away...I'm not going with you." I sit on the edge of my bed.

She gets mad at me. "You're mine too! Don't you miss me?"

I nod my head even though we both know it's a lie. "Yes, Mommy."

She pulls me closer with one arm and lights a cigarette, sitting on the small bed and bringing me down with her. "Well, then...what's the problem here? We can go anywhere you want, kid."

I stare at her face; I haven't seen her for an entire year, and she looks sicker than she's ever looked before. Her eyes are lifeless and her cheeks are sunken in too. "I carried you inside of me for almost ten months—the least you can do is act like you like me."

"I'm sorry, Mommy," I say and hang my head. "Dad says I have to stay here."

Smack!

Her hand sweeps across my small face with so much force that it knocks me backward. I have to brace myself for another blow while my little body is pushed against the corner of my dresser. I hear Mrs. Atchley stir across the hall from us, and my mother's face grows serious and pale. She grabs my arm —harder this time—and growls at me. "Get the fuck out there with Mac."

Mac.

The man with the scary face.

The man who beat me last year and nearly killed me.

He holds his hands open for me to jump into, but I freeze.

"Come on, you little jerk!" he hisses at me, wiggling his fingers. "Let's fucking go!"

"No, I'm not going!" I scream and try to take my arm back from her grip. Her brittle nails scratch me and I cry, hoping that I'm loud enough to alarm Mrs. Atchley. "I'm not going anywhere with you! I hope I never see you again!"

Her face hardens. "You don't mean that. You're being

brainwashed. What about your father is so great? He denies me when I come to him and won't let me see you!"

The door opens and light pours into the dark room from the brilliantly lit hallway. Mrs. Atchley stands in the doorway with a shotgun in her hands, raising it at my mother without hesitation.

"Let him go or you'll be eating bullets," she says with a calm voice. My mother doesn't back down, so Mrs. Atchley raises the gun higher and cocks it, ready to fire. "I won't tell you again, Veronica."

My mother snickers. "You wouldn't dare shoot me in front of him."

Mrs. Atchley's eyes narrow. She doesn't bother looking at me as her eyes grow cold and she stares down my kidnapper. "Try me."

"You bitch," my mother says. "If you don't come with me now, boy, I'll find a way to get you later. I always get what I want. You really wish to never see me again?"

I don't even have to think about it.

I nod my head and say nothing.

She groans and pushes Mac down the ladder and they're both gone. Sirens surround the house and officers command the two of them to get on the ground from their loudspeakers. Mrs. Atchley leaves to put the gun away and then comes back into the room to shut the window and re-lock it.

Police officers are flooding the apartment, asking me questions I don't understand. They rub their jaws in frustration and look at me with sad eyes. The woman that pats my hand, she's nice and she likes to ask me questions I do understand.

"What did your mother want?"

"She wanted me to go with her."

"Did she promise you anything? Toys? Money?"

"No."

"Was there anyone with her?"

"Yes, Mac was with her."

She shows me a picture. "This man? Terrance MacElvaine?"

"Yes, that's him. That's my mom's boyfriend. I don't like him."

She smiles and pats my hand again. When the police officers are all gone, my eyes are so heavy that Mrs. Atchley has to pick me up the best she can to take me back to my bedroom. She puts me back into bed and tucks me in tightly, her warm smile almost making me forget everything that just happened.

Almost.

"We'll deal with the rest of this in the morning, kid. Try and get some sleep—you're safe now." She pats my head and leaves the room.

I never want to see my mother again.

———

"He's crashing!"

"Get his heart back online!"

"We're losing him! Come on, get those fucking paddles on him!"

"I have to repair this tear while he's open...I have to keep going. I said get those paddles on him right now!"

"But, don't you see—"

"I see it, dammit! Do what I tell you to do!"

I think about my mother.

How could she possibly know about this?

Where the hell has she been for twenty years?

The only time I ever heard about her was when my

184

grandfather complained that he was still paying her money because of me.

She's here for money.

Julie is smarter than that—she won't let her in.

My Julie.

———

"Y*EAH*?" *I hear her say from a room at the end of a hallway. I sit in a home office and lean back in a chair so comfortable that I don't want to stand up.*

"Where are you?" I yell for her and hear a shuffle from above me in the attic.

Her sneeze leads me toward the ladder that touches the floor. When I make my way up, I see her taking things from a large chest and throwing them next to her in a frenzy.

"Where are they?" She shakes her head and I step next to her, dodging her flailing arms that come inches within my face.

"What are you looking for?" I ask. She huffs and sits down cross-legged on the floor.

Her eyes are tired as she looks up at me. "I put Colin's journals up here so we wouldn't lose them, and look...I freaking lost them!"

She starts to cry, but I smile and sit next to her. "Don't cry, baby." I wipe the fat teardrops from her cheeks. "The journals are safe...I sent them to be rebound. No need to cry."

Her tears stop and are replaced by giggles. "I just didn't want you to lose the only thing you have left of him."

My chest starts to burn and it feels like someone has punched a hole straight through my body, setting my chest cavity on fire. I feel myself screaming and thrashing around—

I'M FUCKING AWAKE.

———

I THRASH AROUND on the operating table and several pairs of arms try to hold me down. They all yell at each other frantically.

"What the hell? He's awake…he's awake!"

"Get him sedated again!"

I hear a blood-curdling scream fill the room and realize…

It's coming from me.

I can feel the openness of my torso, the chill that surrounds me and tries to suffocate me while I scream. I start gasping for air and I can literally feel the life draining from my body as they all scramble frantically around me, tripping over each other in the process. Dodging my flailing arms, they are trying to save me from more pain, but it's not working.

I still can't see a damn thing.

"He ripped out his IV!"

"Get it back in him! Now!"

"I'm trying! His arms are moving too much—hold him down!"

"Mr. Jackson, please stay still, okay? We need to sedate you again."

"Don't make him have a heart attack, just put the damn needle—"

Silence.

Where is everyone?

Where are all of the voices?

Where are all the doctors and nurses?

Where the fuck am I?

I'm alone…that's where I am.

I miss Julie.

Is she biting her fingernails and anxiously waiting for me to wake up? I have no doubt that she's tried her best not to fall to pieces; I hate that she's under so much stress. That isn't good for her body or the baby.

Our baby.

Is there a baby?

I'm breaking so many rules now that I can't keep up.

Rules between the living and the dead.

I broke my second rule and I took life for granted.

My father is rolling over in his grave knowing that I won't be there for my kid…if there is one.

"Finally, he's back online. Gave us quite a scare there, Mr. Jackson."

"Let's get this over with so he doesn't flatline again."

I listen as they work on my insides but I feel nothing. I'm back to just hearing their voices and wondering what the hell is going on. As long as they can fix me and send me back to Julie, I'm fine with whatever they're doing to me. I laugh at myself—obviously no one can hear me—because this shit is torture. I know I've done some messed-up shit in my life, but this…this is fucking torture.

I don't deserve to die.

Breaking the rules shouldn't have this much punishment.

I have to get back to Julie.

She needs me.

I need her.

We need each other.

I'd like to think that Julie can't even live life without me, but that's a little too real to think about right now, inches from death. I thought death was supposed to be graceful and filled with bright lights and comforting music playing over loudspeakers as you walk toward the white marble gates to meet your maker.

So far…nothing like that has happened.

I'm just stuck in between.

I'm not coming or going.

I'm not living or staying dead.

It's crazy being this alone. I could probably hear a pin drop from miles away with how quiet it is in my head. I can't even hear the doctors around me anymore, but I can feel my life still clinging onto me.

I start to make a mental list of things I'm going to do when I wake up.

A new set of life rules, maybe.

First, I'm going to tell Julie I love her every single fucking day.

Second, I'm going to write Julie into my will.

Third, I'm going to ask Julie to marry me and never let her go.

Lastly, I'm going to run my tragic mess of a mother off without giving her the money that she wants.

I wonder why I haven't had any memories of my grandfather. I think about moving into his house after my dad died, and I hardly saw him the first month I lived there. Anita, the maid, was the only contact I had with him. She would always lie to me and tell me he was out of town on business, but I wasn't stupid. I knew he was shacking up with someone he shouldn't be—somewhere he shouldn't be.

It wasn't hard to figure out Victor Jackson.

There were a few times where I seriously should've been taken away by CPS, but nothing happened that was worse than what my mother did to me. I remember Greta Miller's eighteenth birthday party that I hosted at my grandfather's mansion; I distinctly remember him snorting a line of cocaine and having sex with Greta's married mother in the hot tub—not even a hundred feet from the party and her own daughter.

That was good ol' Vic for you.

I hardly remember his face anymore, really; I do remember the awful stench of his whiskey and cigars that smelled like mint cloves and oranges so badly that I had to have his house steam cleaned from top to bottom before I sold it.

I wonder where Anita ended up.

I know where Mrs. Atchley is; I made sure she was taken care of when Vic died. I bought her an apartment down the hall from mine so she could be close.

I owe Mrs. Atchley my life.

"Okay, let's get him stitched back up."

Beep.

Beep.

Beep.

"That's good, keep going. Be careful not to move him too much; it's imperative that he doesn't rip those stitches."

"There, he's all done."

I hear sighs of relief and cheers from the distant crowd. The doctors and nurses around me laugh with each other and tell me what a good job I did...even though my eyes are still glued shut and they don't know I can actually hear them.

"Mr. Jackson?" I hear the second-voice nurse say to me. "I'll let your wife know you're out of surgery and she can see you soon, okay?"

Thank you, second voice.

It's still cold around my body, but I can hear the beeps of my monitors so I know I'm still alive. He's fixed what he went in for; I might have a fighting chance now.

"You heard the doctor, everyone. He wants us to monitor Mr. Jackson for the next day so he doesn't rip out his stitches. We can take him out of sedation around that time."

Yes! When can I fucking go home?

"I'm going to let his wife know he made it through."

"Sure thing, Mary."

Mary. Second voice's name is Mary.

I'm going to give Mary a huge bonus when I wake up.

When I wake up!

My possibilities might be endless again soon.

"Okay, let's get him to recovery. His heart is still pretty weak, but that will change hopefully as his organs start to heal."

The people transporting me chatter about the surgery and what was going on the entire time. Little do they know I'm aware of everything that happened.

"No one can explain it, man. It was like his body just

said, 'Wake the fuck up,' and then he just...woke the fuck up." A man chuckles. "Poor bastard...I hope he wasn't in too much pain, though. That shit can't be just a bee sting, ya know? He's lucky he didn't code and die in there."

Another man laughs and I shiver inside. I know that laugh from somewhere.

"Yeah, this little shit's lucky, all right."

Mac.

Holy shit, that's Mac.

I pass out as the other guy says something about me having magical powers because I didn't die. I'm more focused on why that asshole is helping transport me into a damn recovery room. This can't fucking be good.

I wake back up in a quiet room; I still can't see a damn thing because my eyes won't function, but I don't hear any shuffling or talking around me.

I really need to wake up now.

EIGHTEEN
CASEY

THE MOMENT NORA told me we were over was it for me—the one moment that everyone has when they realize they've majorly screwed themselves out of something good. No matter what they do—or how hard they try—nothing can bring back that happiness.

I did that to myself.

I self-sabotaged everything with her after chasing her for over three months. I played every little cat-and-mouse jealousy game she managed to throw at me. I learned her quirks and her mood swings, and for what? Nothing feels worse than knowing I stand in the way of my own damn happiness.

Now there's Julie.

And Lucy.

More importantly…*Julie.*

I don't know why I do this to myself; I know I can't have her. I know that I'll always be staring at her when I can and thinking about Oliver touching her when I want it to be me. Even now, as I lie in the darkness of

Oliver's apartment waiting for the sun to rise, I think about her. Oliver doesn't know how lucky he is to have someone like her.

Even in high school, I was never one to dwell on something for too long. Oliver always got the girls while I was left to catch the ones that had time to kill before he got to them. I'm a few years younger than him, which made it even more exciting—and harder to swallow sometimes.

Well, not anymore.

I want someone to just…*love*.

Someone I can get close with and keep for more than a week at my side—someone who I don't have to worry about anything with except for how happy I can make her. I want someone to laugh with and share inside jokes…someone who looks at me like Julie looks at Oliver. Maybe that's my problem. Maybe I'm not jealous of Oliver, but jealous of what they have together. It's hard to see people happy when you're doomed to be miserable.

I know deep down that I have no chance with her. But that's not going to stop me from thinking about it every damn second.

I try and focus on Lucy. Her vibrant red hair is sexy…I *do* like that. Her wide lips pout out without her even trying, and she tantalized me with the way she licked them when she caught me looking over at her in the car.

After we hung up hours ago, she sent me a smiley face and I had to force myself to put down the phone and let her think about me overnight.

Will she even think about me?

Will she even remember me?

What has Nora done to me?

What have I done to myself?

I feel so pathetic and alone right now.

I think back to Lake Reed and how happy Nora and I were.

How happy we were supposed to be.

I can't believe this is who I am now.

I care about everything while caring about nothing at all.

The hours tick by slowly as the sun grazes the halfway open curtains. I email the detective sometime during the early morning and he answers around six with the details of the wreck. I text Harley and arrange for one of his shop guys to fetch the Jeep from the police lot just in case Oliver wants it back for some reason. I get up and gather the things Julie asked for and take a look around the apartment before leaving.

This should all be mine.

There are things that Oliver doesn't know that I *do* know.

My phone rings as I get into my car and my heart skips, hoping it's Julie.

No, hoping it's *Lucy.*

"Hey, it's Harley." I frown because it's not one of the girls. Disgusted with myself for even thinking that, I try and shake them both from my head. "Is Ollie okay, man? I got his Jeep and fuck man, this thing is wrecked. Was he drunk? I know when I left him at The Tavern he was smashed."

My eyes narrow. "When were you guys at The Tavern?"

I can hear his lumberjack fingertips pounding on the front counter of his shop. "Two nights ago, but when I left he was with some chick and she seemed sober enough."

"You left him with some girl? Was it Julie?"

Harley sighs. "No, it wasn't. I warned him, man. I tried to get him to let me take him home, but he wasn't havin' it. So, is he okay?"

"I don't know," I hiss. "I haven't talked to Julie this morning. I've been busy helping her out...you know, since she's his fucking girlfriend."

"Hey, don't be pissed at me. I tried to tell him."

I know Harley likes casual flings, but I know he likes Julie too. He always encouraged Oliver to be with her because she's so good for him.

But she could be good for me too.

"He's getting surgery to repair some tears in his lung, so I don't know. I'll let you know when I find out," I say. I want to throat punch him through the phone. "Is the Jeep too fucked up to salvage? I really want to do something special for Julie right now."

He sucks in hard air and blows it out slowly. I know I slipped and said something that might tip him off on my sudden infatuation with a woman who's not mine. "Yeah, this thing is too messed up. I'll text you the number of my rental guy...they'll need a car. Ollie won't like it if you replace his Jeep permanently for him."

"I know that."

I pull the phone from my ear and get ready to hang up on him. The way he nonchalantly accuses me of being a bad friend grinds my insides. I can't even believe after all the advocacy he's done for Julie that he'd allow Oliver to cheat on her. For a split second, I think about using this to my advantage, but Oliver is still my best friend—no matter how much I think I want her.

"Hey, Casey?" Harley's voice booms. "That other part…can you just forget—"

"—Already forgotten," I say, and I do hang up on him this time. I focus my energy on driving to the hospital and what I might walk into when I get there. My phone makes a dinging noise as I pull into the parking lot, and I don't bother checking it until I walk into the main entrance where it's warm.

LUCY

Good morning. How did you sleep?

A goofy smile grows on my lips. Okay, I can handle this. I blush, looking around to make sure no one is watching me and edging in on my private thoughts. I throw the bag I stuffed all the things Julie asked for over my shoulder to answer her.

I had a lot of stuff going through my head. Sleep wasn't one of them.

The security guard eyes me as I pass him and push the elevator button. When I step inside and look back at him, he tips his gray hat toward me as an indication that I'm doing something right in life for once.

Thank you, random security guard.

> I'm sorry to hear that. Anything I can do to help?

I smile and hear the elevator ding.

> Can I take you to dinner tonight? I'm checking on my friend right now.

> Pick me up at eight?

> It's a date.

I shove the phone into my jeans and smile bigger. When the elevator door opens, my smile fades and panic settles in my bones.

Julie.

She's standing in front of the doors. Her face is pale and stained with tears. I step out to meet her and reach out for her, my fingertips grazing her arm. "What's wrong? Is he okay?" I search her eyes, but they're so tired that I can't tell what's happening. "Julie, tell me he's okay." She lets out a deep breath and falls into me, clutching me around the waist and sobbing into my shirt. "Please tell me what's going on." I stroke her head.

Her grip tightens on me and I know I have to let her go.

"He made it," she whispers. "He made it through the surgery."

I pull away and look down at her; the tears in her eyes are happy ones. I want to use my thumb to wipe them away so damn bad. She flings her arms around me again and I hold her as tight as I can...knowing that

I'll never have this chance again without Oliver's watchful eyes on me. He'll be able to see right through me at first glance.

"I told you he'd be okay." I smile and tuck her hair behind her ear. "He wasn't going to leave you like that."

She wipes her eyes and they sparkle like sunlight on the ocean. "I'm glad you were here for me, Casey. I don't know what I would have done without you. You're one of my best friends; I'm so happy I have you in my life." Her lips touch my cheek and it takes every single ounce of restraint I have not to move my head and let her lips graze mine. I know that once I go there, I won't be able to come back from it. She's not like Heather, though; she won't hold it over my head for years.

She'll just never speak to me again.

Her small, cold hand tucks into mine. "Let's wait for him out here, okay? He's not back from recovery yet."

There's nothing more I want than to sit here and hold her. I let her lead me to the small sofa and pull me down onto it with her; she tucks herself underneath my arm and before I realize it, she's sleeping soundly as she snuggles into my side.

Oh, no. I have to get out of here. Why is she doing this to me?

It takes a few minutes of running through anger and confusion until I'm able to calm down. I know she's not intentionally leading me on…it's not her fault she needs someone to comfort her. Honestly, I lie to myself because it makes me feel better—she's just clutching onto the first person she can. If Nora were still here…

Julie wouldn't think twice about asking me to be her errand boy instead of white knight.

Her arm snakes around mine and she pulls it tightly into her, seeking the undying comfort I know she's longing for. I like the fact that she called me one of her best friends; it's nice to know that someone can see the good in you even when you can't see it yourself. She knows what I need to hear before I do.

"I want to do something special for Oliver since his Jeep is totaled. Do you think you can find one that looks like his old one?"

I nod. "I can try."

"Casey?" Her voice is suddenly sleepy. "Why do you smell like women's perfume?"

I make a weird face, but she doesn't see it. "Oh, I hung out with someone last night and gave them a ride home. Her perfume must have stuck on my clothes. I stayed at Oliver's last night so I could come straight here with your stuff. Does it bother you?"

She doesn't answer right away. "No, it doesn't bother me...I was just wondering."

Her body starts to shift away from mine and it's confusing. Is she really upset that I smell like another woman? No...that can't be true. My arm tightens beneath hers, warning her that if she lets go now, I don't know when we'll be able to be like this again.

"What's her name?"

It takes me a few seconds to remember because all I'm thinking about is her. "Lucy."

"She must be pretty special. I'd like to meet her someday."

I take my arm back and her eyes flick to mine. "Uh,

here's the stuff you asked me for. I have some things to take care of—can you call me when he wakes up?" I pick up the bag from the floor and put it on her lap.

"Sure, Casey."

Her eyes cloud over again and I know it's because I'm acting like a fool. I'm not stupid. There's a small part of her—no matter how small it is—that has some sort of feelings for me too. I'm not making it up...I know I'm not.

"Hey." I smile at her and wink. "I'm just a phone call away. You're not alone."

She shrugs. "I know. I just don't like waiting."

"I know you don't," I blurt out, and she looks at me, confused. "I mean, no one does."

I nod at her and get into the elevator as fast as I can, shutting her out.

No one likes to wait.

But I will wait for someone like you.

NINETEEN
OLIVER

I'M NOT AWAKE YET.

What the hell is the problem here?

I can only still see darkness, and it pisses me off with each second that passes. I'm so worried that Mac and my mother are both here with Julie that the machines are picking up my anxiety.

I'm thirsty.

And I can't hear anyone—especially Julie—and I don't fucking like it.

I scream but I'm the only one who can hear it. I hardly notice someone walk into the room and start shuffling things around in the drawers and cabinets. They knock over some bottles and when the door opens again, they're startled and knock over a few metal objects. I hear Mary's voice call for help.

"What do you think you're doing in here?" Mary asks the intruder. She sounds like she's across the room and the intruder is breathing down my neck. "You need to leave before security gets here and escorts you out again. Mrs. Jackson has ordered you not to be near her husband."

The intruder laughs. "They aren't married, you stupid twit. Open an internet search and use your pretty little head, you dumb broad."

My mother.

I would know her cigarette smoke-filled rasp anywhere.

Mary isn't having any of it. "You can either leave now or get arrested."

My mother's laugh is like long fingernails on a chalkboard. "I signed those damn DNR papers and I hear that he had complications during surgery, so why is he alive now?" Several people run into the room, and there's so much chatter that I can't make any of it out clearly.

"*He* knows! That fancy doctor my son's fake wife ordered from another state! You there! I said don't resuscitate him, and now look! He's a vegetable and I'm going to sue your ass!" Her voice cuts out on her when she runs out of breath. "Why did I sign my name to those damn papers if they meant nothing?" Her whisper is hoarse and filled with the puffs of smoke left in her lungs.

Dr. Osmond comes closer to where she hovers over me. "Ma'am, those papers are for severe incidents requiring CPR or life support. That wasn't the case for your son. He woke up during surgery…that's all."

My mother's deep growl thickens as he gets closer to her. "I still don't want that little gold digger near my son. She has no business being here."

Mary's voice wafts through the crowd. "She's the

wife—what she says goes. Remove her from the room, please, before Mrs. Jackson finds out she's here."

My mother kicks and screams as I hear how much of a fight she's putting up while they try to drag her out. Once it's quiet again, I can hear Mary and Dr. Osmond talking at my side about the situation.

"*Is* she his wife?" Dr. Osmond asks.

Mary clicks her tongue. "No, she's not. But I know that woman has no business being here. I knew the Jackson family a long time ago in middle school; his mother is bad news."

He sighs. "Well, keep her out of here, then."

"I will try. I'm going to wake his wife—or whatever she is—up and let her know he's in recovery now."

"Okay, go ahead. I'm going to check his vitals one more time before I head up to sleep for a few hours. You're a lucky man, Mr. Jackson. It could have been much worse for you." He chuckles, and it makes me want to punch his lights out.

Someone opens the door and leaves.

I *felt* it.

I felt the breeze from the door.

I'm waking up!

I feel like I'm trying to kick and push my way through a dozen brick walls.

Dr. Osmond's hands are poking and pushing into my skin and there's no way he can't see the smile on my face from being able to feel something again. The door opens again and I can smell her strawberry shampoo before she even speaks. When she leans down to my ear and I can feel her hot breath on my skin, the machines start beeping faster. "I'm so happy you made it...I would have been so lost without you. I love you, Oliver." Her breath tickles my ear and no one notices, but a teardrop falls from my eye onto my neck.

I want to hold her and never, ever let her go again.

When I wake up, rule number two will be obeyed. I'm not taking anything for fucking granted again: not Julie, not life…not even Casey.

"Your husband made it through surgery with a few complications, but nothing that wasn't quickly managed," Dr. Osmond says to Julie. "You're lucky you contacted me when you did, though—any more movement and the tears would have required a much more complicated surgery. But for now, he's breathing well enough that we were able to remove his tracheal tube."

"How is his heart?" Her small voice is nuzzled against my ear. "Will he be okay?"

"His other organs will grow stronger as he heals. It's a matter of keeping him sedated for now and letting him push past that first wave of healing pain. He will need around six weeks for those stitches to heal properly."

"I'll take care of him."

"I'll have a nurse draw up after-care paperwork now so you can see what you're in for."

"Thank you. Can I be alone with him now? I'd like to be the only one here when he wakes up."

"Of course. I'll stand by for a few days, but the hospital will call if they need me."

I feel the rush of the door again and squirm inside my body.

I want out of here!

She lays her head down on my lap again, and it's the

most amazing fucking feeling I've ever experienced. Her warmth heats my cold skin and I scream at myself to bring my arm up and capture her, but I'm still immobile. "Can you come back now?" she whispers then yawns, nuzzling into my gown. "I'm exhausted and I need you here with me."

I'm here, baby.

I'm so tired from hitting against the brick walls, but I won't give up. Not while she's overwhelmed with sadness and hovering over me. My sad excuse for a mother isn't going to kill off the last Mr. Jackson, that's for damn sure.

I try and make my body move, but the effort drains me of whatever energy I have left. Julie puts her hand in mine and intertwines our fingers, lightly snoring as she cuddles into me and falls asleep.

I can feel her hand in mine.

I can feel her hand in mine!

A blinding light seeps into the cracks of my eyes and it burns so bad that I have to shut them tighter immediately. I pry them back open and it looks like glow-in-the-dark slime oozing though my brain.

Am I walking into the light?

This isn't fair! I thought I was going to be okay?

My body starts to panic and the machines start beeping faster, but Julie doesn't wake up. I see squares of some sort—grayish and spotted squares—that look like ceiling tiles above me. I blink a few times before letting my eyes adjust to the light I haven't seen in days. I don't know what else on my body is working and I don't want to alarm Julie until I know for sure.

The desire to touch her burns inside of me; my body

is so weak that I can barely move the arm she isn't clutching. Trying several times, I finally manage to slowly move it up and down on the bed without waking her. The room is a private suite, and as my eyes scan everything around me, I start associating the sounds with the objects when they were used.

My toes wiggle and I can move my legs just a little; it's enough to make me smile and this time, I can actually feel my own smile so I know it's there.

I'm alive.

I. Am. Alive.

And everything fucking hurts.

My throat is so dry that I cough, and I expect dust to puff past my lips. It takes a few tries but I manage to croak out her name loud enough to wake the sleeping beauty. She takes a few seconds to lift her head; I can tell that she thinks she's dreaming. When her eyes follow my torso up to my face, our eyes meet and the fire between us captures us in a whirlwind.

"Good morning, sunshine." My laugh is weak, but I try. "Don't cry, baby."

"Oh my god!" She bolts up and throws her arms around me. She feels my body tense from the pressure and her grip eases, but she doesn't dare let go. "I was waiting for you to wake up. I knew you wouldn't let me down."

Her lips find me and she's devouring my mouth so hard that I can't breathe. I don't want to let her go, so I find enough strength to raise my hand to her cheek and pinch her chin between my fingers. "Water." I smile against her lips. "I need water."

She immediately stands up and pours me a glass of

water, hitting the call button next to the bed. I drink the cold liquid so fast that I nearly choke. I hand the empty cup back to her and really take a good look at what I've missed. She's fragile looking and her skin is so pale that it looks like paper. Her eyeliner is smudged all around her eyes in several different directions from crying and wiping away her tears.

That's my *job.*

I get angry and look down at my lap. "I missed you," I whisper, and tears form in the corners of my eyes. "I missed you more than I've ever missed anything in my life." I hear her gasp so I look up and see the mascara-stained tears fall down her cheeks. "Come here."

She moves toward me and lets me pull her as close as I can get her without hurting myself. I still have tubes and other shit hooked up to my body, but I try and pretend that it's just Julie and me without any other bad shit getting in the way. She lays her head gently on my chest and tries to hide her small sobs, but she isn't fooling me. I know her too well to even think she isn't going to cry about this randomly for the next year of our lives.

I smile when I think about that.

It feels good to have a future again.

"Hey, sunshine, it's okay. Don't cry…I'm right here." My breath is ragged, like I've smoked a pack of cigarettes through a breathing tube. I run my fingers through her soft, honey blonde hair; I almost forgot how silky and addicting it is to touch. "I need to ask you some questions…can you handle that?"

She nods and wipes her cheeks. "I can do that."

"Did the man die? The man that I hit?" I brace myself for her answer. I realize I should have waited a few minutes before asking anything like this. I'm already feeling like I'm going to puke just thinking about it. Her eyes glaze over and she looks confused. "The man in the car that I hit before rolling the Jeep... did he survive?"

She slowly shakes her head. "No, I'm sorry. He didn't make it, Oliver."

I have to hold onto her hands so I don't fall off the bed from how dizzy I'm getting. "I killed him? I killed him and I'm alive? Are you sure, Julie...are you sure he's dead?"

The door of the room opens and a woman with short brown hair and green scrubs comes into the room. A smile spreads across her face when she looks at Julie and then back at me.

"Mr. Jackson! You're awake!"

"Nurse Mary." I nod and she looks confused how I know her name. "Is he the only person that died?" I watch her nod her head and I can tell she feels sad for me. "Does he have any family? I'd like to pay for his funeral and whatever else they need."

"I don't know, Mr. Jackson, but I can find out."

I shiver and choke back tears. "Please do." I look at Julie, who can't take her eyes off me. "I was rushing over to see you, Julie." I try and soothe her before she has an anxiety attack like that last time she was under too much stress. "I ran a stoplight—I *know* I did."

Julie shakes her head and her hair falls around her angelic face. "No, the man behind you slammed into you and made you go into the intersection, Oliver." Her eyes darken and I can't help but keep noticing how sick she looks. "Are you saying this is my fault?" Her whisper is sharp and laced with hurt.

"Of course not." I squeeze her hand. "I'm just angry. This isn't your fault. It's going to take me a long time to even believe that it's not mine, either." Her smile is weak; I want to take away her pain so fucking bad that it's consuming me. I pull her down and kiss her lips, not caring that Nurse Mary is still in the room. "I missed you so bad...*wife*." She blushes and her hand squirms inside of mine but I hold on tight. "What's wrong, Mrs. Jackson? Are you *blushing*?" I tease her and tug on her arm, pulling her lips back to mine. I can feel her quick heartbeats as I glide my lips across hers, and she blushes so hard I can feel the heat on her mouth.

Her eyes widen when she sees my hospital gown raise where my hard-on grows. "You just got out of surgery—and nearly died—and you're thinking about..." Her beautiful head turns to glance at Mary and she whispers, "sex?"

I laugh so loud it echoes in the room. "There isn't anywhere I won't want you. I nearly died, Julie—it only makes me want you more now that I can have you again." I bite my inner cheek as Mary puts something into my IV and my head starts getting fuzzy. "At least tell me if you're pregnant or not. I didn't get to read the results."

"You didn't? I thought that's why you were coming over."

"I was coming to see you. I didn't like how things ended."

She whimpers and her body is out of focus for me. "We weren't ended."

A goofy smile spreads across my face and I nearly start drooling on myself. "Tell me. I want to know what my future holds."

"I'm not pregnant, Oliver."

I study her face and I don't see as much sadness as I thought I would see.

But *I'm* sadder than I thought I would be.

"Are you okay?" She squeezes my shoulder in comfort. "Are you upset?"

I shake my head. "I'm just tired."

"I put a light sedative in your IV, just to help you sleep," Mary says. She smiles at Julie like a big sister would. "You need more rest before you can get out of here, Mr. Jackson."

Julie hiccups, more tears streaming down her face, and pulls my blanket over my chest. She kisses my cheek, then backs away before I can grab her and pull her into this bed with me.

"You should get some sleep. I'm going to run home to shower and change. Is there anything you want from the apartment when I come back?"

"No, just hurry back. I don't care if you shower. It's not like you're letting me touch you." I pout and both of the women laugh at my stubbornness.

"Okay, you big baby. I'll see you soon. I love you." She winks at me and nods at Mary before closing the door behind her.

She's gone again.

Mary mumbles something and leaves me too.

The room is silent again, just me and my machines.

I rest my head back onto the pillow and breathe out deeply.

I close my eyes and I'm too afraid to fall asleep. I don't want to lock myself in the prison inside my mind again.

Sleep wins quicker than I thought.

Now let's just hope she lets go of me quicker than she did last time.

TWENTY
JULIE

AS THE ELEVATOR slowly goes down into the hospital lobby, I have a smile on my face. An actual, honest and real smile. He didn't die and leave me here alone; I'm thankful for that. Oliver has become a part of me that no one would ever understand—or even compare to.

How would I be able to live without him?

I don't have to worry about that now. Still, I almost lost him and that doesn't feel good at all. I surely didn't want to meet his mother the way I did; just being in the same room with her made me feel itchy and bizarre. Her intentions were crystal clear before she even opened her mouth; my parents weren't the best, but at least they cared if I lived or died. Regardless, I never want to see her ever again.

But there she is.

In the lobby.

She's red-faced now and her fingers are twitching as she sits in the general waiting room. I swerve around the people entering the building and think I've made it out without her seeing me. I glance over to where she was sitting and her gaze locks with mine. Despite her frail body, she bolts up and runs toward me. The security guard sees her, too, and he goes on full alert as she approaches me.

"You there, little girl," she snarls. "Let me ask you a question. Who do you think you are, throwing me out of my own son's hospital room?"

I don't answer her, and it pisses her off more.

"Answer me, you little slut!" She seethes and looks the guard square in the eye. "Don't worry, I ain't touching her." The guard looks like he lets out a deep breath, but he still keeps his eyes locked on her. "I want to see my fucking son," she tells me.

I stare at her mangled tennis shoes and trail my gaze up her skinny, pale legs that peek out through tattered jeans, and her t-shirt that says, *Don't hate me because I'm rich and beautiful*." I scoff when I read it and her lips curl into a snarl. She's changed her clothes since being thrown out of Oliver's room, and I wonder where she lives; she'd have to live close by to be able to change and get back here this quickly. The feeling of pity rises in my throat, but my anger toward her pushes it way back down where it came from.

"What the hell are you looking at?" Her teeth snap together. "Oh, I see what this is. You think you're better than me, don't you? I know all about the trailer trash my son likes to sleep with. I'm sure you're no different than the last little bitch he thought he loved."

My mouth opens, but I'm not even sure what I'm going to say to her at first. "Well, your wish is my command. He's awake and he's alive, not that you care about either. You can go up and see him while I make arrangements for him to come home." My voice is cold and I try to move past, but she grabs my arm with her thin, bony fingers.

"I *know* my son. He will throw you away like the trash you are."

I let a snicker sneak past my lips. "You don't even know me. Oh, but I know you. I know all about you and what you were like even before Oliver was born. Colin has been filling me in on some details that even your own son doesn't know."

"You don't know me, either." I hear her teeth grinding and it sounds like metal on metal. "You don't know what I'm capable of, and I would watch your mouth before something you say gets you in some big trouble, little girl. I wouldn't want something happening to that pretty little face of yours." I feel a heavy chill in my spine as she lets go of me. "And Colin Jackson is dead, so I guess that makes you a gold digger and a liar." She snarls as she races toward the elevator. She flips her middle finger at the guard, who looks at me for silent confirmation that she's okay to go up.

"Can you have someone follow her up?" I ask him when I pass his station. He nods and gets onto his walkie-talkie, watching me as I leave through the hospital doors.

I find a taxi and tell the driver the address of Oliver's apartment. The drive is somber as the aftermath of the recent rains glistens on every surface of the city. People rush through the streets to get on with their lives, but not me. I'm gliding past those frantic few because I need the mental break.

I need a release.

I try not to think about anything until I stand in front of Oliver's door. It feels weird to be here without him, but I find solace in the fact that he's alive and awake now. I wonder if I should call Randy and tell him that I'm okay. That's more than I would do for my parents—those people are the root of everything for me. The way they treated me when I was a child was always more than anyone could bear to hear, so I stopped talking about it. I thought about telling Oliver loads of times, but I didn't want to upset him any more than he already was about Brandon.

My heart sinks.

Brandon.

The man twisted from innocence to downright malice. Soon every sentence he said to me was sour, and I just let him do it to me for years and years. I let him take possession of me and own every fiber of my being. My parents taught me that I wasn't worthy of being loved as anything other than an object, and Brandon verified every dark thought they'd pushed into my head.

Luckily, I don't care enough about him to keep wondering.

Then, there's Oliver: my knight in a Jeep.

The way he moves with me…Each step I take, I find myself wondering what he would think or how he'll react. Not out of fear, but out of respect. I respect him more than I respect anyone I've ever met.

The apartment is fairly dark—Casey must've drawn

the curtains when he left earlier. I make my way to the bathroom without turning on any lights. Everything around me makes me think of Oliver, and not just because I'm in his apartment. I wash my hands in the sink and look at his toothbrush. I think of his perfectly lined, perfectly white teeth shining at me when I've said something dorky that he thinks is adorable. His clothes on the bathroom floor make me think about wearing his t-shirts when I sleep at night next to him, and I can almost feel his hot breath in my hair as I look at myself in the mirror.

I need a haircut, along with many other things. Worrying for days on end doesn't suit me well, and I'm in desperate need of a shower.

I hear footsteps in the hallway and I immediately back away from the open door. I hear someone stop at Oliver's bedroom door, open it, and walk inside. I take my phone from my pocket and dial 9-1-1 but don't send the call just yet. I'm thankful I didn't strip down for my shower yet as I tiptoe around the corner and see Oliver's door wide open, but no one is there.

I make my way to the bedroom and peek inside, and Casey is picking up things from the floor, throwing laundry into a basket and straightening up.

"Casey?"

He jumps three feet off the ground. "*Julie*! Holy shit." He clutches his chest and starts to laugh uncontrollably. "You scared the shit out of me."

Suddenly, all the emotions I've been harboring since I found out about Oliver's condition come rushing out of me. I match Casey's laughter and clutch my stomach because it's sore from all the short breaths I'm taking to try and stop. Even when his laughter stops, mine continues louder and forced.

I am making myself believe that I'm happy.

I *am* happy.

Oliver is alive and that makes me happy.

"What are you doing here? Is Oliver okay?" He tries to cut through the small hiccupping giggles that I've been reduced to. There's something about Casey that just *feels* good. It's like the same warm aura that Oliver has, only subtler and a bit self-conscious. His chocolate-colored eyes have the same shape as Oliver's too.

I *must* be exhausted.

"Oh, I came home to shower. Oliver is awake." Our smiles broaden as we stare at each other. There's something about him that I can't describe and can't figure out. He towers over me just like Oliver and Brandon, but they are on opposite ends of the figure spectrum. Oliver is broad and has biceps for days, while Brandon is more slender and solid.

Casey is just…*normal*.

A normal, uncomplicated guy.

He says something to me, but I'm too busy trying to figure it out that I don't hear him.

"Hey!" His fingers snap in front of my eyes. "Your phone is ringing!"

Without hesitation, I click the answer button on the phone and put it to my ear.

"Hello."

Oliver's syrupy laugh snaps my focus back where it needs to be. "Miss me yet? I miss you like fucking crazy. When are you coming back?"

I don't meet Casey's eyes, but I know he's staring at

me. "I just left you less than an hour ago. Of course I miss you. I'll be back soon, okay? Casey…is here." I say it because I feel like I'm doing something wrong.

I *am* doing something wrong.

I'm in my boyfriend's apartment alone with his best friend.

My friend too.

That eases my worry a little. Casey is my friend too. We're not doing anything wrong.

"Why is he there?" Oliver snarls. "Let me talk to him."

"No, you need rest. He's here helping me with something for you. Don't worry."

Casey's gaze meets mine; he nods because he knows what I tell Oliver isn't a lie…but it's not the whole truth, either. I think Casey has feelings for me and I don't know where I went wrong to make him feel that way. Then again, I don't even know what I did to make *Oliver* fall in love with me.

He sighs. "Fine."

"I'll be back soon, I promise. Is there anything you need?"

"Yeah, *you*. I fought like hell to come back to you…I don't want you away long."

I blush because Casey is watching me. Maybe it's a better idea to remove myself from the room and have this private conversation. He doesn't stop me or follow me, which is a relief. "I promise I will be there."

"Casey needs to leave." He yawns loudly. "I don't want him there alone with you."

"Don't you trust me?" I whisper. "I think you just need sleep."

"I had sleep when I was dying, remember?"

The fact that he keeps throwing that in my face doesn't appeal to me. I don't want to keep being reminded of the horrible accident that almost destroyed everything around me. Yet, he can't stop talking about it like it's not even real.

"I'm sorry, I shouldn't have said that," he murmurs. I smile because he can read my thoughts even from miles away.

"I'll be back by nightfall, okay?" I clear my throat and speak a little too loudly, hoping that Casey will hear this part. "I'll tell Casey what you said."

He doesn't question my voice. "Thank you. I love you, Julie."

"I love you too."

Now that Casey has heard his name, he comes up behind me in the hallway. He's so close to me that I can smell the whiskey on his breath; it circles the air around me. I make sure to hang up the phone before turning around. He's frowning. "He wants me to leave, doesn't he? He doesn't trust me here alone with you."

I cross my arms. "He trusts *me*."

"Julie, I think we need to talk." His sandy blond hair tickles his forehead. "There's something I think you should know."

I follow him into the living room and sit next to him on the deep mahogany leather sofa, ready to hear whatever he has to say to me. The way he searches for words in his mind is like watching a ping-pong game; his eyes dart right and left as he fights with his heart.

"I don't think it's a secret that I have some sort of feelings for you—"

"Wait, what?" I hold up my hands. "*This* is what you wanted to talk about?"

He doesn't have any remorse for how insensitive this is. Regardless of what his feelings are…this isn't the time or the place. Actually, there *is* no time and place because I don't have feelings for him like I do for Oliver.

"Julie, please. Can you just listen to me?"

I shake my head so hard that I instantly get a headache. "I can't believe this. You're *really* doing this right now?" The steam from my rising anger radiates from my skin, reaching out to grab him and give him a good shake. "Oliver nearly died a few days ago and you do this? I can't believe that everyone around him is such an asshole."

"I'm not trying to be an asshole—"

I snort loudly. "That doesn't mean you're not being one. I can't believe this!" I stand up and cross my arms over my chest. "What's your problem? I've been nice to you—even trying to convince Oliver to forgive you for something as horrible as sleeping with his girlfriend—and I even told you I consider you one of my best friends. There's a key word in there, Casey. I'll give you a hint. It's the word *friend*." I know I'm being mean, but I feel justified.

Casey looks sick. "Don't do that. Don't act like there isn't something here."

My eyes burn into his on purpose. "Look, you listen to me right now: Whatever you think you're feeling for me, you aren't. It has to be some kind of remorse thing, because of the accident. Maybe you feel like you have to do something or take care of me because Oliver can't…I don't know. I just know that whatever you think you're feeling isn't real."

I've hurt him, but I hardly care. I thought we were friends, not—whatever else he has in mind. I don't fear Casey, but I know that it's time for him to leave.

"I think you need to really go."

His gaze finds his lap, the same way Oliver's does when he knows he's defeated. "I'm sorry, I didn't mean to upset you. I'll go." He stands up and smooths out his jeans before walking slowly toward the front door. "I just wanted to talk, Julie. I don't *want* to feel things for you—did you think about that? I don't know what my problem is."

The regret in his voice captures me. I close my eyes and sigh, sitting back down on the sofa. "Casey, wait. I'm sorry, I shouldn't have freaked out on you. That's so unlike me, and I'm really sorry. I know you're just trying to be truthful with me."

He's back on the sofa next to me before I can open my eyes again.

"I love Oliver." I take a deep breath. "And this is too much drama, once again. You and Nora just broke up. You're not in a good place to be making decisions like this."

He nods. "I think I'm just jealous of what you and Oliver have. Plus, you're easy to talk to and be with…I don't feel like I'm overcompensating to be something someone *wants* me to be."

I think about holding his hand to comfort him, but I don't want him to read too much into it. "Casey, you'll have that someday. You just told me you met some-one…Lucy, right? Maybe she's the one you can have that with. Whatever Oliver and I have…it's even still new to us. I don't know why we fit so well together— we just do. I just know that I'll always be able to depend on him, and that makes everything else just fall into place."

He points at me and smiles. "See, I want that."

"Well, I can't give that to you."

"I know that." His jaw clenches tightly. "I'm not in love with you or anything. I just like being around you. At least, I'm pretty sure about that."

I think of something to ease the tension. "Maybe you can make life rules for yourself like Oliver has…maybe that will shake things up a bit for you."

He scoffs. "What rules? He never told me about any rules."

My eyebrows rise. "He didn't? That's interesting. He's pretty vocal about them to me."

"What are they?"

I shrug my shoulders. "You'll have to make some for yourself…it's your life."

He smiles at me, but I know this isn't over.

I know I haven't made him feel better or any differently.

This is going to cause a problem if I can't be any clearer than I just was.

Oliver is going to kill him.

TWENTY-ONE
OLIVER

IT'S DARK AGAIN.

No, no, no!

Wait, I'm just asleep.

Okay…I'm okay.

I see Julie humming to herself and wearing the most hideous Christmas apron known to man. It doesn't even matter—she's so damn intoxicating and sexy that it kills me every time I lay eyes on her.

Okay, poor choice of words right now.

No…she literally kills me.

I smell bacon and it makes my mouth water. The sizzle of the pan whispers in my ears as I reach her and pull her body against me. I tighten my arms around her as much as I possibly can without forcing the air from her lungs. She eases into me, the backs of her thighs touching mine.

"I knew as soon as I started the bacon that you'd wake up, sleepyhead." She giggles and takes the bacon from the pan, putting it on a serving tray before facing me.

Whoa.

The sunlight from the open windows behind her glows around her face and I have to remind myself that I'm not in heaven and she's not an actual angel. She thrusts a coffee mug at me and fills it as our eyes meet—I want her so fucking bad even in my dreams.

"Are you hungry?" She winks and bites her bottom lip.

How can I answer you, Julie?

I am hungry for you.

So, so hungry that it never goes away.

I cough the perverted comment back down my throat before my lips unlock and I take her right here in the kitchen. I'm pretty sure she knows me well enough by now to feel my desire for her. I don't care where we are—I want her.

"I could eat." I give her a small smile and she hands me a plate of bacon, eggs, and chocolate chip pancakes, gesturing me toward the dinner table.

I smile, and she knows.

She knows that chocolate chips are our thing.

She knows that I will give her everything she ever wants or needs.

I take her hand and kiss her fingers, making sure I soak in every ounce of happiness that she gives me. I've never felt this strongly for anyone before and at first, I didn't like it.

Now I can't ever think about not having her love.

She deserves someone that can take her pain away and make her smile.

I'm that person for her.

All of these perfect dreams of what our life could be—or might be—are just teasers to what our future must hold. I'm going to do everything in my power to give her the future she deserves...the future we both deserve.

I'm going to ask her to marry me. I know it's completely

insane and way, way too soon. I just have to wait for the right time to do it, so it won't push her away.

She was made for me…I know she was.

I just need her to start believing it too.

She has to stay for more than a few days before I can trust her not to break my heart with an actual commitment attached. I feel bad because I'm lying to myself. The truth is, I do trust her. I trust her with everything—my life, my heart, and my future.

I just don't trust myself to not get in my own way and ruin it all.

————

"You assholes better let me in there! She said I could see him! Ask that guy, he's knows! He's my son—that gives me rights!"

My mother's horrendous voice breaks through Julie's sunshine in my head, and she disappears. "You go in there and ask him. He wants to see me! Oliver! Oliver, help me!" My eyes flick open and I cringe at her scratchy voice, making me wince in pain from the sudden movement. I think about closing my eyes and pretending I don't know who she is, but the screaming outside finally forces me to push the call button for a nurse to come in. Nurse Mary is flustered as she enters the room and shuts the door behind her.

"I'm so sorry, Mr. Jackson. We're trying to make her leave. She says that your wife gave her permission to see you."

I wave her off. "Just let her in. She only wants money."

Mary does what I ask and opens the door for my mother. I prop myself up so I can get a better look at her when she saunters in and gives Mary a dirty look. "I told you so, little girl."

"I thought you were dead," I say to my mother, not ready for niceness. "Or maybe I just hoped you were dead, I don't know." At this point, I don't have the patience for a conversation that doesn't get straight to the fucking point. I know what she wants—I'm just not going to be like my father and grandfather and give it to her.

She scoffs and looks around the room nervously. "I'm sure you wish I was dead, kid. You always did have shitty luck, didn't you?" Her snarl is unnerving; she sits down in the chair Julie planted herself in for days. "You almost died chasing after some bitch that doesn't even deserve you, didn't you?"

"More like I don't deserve her. What do you want... why are you here?" She is so far gone it's sad. She doesn't even look like the woman I remember anymore —everything about her has changed and gotten worse. "The last time I saw you, you were climbing out of my window after trying to kidnap me. I distinctly remember telling you I never wanted to see you again."

She laughs.

Laughs.

"Well, I paid the price for that. As for never wanting to see me again...you don't get to make that decision. I do what I want and go where I please." Even though she licks her lips, they are still cracked with deep splits. "Why do you *think* I'm here? I need the money your grandfather left me in his will. I know what I'm entitled to. Don't fuck around with me."

Her face is sunken in from the long-term drug use, and the eyes that we shared—the wide, emerald green eyes—are now a mismatched pair. Hers are dull and lifeless. It would be easy for me to take pity on her like my father and grandfather did all those years ago. Unfortunately for her, I don't pity her as much as I fucking hate her.

"Like I told you, Vic didn't leave you any money. So, if that's the only reason you're here…you can leave the same way your sorry ass came in. Oh, and don't ever fucking talk to Julie ever again, you understand?"

Her laugh is really annoying the shit out of me. "Like I said, I do what I want. If I want to wait for her downstairs, I will. Mac is doing just that right now."

Fire-red heat flashes through my body. "You're not going to intimidate me, Veronica. You think you have all the power, but trust me, if you even come within a hundred feet of Julie, I will eviscerate you and your little drug dealer boyfriend."

Our scowls match even if our eyes don't. It's going to take nothing for her to reach out and choke the hell out of me while I'm incapacitated. Wheels turn inside her head and thinking too hard is making her eyes roll around like a crazy person.

"Just give me what I want and I'll leave her alone. You'll never see me again."

I scoff. "Yeah, because I was fucking born yesterday. I know you, *Mother*, and you're not one to keep your fucking promises. Exactly how much are you trying to extort from me?"

"Three million."

I laugh so loud that the guard standing outside the door looks into the window. I nod toward him to call him off. "Three million dollars…wow. You really are a piece of work, aren't you? Look, this has gone on long enough. I'm not giving you shit, so you can leave now."

The anger rises in her throat and blows out of her mouth like invisible fire. I realize that I'm still immobile enough not to be able to defend myself if she gets too crazy. I hit the call button and Mary comes back into the room with the guard that was looking into the window only moments before. My mother fakes a smile and calms herself down enough to hover over me, pretending to tuck her beloved son into bed.

"You will give me what's mine one way or another, *son*." The hiss from her lips reaches my skin and burns my flesh. "Just give me the money and I'll walk away. I'd hate to see anything happen to that little blonde tart that's been crying over you up here…what did you call her? Julie? Mac likes young blondes, you know."

"You fucking bitch! I said don't touch her," I hiss back at her. "If anything happens to her because of you, I'll spend every penny I have making sure you rot in jail." If I could move my arms quickly, I'd catch her neck and squeeze the life out of her. She's already dead to me and now she's threatened Julie again. The security guard pulls her away before I can get to her. This time she doesn't go kicking and screaming—she has a wicked smile on her face.

"Wow, she's really crazy." Mary snorts. "Like psycho thriller movie scary."

I exhale deeply. "You have no idea. I haven't seen her for twenty years."

Her mouth falls open. "*Twenty years*? How can you even recognize her?"

"It's hard to forget someone like that when they make such a huge impact on your life." I pick up the phone from the bedside table. I need to talk to Julie; I need to make sure she's okay. I need to hear her voice and know that she's coming back to me soon. "Like my wife." I smile at Mary because she knows better. "I've only known her a short time and there's nothing about that woman I will ever, *ever* forget."

My Julie.

The phone rings a few times before she answers. "Hello." Her voice is drained and I feel bad for her exhaustion the last couple of days.

I try to laugh and get her in a better mood. "Miss me yet? I miss you like fucking crazy. When are you coming back?" My lips move so fast that I don't realize how clingy I'm being; I just want her to be safe. I want to make sure she knows to stay away from my mother and her drug dealer boyfriend.

"I just left you less than an hour ago. Of course I miss you. I'll be back soon, okay? Casey…is here." She trails off and I know it's to make me aware that she has no secrets. I can't trust Casey with her—I couldn't even trust him with Heather, and she didn't mean as much to me as Julie does.

But I *do* trust Julie.

I make a quick decision not to tell her about the scene my mother just caused. Instead, I take the jealousy route so she doesn't suspect anything else is wrong.

"Why is he there? Let me talk to him."

"No, you need rest. He's here helping me with something for you. Don't worry."

I know I'm not going to win this. "Fine." I pout, but she can't see me.

"I'll be back soon, I promise. Is there anything you need?"

The medicine that flows through my IV is making me sleepy again. "Yeah, you. I fought like hell to come back to you...I don't want you away long."

"I promise I will be there."

My yawn stretches my entire face. "Casey needs to leave. I don't want him there alone with you."

Her whisper is so low that I can barely hear her. I press the phone deeper into my ear. "Don't you trust me? I think you just need sleep."

"I had sleep when I was dying, remember?"

She stays silent, seething at me for bringing it back up.

"I'm sorry, I shouldn't have said that."

I can hear her smile from miles away. "I'll be back by nightfall, okay?" She clears her throat. "I'll tell Casey what you said."

"Thank you. I love you, Julie."

"I love you too."

Then, she's gone.

It's just me again.

I want her to hurry up and come back.

I want to fucking go home.

I wish this accident never happened.

Julie has twisted me into someone I never dreamed I could be.

There's a knock on the door and it opens slowly; someone doesn't know if they should come in or not. I see Nora's soft, curly black hair and gold hoop earrings before anything else. She's still walking with crutches, so it takes her a few tries to open the door and come through without tripping herself.

I laugh as she blushes, nearly falling flat on her face. "Hey, be careful. If you fall, I can't help you up. Then we'll need to get you a bed next to mine." I motion to the wires and things running from my body. "Do you need me to call a nurse to help you?"

Her forehead wrinkles. "No, I'm fine. I just need to sit down." Her small body falls into the chair next to me and she takes in a deep breath. "Not that I wouldn't want my own private suite. They stuck me with a room-mate who coughed so hard I thought parts of her were going to come out and splatter on the floor."

I laugh. "That's fucking gross. Why didn't you tell me? I would have seen that you'd gotten a private room."

"Oh, that's too much trouble." She waves me off. "I just wanted to come and see if Julie needed anything." Her hoops make a clinking noise as she looks around the room. "But I see she's not here right now."

"No, she's not. She went home to shower. She's with—"

Nora's eyes meet mine and I don't want to finish the sentence, but I have to.

"—Casey."

"I can talk about him." She rolls her big eyes back

into her skull. "He's a real-live person...he'll come up in conversations." She laughs to herself and looks at her lap nervously. "It's just sad that we were so good and then...well, you know."

I can't help but smile at her. Nora isn't the person I thought she was: She's kind and hopeful enough to be unapologetically vulnerable. "Nora, I don't have to tell you that Casey is a mess. I mean, fuck, *I'm* a damn mess...you're a mess...everyone's a mess." I start to laugh, and her lips finally turn up into a smile. "No one is perfect. I'm not saying that you should forgive him for what he's done, but...I guess I'm saying that you don't have to be sad about it. It's not your fault. He didn't do it because of *you*."

Her laugh is comforting; I really needed someone to talk to like this. "I guess you're right," she says. "I mean, it's not like we were in love like you and Julie."

"*No one* is in love like me and Julie are."

Her smile is warm, and she wipes a few stray tears from her flushed cheeks. I obviously didn't think very highly of her when we first met—hell, I didn't even remember her—so I never really noticed how pretty Nora is, with her thick and curly jet-black hair and light-brown skin. Her eyes are really expressive too—they're sparkling even while she's trying to choke down tears. Not for the first time, I think how much of a jackass Casey can be. He fucked up big time...again.

"I just really thought Casey would be the one, you know?" Even though I get it, her sudden outpouring of emotion makes me a little uncomfortable, because we hardly know each other. But it's not like I can go anywhere, so I listen to her and try to help her the best I can. "At first, I thought there was something wrong with me. Maybe I wasn't pretty enough or sexy enough —" Her eyes dart to mine and she blushes. "—for him to have to sleep with Heather. But really…it's *her*. She's just not a good person."

I nod. "I can agree with that. Heather is a succubus."

Nora's laugh is free and easy now. "I wish I never met her. I still feel responsible for bringing her to Lake Reed and causing so much drama."

"Nora, it's nowhere near your fault. Heather knows how to work the game—she knows how to get what she wants, trust me. I was in love with her at one point in my life, but it felt nothing like what it feels like with Julie."

She bites her inner cheek, embarrassed. "What *does* it feel like?"

I suck in air and notice the hope in her eyes. "With Julie? It's hard to explain. I pushed her away so hard at first because I didn't *want* to want her….and I wanted her so fucking bad it consumed every single thought I had. But I had to make sure it was real and it wasn't going to go away. The feeling only got stronger the more time we spent together, and it was literally unlike anything I've ever felt before in my life. Like I said…it's hard to explain. I just…*knew* she was the one."

She gives me a doe-eyed look—if she were a cartoon, little hearts would've popped up in them. "That's beautiful." She sniffs and wipes her cheek. "I'm glad you two found each other."

"It was because of you and Casey—never forget that. I owe you, Nora."

She smiles and relaxes in the chair. "Good, because

I'm too exhausted to walk all the way to the elevator right now." We both start to laugh, and the air between us gets easier to navigate.

I never thought about things like that—Julie and I are together because of Nora and Casey.

Now I just have to keep Casey away from my girlfriend.

Again.

TWENTY-TWO
BRANDON

EVEN BEFORE I wake up completely, I know my arm is clenched tightly around someone. I don't even have to open my eyes to know it's not Julie. It's never Julie. It will never be Julie again, and that is something I will have to face in the long run. For now, I keep my eyes closed and think about her golden hair and how sweet she smells in the morning.

I feel my good morning mood float away from me as I relive my stupid decisions with her. The hate I have for myself creeps back into the sunny room and taunts me, letting me know again that it's not Julie next to me.

I'm with Heather in her bed.

This purple monstrosity of a bedroom.

I screwed my life up so bad that it won't ever *not* bite me in the ass.

I wonder if Heather even really likes the room and think maybe she'll be more comfortable in my bedroom with me. Thinking that makes me groan, nearly waking the woman clinging onto me. The sunlight is burrowing into my still-closed eyes and I have to make myself calm down a little as Heather starts to yawn and stretch against me.

She isn't Julie.

I need to be everything with Heather that I wasn't with Julie.

That's how I survive this.

The first rule is: Treat her differently.

I don't know how I'm going to fake loving someone when I'm yearning for someone else, but I have to try. I tighten my grip around her body and let her relax into me. She lets out a small sigh and it actually excites me as she stretches her body against me on purpose.

I open my eyes and whisper into her ear, "Good morning."

She doesn't open her eyes to greet me, but she snakes her hand down my body and into my boxers. "Whoa, hey!" I say in surprise. She starts to giggle but keeps her hand in my shorts. She turns to face me and I see her in a whole new light. Half of her makeup had smudged off during sex last night, but she just looks like a normal girl—fresh-faced and naturally beautiful.

Her long nose perks up at me as she grins. "I thought you would've gone back to your room by now." She blushes, and it's nice to see her act like she has normal feelings for once. "I'm surprised to wake up with you."

I breathe in deeply and let it out slowly, brushing hair from her eyelashes. "Do you not want me here? I can go back—"

"Don't you dare." Her smile is amazing.

And it's just for me.

That's a nice fucking feeling to have.

"I thought it would be better for us to stay together sometimes, is that okay?"

Her eyes grow so wide they remind me of Julie, and that's not okay. "Better for us? So…there's an us?" I didn't realize that I'd said it like that, but I don't want to take her happiness away from her. I roll onto my back and pull her closer into my chest, letting her lie with me so she can't see the fear in my eyes. She takes her hand back and cuddles into me with so much hope that it's hurting my head.

I don't like this immature flirting dramatic shit.

"Isn't there an us?" I ask and try not to cringe. Surprisingly, it isn't as horrible to say as I thought it would be. I could see myself with Heather—but I'll have to give up Rachel too.

I almost forgot about Rachel.

Young and willing, the boss' daughter.

No responsibility or commitment.

I wasn't strong enough to give her up when I was with Julie…and it cost me more than I'll ever be comfortable with. "Is this room okay? I wasn't sure if you liked purple. We can go and you can pick another color out and I can repaint it for you."

She places her finger over my mouth to shut me up. "I like the color—it's nice that you painted it for me, and it's nice that you want to make me feel comfortable."

But I know how she was before inviting her to stay here.

"I'm not as rich as Oliver." My gaze drops. "I make

good money, but he has so much money that it's unreal."

"How do you even know that?" She giggles and sits up, pulling me up with her. "Did you research him or something?"

I blush. "When I first found out he was sleeping with Julie."

She cringes when I say Julie's name now. "Well..." She raises her eyebrows, looking for her clothes around the room so she can run away from me. "There's a constant reminder I don't care to have. You talk about her so much, it's like she never left."

I wish she never did fucking leave.

I scoff. "Do you think I want to be reminded that you're sizing me up next to someone like Oliver Jackson? He's never worked a day in his life, I bet. At least I work for my money."

"Okay, calm down," she soothes me almost instantly. "Let's just try harder."

She watches me climb out of the bed and follows me like a puppy dog. I catch her hands and put them around my body. "I'm sorry, I'm not used to trying this hard to make someone happy. I won't compare the both of you, okay?"

"What about her stuff in that room upstairs?"

Who the hell does she think she is?

That stuff isn't just stuff in that room—that's everything in my life from the past five years that ever mattered to me. I grit my teeth and pull her closer to me, squeezing her tight. "I'll call her later and see if she can send someone to pick up her stuff." Heather tightens her long arms around me in a possessive gesture, and it turns me on.

I like that she's ready to fight for me.

She pulls her body from mine and glares at me. "Another thing too. Enough with this hot-and-cold shit. Either you want to be with me or you don't. I don't have room for another asshole in my life." Her eyes glitter with fire and I can tell she's waiting for me to grab her and throw her back onto the bed, but I have to get ready for work.

Oh, but make no mistake: *I want her.*

I want her *bad*.

"I have to get ready for work, okay? You just make sure you'll do anything for me…and I'll do anything for you. Is that a deal?" I whisper in her ear and smack her ass and she gasps, slapping my shoulder playfully. "You're lucky I have to work or you'd be tied to that bed all day." I let her go, running from the room before I make good on that statement. I notice the time and I'm able to quickly shower and change into dress slacks before Heather knocks on my bedroom door.

"You don't have to knock, we're not strangers." I laugh at her and open my closet door. She notices my slacks and licks her lips. "Did you need something?" I hold up two different button-up shirts—one light blue and one steel gray—and she points to the blue shirt and smiles. I take it from the hanger and pull it on, watching her bounce toward the bed and sit cross-legged while I dress for work.

She pushes her lips out, trying to figure out what to say to me. "I was just wondering if I could take some of those college courses we talked about before."

The fact that she's asking my permission really, really excites me.

I try not to show her my victorious smile. "Of course you can. You can use my laptop downstairs if you want to do that while I'm at work today, if you want. Just let me know how much the tuition is and I'll work it out, okay?"

Her mouth forms a small circle. "*You're* paying for it?" She stands up and smooths out the collar of my shirt. She trails her long fingers over the row of neckties that are revealed when I open my top dresser drawer. She pulls out a silky, black tie and I let her tie it around my neck gently. She knows if she gets a little too rough, I won't want to go to work and leave her here alone. "I don't want to owe you anything except for my attention."

I grab her hands and hold them against my chest. "You are my chance to make shit right in my life. I'm not going to fuck this up on purpose. You just make sure you're doing the same and I'll give you whatever I can give you."

Her smile is bright; I can feel the love that grows for me reaching from her skin to touch me. "Okay, I'll look at some classes today. Thank you." I have to pull my hands from hers because I don't want to leave her here alone. I don't want her away from me because she might change her mind and go running back to Oliver.

Julie's in her way with Oliver and with me.

I know she watches me drive away, as I make it a point to drive slowly so she can see me leave. I come to a stop sign and dial Julie's number. My heart skips a few beats waiting for her to answer.

Voicemail.

"Hey, Jules. It's, uh, Brandon. Look, I have something to tell you. I met someone...you know her. Her name is Heather Michaels, and she's Oliver's ex...but you know that. She's living with me now, and I still have some of your stuff at the house. It's just...Heather doesn't really want reminders of you lying around the place while we're together, you know? I'm sorry, I know this is bad timing with..." I hesitate; I don't want her to know I was watching her and overheard about Oliver, "...you know, life and all." I clear my throat and try to save face. "Just call me back and we can work something out."

I hang up. I'm such a pussy.

I almost said, "I love you."

I can't stop thinking about her the rest of the way to work. When I park the car and pump myself up to try and make it through the day, my phone rings and Julie's name pops up on the screen. My body ignites when I realize I'm about to talk to her for the first time in weeks. She saw me at my absolute worst the last time we spoke in Oliver's parking garage and by now I assume she's been told I'm innocent.

"Hey, Jules. I'm really glad you called me back. I miss talking to you."

"Brandon," a man growls at me. His hatred seeps through the phone like invisible waves of destruction around my throat.

"Oliver," I snap to show him I'm not intimidated.

"I'm going to need you to fuck off and stop calling Julie."

I snort. "And if I don't?"

His laugh is scary, even to me. "If you don't, then you won't like what happens to you."

"You don't scare me, Jackson." I try and convince him that I'm not actually shaking. As rich as he is, there's no limit to what his money can buy. He could probably make me disappear if he wanted…and I'm sure he wants to.

He clears his throat and lowers his voice. "Now you fucking listen to me, you piece of shit. I'm only going to say this once and you better get it through your fucking head. Julie isn't yours anymore, she's mine. She loves *me*, she doesn't love you anymore. I don't know how much fucking clearer I can be with you."

"It's crystal clear, don't worry about that."

He laughs at me again, pissing me off more as my co-workers pass me in the parking lot and eyeball me sitting in my car with a fucked-up look on my face. "I hear you're living with my sloppy seconds, so all I can tell you is good luck on that. She's a pistol and not the shiny kind. So, play by my rules or you'll regret it." He hangs up the phone and I'm left with nothing except our anger fighting in the car.

How dare he order me around like that?

How did he know about Heather living with me already?

I don't take orders from anyone. I know Julie better than he ever fucking will.

He doesn't know me very well, but…

I love to break the rules.

TWENTY-THREE
OLIVER

I HANG up the phone and Julie glides into the room. Her eyes are bloodshot from serious lack of sleep. She arrived a few minutes earlier with Casey in tow—and he looks like he feels awkward to be in the same room as the two of us. They didn't come back until this morning, but I wasn't aware until I finally woke up and they were already in the room.

"Did you talk to your lawyer?" she asks, looking directly at me. "Do you need more privacy?" I hate lying to her, but I'm not telling her about Brandon's call. I erased the voicemail and handed her the phone. I just want to get out of here, but that isn't happening until I can walk around the entire hospital wing floor by myself a few times to prove my strength. I don't know how it happened, but after my lungs were repaired, the rest of my body just…gave up. I did manage to sweet talk Nurse Mary into letting me change into my own clothes, but she insisted that someone help me, and Julie isn't strong enough to hold me if I fall.

"No, I didn't. My mother isn't going anywhere, trust me." Her face is dark and worried. "Come here, I won't let anything happen to you. You trust me, right?"

I feel her smile on my chest. "Always."

Damn.

That feels good.

Choking back some stray tears, I look at Casey. He came back to the hospital with her, and the thought of them riding in a car together isn't a good one. His face is disturbed as he watches Julie and I interact. I know he's hiding something.

"Casey, can you help me change into my street clothes? My abs are still really sore." He frowns because he hates when the fact that I'm built better than he is comes up. "I promise you won't see anything you shouldn't see."

"I'm not worried about that." He looks at the ground. "What happens if you rip your stitches?"

Oh. I hardly thought he was worried about me.

I snort. "I won't. We can go slow. Maybe Julie can find Nurse Mary for me and tell her I'm ready to walk the floor."

"Oliver, you've been in recovery for one day," Julie scolds me. "What's the rush?"

I squeeze her hand and hold it over my heart. "I want to be able to touch you without tubes and wires in the way. I want to be able to sleep with you in the same bed." I rub the sleeve of one of my sweatshirts she's put on and smile. I like when she wears my clothes. It warms my insides knowing she wants a part of me with her always. A stretch maybe, but I don't care. Right now, it's not about what looks right; it's about what *feels* right.

"I have some rules for you." Julie's eyes narrow at me. "You like rules, don't you?"

I lick my lips and think about what I'm going to do to her once I'm fully mobile again. She's playing with my dark side; she knows that breaking the rules are what started everything in the first place. "What are your rules, Mrs. Jackson?"

Casey coughs. "I think I better help you get dressed, man. I gotta check on something." He looks over at Julie and raises his eyebrows. They have something going on...and I'm going to find out what it is. "If you want to find the nurse, I'll help him."

Julie nods but doesn't look at him. "Okay." Her smile pops back on her face when she looks at me. "I'm going to find Mary." She lowers her voice and hisses at me, "Play nice."

I know what she's talking about, but I'm not saying one word about it. I'm not going to play nice with Casey...I know his game.

He chased Heather.

He's chasing Julie.

When she closes the door, I scowl at him. "You better get over whatever the fuck you think you feel for her." My voice is shaky because I'm so pissed. "I don't know what it is with you assholes thinking you can take her from me—"

"You need to calm down," Casey says, taking my clothes from the bag on the chair. "You're extra emotional right now, so you're reading into nothing. I'm helping her with something."

I let him throw the clothes next to me and he helps take my gown off. Nurse Mary had already had another male nurse help put boxers on, so Casey takes note that he really won't see anything he doesn't want to see. "What are you helping her with?" I demand. "I want to know right now."

He puts the t-shirt over my head and sighs. "Then you'll ruin the surprise she has for you."

"I don't fucking care. I want to know."

I put my arms slowly through the sleeves with his help and he shakes his head. "Dude, why can't you just let her surprise you? I know you don't trust me...but you trust her. Just let her do this for you...don't fuck it up."

He's right.

I don't like it, but he's right.

"I'm going to ask her to marry me," I tell him, looking in his eyes. They only darken for a few seconds as he thinks about this. "I want her to be my wife."

"You left The Tavern with another woman. I hardly think that's true."

I push his hands away and take the sweatpants from him. "What the fuck do you know about it?"

He steps back so I can't swing at him. "Harley told me about it. How could you do that to her? I thought you supposedly love her?"

I don't like the way he's talking to me, but he's right. "I want to marry Julie. Whatever you think happened at The Tavern, forget about it. Nothing happened. Not that I have to explain myself to someone like you."

"Someone like *me*? What's that supposed to mean?"

I manage to pull the sweatpants on by myself; I have

246

to shimmy my body around on the bed to pull them over my hips. I've lost some weight, but only I'd notice it, so it doesn't bother me too much. "I mean that you always want what you can't have...and you can't have her."

"Like I said...you're emotional right now because you almost lost her."

He glares at me as Julie walks back into the room with Nurse Mary. She notices our showdown. "What are you two up to?" She eyeballs me but doesn't even bother looking at Casey. I know she wants to comfort me by showing me that I'm the only one she has eyes for, but something doesn't feel right. There's something else going on here.

I shrug and give her my best adorable face. "Just catching up. Casey is leaving. He has somewhere to be." I look over at him and his eyes are glued to Julie. "Right?"

"Actually, Casey—" Julie interrupts and forces herself to look at him. "—can you stay for a bit and help Oliver walk the floor?"

His eyes brighten and it pisses me off. "I can do that."

Anything for you, Julie.

That's my fucking job.

I'm going to kick his ass.

Julie kisses my forehead and they each take one of my hands and gently pull me to a standing position. The pain of my stitches doesn't compare to the pain Casey is going to feel when I throat punch him for looking at Julie as anything other than a friend.

She's mine.

My Julie.

We make it out of the room with no problems. My hand is clutching Julie's so tightly that it turns a little red. I don't dare let go of either of them; I want to get the hell out of here. I wonder if I can steer them toward the elevator and just escape, but Nurse Mary isn't far behind us. The tension is too much for Julie to handle, so I hang my arm over Casey's shoulders and squeeze.

"Are you okay?" Julie whispers so Nurse Mary can't hear her. "Do you need to rest?"

I shake my head. "No, let's keep going. I can do this."

She smiles and it gives me an extra jolt of adrenaline. "I know you can. You can do anything; I believe in you." The moment that she says this, I feel strong; I feel like I'm invincible, so I let go of Casey's shoulders and push off him, walking slowly down the hall on my own. My abs hurt a little from the sudden usage, but I manage to walk a few steps and turn around to smile at the group.

"Well, look at this." I raise my eyebrows in amusement. "Let's sign those release papers."

Nurse Mary laughs. "Not so fast, Mr. Jackson. You need to walk around the entire floor a few times without help before anyone feels comfortable releasing you. Twenty-four hours ago you were closer to death than life, remember that."

I scoff and walk the circle of the floor by myself as the three of them follow closely behind. I just want to fake it enough to be able to get out of here, so I don't look back at anyone in fear that I'll lose my footing. He better not be touching her, I do know that. I try my best not to lose my focus, but once we are back at the open door to my room, I have to stop and make sure.

"He needs to rest," Nurse Mary says and nods her head toward the room. "Let's get him back into his bed."

"No." I wave her off. "I'm going again."

"Mr. Jackson—"

I snap my head toward Casey and he can tell what I'm thinking. "I think he just wants to get out of here... can we just sign him out?"

Julie looks at him and then back to me. "Absolutely not! You're not going anywhere unless the doctor says you can. You almost died, Oliver!" Her voice rises and I smile at how cute she is when she's angry, which makes her even angrier. "Stop it, Oliver! This is serious! If you don't follow the doctor's rules...you're not going to recover fully."

I scoff. "I don't follow anyone's rules but my own."

I don't even follow my own *rules.*

Julie's phone dings in her pocket as she scowls at me. "Mary, if the doctor says he can leave, then I'll take him home. But—" She looks at the phone and then glares at me. "—if he says you can't go home, then you stay here."

"Yes, baby." I lower my eyes to the ground and pretend to pout. She laughs as I start walking around the circular floor again, this time with a little more speed than before. Her eyes are glued to her phone so I motion for Casey to come closer to me so we can talk.

I don't bother looking over at him. "Brandon called

—that's who I was talking to on the phone…not my lawyer. He wants to see Julie and she's got stuff at his house he wants her to pick up. We need to make him go away."

"I have my hands full already with Julie's surprise." He shakes his head, paying no attention to the rules of brotherhood. "I don't have time to worry about someone trying to take her from you, brother."

"You better start fucking worrying about it, *brother*," I snarl and look quickly behind us to see who's listening in. "If he gets her alone—which we know he can do, *remember*?—there's no telling what the hell he will do to her. For some fucked-up reason, she still trusts him."

Casey nods. "And you don't?"

I give him a stupid look because that was a stupid question. "You're kidding me, right? The guy destroys her life and lays his hands on her, tries to take her *in front of you,* and you can stand there and ask me that?"

"Okay, you're right." He shoves his hands into his pockets and now he's looking at the women behind us nervously. "What do you want me to do?"

I lick my lips and try to bite my tongue before I actually say what I'm thinking.

"I don't ever want her to be alone. There's going to come a time when I'll have to fly to New York City and take care of some business." I bite the flesh of my cheek and feel the pain I deserve. "And you're going to have to look after her."

"Why don't you just take her with you?"

Because I don't want her involved in anything that will make her leave me.

I have secrets just like any normal person.

That's why I have rule number three: Keep your secrets safe.

There are just some things about me that Julie can't fucking know: things that I don't even want to know myself.

Julie catches up with us and I have to end the conversation as she places herself in between our bodies. Her soft arms wrap around my waist and she smiles friendly at Casey, glitter in her eyes. "The doctor says you can leave tomorrow morning if you're feeling up to it."

I stop and turn to her, pulling her into a tight embrace. I push Casey back a little at the same time... he's a little closer to her than I'd like right now. Regardless if we agree on the Brandon problem, we still don't agree on the fact that he doesn't recognize he can't have her.

"That's fantastic," I say into her mess of hair; I don't care that it surrounds me. I missed it more than anything else when I was nowhere.

Nowhere.

That's where I've decided I was.

"There's something else." Her voice grows somber and she shows me her phone.

BRANDON

I have some of your things still. Come
get what you want soon please.

What things?

Some sentimental stuff you might want.
Whatever you don't take, I'll get rid of.

> I'm with Oliver at the hospital right now. He had an accident.

> I know. I talked to him earlier.

> I didn't know that. I will be there in the next few days, is that okay?

> Just hurry. Heather wants it gone.

Her eyes narrow at me. "Care to tell me what this is?"

My eyes get dry from how wide they are. She caught me. "He called you when I borrowed your phone. I told him to fuck off."

She rolls her eyes and Casey tries to hide a laugh. Once she glares in his direction, she directs it back to me. "Oliver, you might have made a mistake! I have some really sentimental things there still, and your little male ego tug might have caused him to destroy them!"

I feel bad.

No, I feel *really* bad.

"I'm sorry, baby, I didn't realize. Look, just call him and tell him that Casey will take you over there now."

Casey clears his throat. "Again, I'm still pretty busy."

I grind my teeth. "Fine, then whenever we get out of here...we'll go."

"Fine." She enters my room when we get to the open door. Casey excuses himself and Nurse Mary goes to fetch some paperwork. I look at Julie through the open door and let my body relax against the doorframe.

She sits in the chair next to the bed, waiting for me.

Her skin is so milky that it's almost impossible not to want to touch her. Her bright blue eyes meet mine and they twinkle at me, revealing the swirl of her emotions from anger to amusement.

I belong to her.

TWENTY-FOUR
JULIE

THE ENTIRE NIGHT, it was hard for either of us to sleep. I think we were both too excited to get out of this hospital and back to a real bed.

Together.

Halfway through the night, I let it slip that I brought some of the journals with me. He wasn't surprised and let me crawl as close as I could get to him so we could read some together. I'm sure he doesn't like reliving his past, but in my jumbled mind…I'm helping him get through something he doesn't know is holding him back. He needs the distraction right now, regardless of what the distraction is.

September 12th, 1992

Four incredible months.

I've had a complete, loving, and full family for four amazing months.

Veronica wasn't sure Oliver was going to make it, and it's all my fault. If I'd kept a closer watch on her during her pregnancy, he wouldn't have been born with so much hurt in his veins. She pushed so many things through her body that my son paid the price for.

I felt her pulling away from us these last few weeks, but I chose to ignore it and shower them with my love instead. She says it's what's made Oliver pull through like he has.

I think he's just strong...like his dad.

Or maybe it's a miracle, like Veronica says.

I shut the book and look at Oliver's sad eyes. "I know this can't be easy, learning the harsh truth about your own mother."

He shrugs. "It's nothing I didn't already know or suspect. She's not a good person, baby—I already know that." He smiles and touches my cheek. "She never had the light that you have...at least, *I've* never seen it."

My cheeks flush with heat. "I'm not an angel, Oliver."

He leans as close into me as he can without cringing from the pain. "Sunshine, you are my angel. Don't you ever forget that. Now..." He looks down at the closed book in my hands. "Let's read some more."

"That's all for this one." I hold up the book and shake it. "That was the last entry."

He scratches his jaw. "How many have we been through now? Three of them?"

"Yes, but I think I have the fourth in my bag." I rummage through the bag and find the faded green book, putting the finished one back inside for safekeeping. "Here it is."

Oliver breathes in deeply, but I don't hear him exhale as I start reading to him.

December 25th, 1997

"Wait, where are the books from the last five years?" Oliver interrupts me. "Did you grab all of the journals from the cabin?"

I shake my head. "No, this is the last one I took. They were all in order when I grabbed them, though. Maybe they're still in my library, and when you're better we can go look." I narrow my eyes at him, because he wants to argue and suggest that we go back to the cabin now—I can tell.

I start reading out loud to him again.

December 25th, 1997

Life is rough and hard.

I gave up on Veronica long ago and vowed my undying love to my son. Even my father is coming around and showing interest in being a grandfather. I'm grateful and happy for that, if for nothing else.

Last week was the last straw. I called Mrs. Atchley and explained everything to her before I had to leave town. I knew something was going to happen...deep down, something wasn't right. The air wasn't right, Veronica wasn't right. Mrs. Atchley raised me, and the very best thing I can do for Oliver is let her help me raise him.

I suspect that my father knows that I know Mrs. Atchley is my birth mother. I've known for some time, but there's a reason neither of them has come forward with the information. Regardless, I need her help in making Oliver into a functional member of society instead of the mess that Veronica almost twisted him into.

That's why I called her. I knew she would take Oliver if I couldn't make it home in time. And when she called me and told me about what Veronica and her friend, Mac, did to my son... that was the first time I'd ever felt hate for her.

Hate. For the mother of my son.

Even thinking it makes me sick.

I close the book and wait. Oliver doesn't speak—he's too busy remembering one of the worst times in his life, the day his mother left him for good. I hate myself for even telling him I had the journals, but in a way... it's a good thing he's facing this now when she's lurking around in the shadows.

"This is some heavy shit," he says with a quick exhale. "I think I'm done with that for a while."

A smile spreads across my face. "I'm proud of you for sitting through that. Your father kept a pretty detailed recollection of your life."

He nods. "Yeah, he was always a sentimental guy. Let's talk about something else."

"Well, we can talk about how you're going to behave at Brandon's house."

I agreed to let Oliver come with me to Brandon's house; some of the things that I want from there, I honestly never thought I'd see again. I gave Oliver some conditions about going with me, but all he did was smile like a schoolboy and mutter something about following the rules before falling asleep mid-conversation.

The rules.

I can't even think about those right now.

The rules of living.

The rules of breaking up.

The rules of not letting your boyfriend's best friend fall for you.

The rules of keeping your boyfriend *in* love with you.

Oliver is snoring softly next to me in his hospital bed. As his eyelids flutter, he finds my hand and inter-twines our fingers, sending jolts of electricity up my arm. I can't stop examining him like he's not really here. I can't help but wonder what substance we really have between us, not to question our love but to really figure out where it came from.

He *saved* me.

I saved him.

I found a new confidence in myself when Oliver started chasing me. There's a balance between us; he's rough and tumble and I'm the calm he seeks when life gets too messed up for him to process.

My classes start in three days...who will help take care of him when I'm away? I felt the tension between Oliver and Casey...Oliver knows something. He isn't stupid. He knows his best friend well. He knows that Casey is struggling with something inside of himself that no one can fix but him.

A few months ago, Oliver and I disgusted each other...or so we thought. He always seemed so angry, but that's because he was fighting an ember of feelings growing inside of him for me. We became so addicted to each other that it's probably not even healthy.

How can I be so in love with someone I barely know?

This isn't Brandon love—Brandon love was forced and broken.

Oliver love is pure and unexplained...heated and passionate.

He stirs next to me and I squeeze his hand to let him know I'm still here; he smiles in his sleep and continues to snore lightly. I don't know why I'm sitting here questioning everything—like usual—while this man who loves me sleeps soundly just knowing that I'm next to him.

A small knock on the door startles me and Mary pokes her head inside.

"I have some paperwork for you to sign if that's okay," she whispers. "Only a legal guardian or spouse can sign these, though." Her fingers scrape across the pages and it sounds like sandpaper.

I glare at her. "What are you saying, exactly?"

Her lips stretch into a thin line. "I'm saying that it was okay before when he was in trouble, but now, legally you can't sign these if you're not his wife."

I grit my teeth and start to seethe. "He told you I'm his wife."

"That doesn't mean you actually are, honey." Her voice is condescending enough to make me take a deep breath. "Just because you wish for something doesn't make it real."

I could pounce on her.

"Get out," I whisper, trying not to wake Oliver up. "Get the hell out of here."

Her laugh is louder now. "I could just have you escorted out of here, since it seems you aren't who you say you are."

"Yeah, but then I'll have your job, now won't I?" Oliver's tired voice chimes in as he sits up and stares at her. "I'd listen to my wife if I were you, Nurse Mary, and get the hell out of here before she kicks your ass." He starts to get up from the bed, but I place my hand on his shoulder to keep him down.

I turn to Mary and she's still frowning. "What's your problem?" I spit.

She grabs me by the arm and squeezes hard. "I think it's time for you to leave." Her voice is rough. Oliver rushes off the bed now and heads for us, yanking her arm free from the hard grip she has around mine.

His eyes are dark and scary. "Don't ever fucking touch her again," he growls. "What the hell is your problem?"

"I knew you wouldn't remember me, even when you were coherent enough. I tried to let it go and tried to be professional, but I can't do it anymore. You met her three months ago and already you're calling her your *wife*? We dated for six months before you dumped me for that Heather bitch, and all I got from you was a text message!"

Oliver laughs. "Oh, shit. I didn't even recognize you. Wasn't your name Mary *Braxton*?"

Nurse Mary scowls. "I use my mother's maiden name now."

Oliver laughs harder now. "I remember our relationship as more...casual than anything else. We weren't actually together."

My body squirms from how much he's shaming this woman. Clearly, she's been holding a torch for him for a long time, and I don't like the way he's talking to her. But that's a conversation for another time.

"Oliver—" I begin, but he cuts me off.

"I'm sorry that you feel like I treated you wrong, but I'm not that same person anymore. I also don't know what you want from me, since I'm in love with someone else."

Mary runs from the room, leaving us alone to look at each other and figure out what the hell just happened. When the door opens again, both of us hope that Mary isn't coming back for more.

"Hey there, you two," Dr. Osmond says loudly as he walks into the room. "How are you feeling today, Mr. Jackson?"

Oliver shakes his head and pulls me closer to him. "I'm actually doing better than I ever have, thanks to my nurse right here." Dr. Osmond chuckles as Oliver smiles at me. "I don't want Nurse Mary back in this room. She's not welcome here."

Dr. Osmond doesn't seem surprised. "That's not a problem. Now…" He waves his hands in the air. "Let's talk about getting discharged. If you feel strong enough, then you can sign out and go. I'll be flying back in six weeks for a follow-up, but in the meantime, you have to promise me that you'll do your physical therapy and get enough rest. Think you can handle that, Nurse Jackson?" The doctor winks at me, and I look at Oliver to make sure he isn't going to blow a gasket. I sweetly smile at the doctor and nod my head. "Good, then you are free to go. Normally we would keep you for longer, but you've seemed to heal very nicely. It's uncanny. You can call my personal phone if anything goes wrong, and Mr. Jackson…" His eyes burrow into the space between me and Oliver. "*No* working out."

"But—"

I raise my eyebrows. "You heard him."

"And no sex for at least six weeks."

Oliver's sigh fills the room. "You're fucking kidding me."

Dr. Osmond shakes his head. "I'm afraid not. No sex, no physical activity." He winks at me and shakes Oliver's hand before leaving the room. I forgot how peaceful he looks when he towers over me—how much he preys on my emotions when he does normal, mundane things like pick me up in a tight embrace.

I have to cross my legs and force myself to think about something else as he gathers his things, excited to finally be free. He runs some water through his now-longer hair and frowns into the mirror. "I need a haircut…wanna stop on the way home?"

Home.

I blush. "Anything for you, Mr. Jackson."

His broad smile finds me in the reflection of the mirror. "And anything for you, Mrs. Jackson."

Eek.

Double eek.

The feeling that I got when he first smiled at me months ago comes rushing back into my blood, making me dizzy. "First, we go to Brandon's to get my things." He jokes like he's having a heart attack as he turns around, and all I can do is laugh. "I promise we'll be in and out."

His deep emerald eyes find mine. "Promise?"

"Have I ever lied to you?" A nervous laugh escapes my throat because…yes, I have.

I've lied through my teeth.

His groan fills my head. "Fine. Let's go to Brandon's, but I get something in return for you making me see those jerks again." His smile is playful, and his thick fingers tug at the end of my t-shirt.

"Like what?"

Don't be stupid, Julie. You know what he wants.

He licks his lips slowly. "Cheeseburgers."

"Cheese—wait, what?" I have to hold down the vomit in my throat. He scared the hell out of me on purpose and his hearty laugh isn't making me feel any better. "I'll get you some cheeseburgers." His eyes are happy and they dance with mine; I take his waiting, outstretched hand. It's like we're back on the same wavelength as he tugs me into the elevator and nods his head at the on-looking nurses.

A fire burns in my stomach when I think about Mary.

What was her problem? How can someone hold onto something for that long?

Casey texts me that he got us a rental car that's waiting for us in the parking lot. I answer him with a quick "thank you" and make sure he can't read anything into it. I find the small blue car without a problem and watch Oliver cringe.

"Is the Jeep gone?" His sadness reaches out to me and I can't take the pressure.

I wrap my arms around him and he lets me hold him against the new car. "That's what Casey is working on for me."

He kisses my ear and pulls away quickly. "Call him off the case; I'll buy my own car. I love you for thinking of that, though. Plus, I want to drive."

I shake my head. "No way, get in the car. I'm not taking any chances."

He doesn't like it, but he gets in the passenger side. I really wanted to go to Brandon's alone, but Oliver was never going to let that happen. He buckles his seatbelt and folds his arms over his chest. "So, we're going to Brandon's. What do you have there that you want so badly? I can replace anything you've left behind."

My mouth moves before I even know it. "I don't like

when you throw your money around. There are some things that money can't buy, Oliver."

I've hurt his feelings, but there isn't any other way to say it. I've tried to ignore the comments he makes about buying me things and giving me whatever I want. While I appreciate the gesture…I don't need anyone to take care of me anymore.

"I have pictures and things. There's a ring that my Aunt Shelley gave me before she passed away. I want that back too."

He finds my hand and caresses my fingers. The roughness of his thumb excites me as it glides over my knuckles; I almost forget where we are and what we're doing. I know the way to Brandon's house like the back of my hand—I lived there, and I'll never forget the endless, tear-filled drives home I had going back there.

"You're quiet." Oliver's voice cuts through the silence as I turn onto Brandon's street. My heart races—I'm nervous. "Are you having second thoughts? I can send Casey back here and get your stuff."

I pull into the driveway and park the car. "No, I need to do this. I'm glad you're here with me. I don't think I could do this alone."

"Baby, I'll do anything for you. You know that, right?"

His sexy smile punches me in the stomach. "So, do you think you can handle this?" I motion toward the front door of Brandon's house. "It's a pretty stressful situation, and you just got out of the hospital…"

"Oh, I can handle this." He unbuckles his seatbelt and opens his door. It takes him longer than me to get out of the car. "The question is, can *you* handle it?"

I say nothing.

I know what he's talking about, but I still say noth-ing. The truth is...I don't *know* if I can handle this, but I'm glad he's here with me.

I'm going to try my best to fake it until I make it.

TWENTY-FIVE
CASEY

I DRIVE AWAY from the hospital parking lot after signing for Julie and Oliver's rental car; Julie is still on my mind even worse than before. I try not to think about her, but her pale, milky skin and bright ocean blue eyes haunt me.

What the hell is wrong with me?

I park outside my own apartment—a mile from Oliver's fancy one—and lay my head back on the headrest. I have to start thinking about Lucy. I still owe her dinner, and I'm exhausted. The guilt of not making more of an effort bothers me enough to make a better plan. I wonder if she'll want to come over to my place instead. I take out my phone to text her, but I don't know if I even want to...but I have to.

I have to get over whatever this is with Julie.

> Hey, do you want to come to my place for dinner tonight?

Her red hair fills my mind and it's nice to have something in my brain other than Julie for the first time for days. Lucy is sexy too…but she's not sneak-up-on-you sexy like Julie is. No, Lucy *screams* sex appeal and that's not a bad thing, either. I like women who leave a little mystery to themselves and Lucy wasn't exactly an open book when I spoke to her.

I'm not capable of a love triangle.

I can't even keep one woman interested in me.

I still want the instant chemistry and deep love that Oliver and Julie share.

LUCY

It's a date. What time?

Six o'clock. Wear something comfortable.

What do you mean? Like pajamas?

I laugh as I open my apartment door and step inside. I graduated from state college last year and my parents congratulated me by paying my rent until I find a job. I'm sure my father wasn't impressed that it's been over a year and I haven't found one.

I've been too focused on other things.

We can have a slumber party if you want. Dinner, movies, and popcorn?

I send it before I think about it. I know it was a stupid, cheesy thing to say, but it's too late to take it back now. I look around the apartment and feel more alone that I have in months.

Sounds amazing. Text me the address
and I'll see you at six.

My heart skips as I send her my address and look around the apartment again, scanning the room to see what needs to be done before she gets here. I keep a pretty clean place; I don't like a lot of clutter, and I haven't been here much lately to even make a mess if I wanted to. I've been chasing Julie around and being there for her.

Dammit.

I growl as I straighten the pillows on the sofa. It takes nothing to put me in a bad mood these days, but I have to get happy before Lucy gets here. I order pizza from my phone and decide to take a shower just in case something exciting happens and Lucy lets me sleep with her.

I'm disgusted with myself for thinking of her like that.

I don't want to sleep with her on the first date, I just don't. That's not the person I am. I like to know people before I do something that intimate with them. Except for Heather—she was just always...there. I don't feel bad about the way I treated Heather, because she treated herself the same exact way. She hates herself, I can tell.

The shower sounds like a heavy rainfall when I turn it on; big, fat drops of water splash on the walls and welcome me inside. I turn the temperature up and step in. The heat from the steady stream rises around me and clears my negative thoughts away.

No Julie.

No Heather.

No Nora.

Lucy.

There she is.

Wild, red hair.

Subtle freckles on her cheeks.

Thin lips that pucker when she's annoyed.

Olive-green eyes.

Perfectly shaped ass.

Okay, there we go. I smile and I'm finally able to let go of whatever's holding me back and start washing myself clean. It's not going to be fair to Lucy if I'm with her and thinking of someone else, especially if that someone else isn't available. I make sure I scrub every inch of my body to ease more tension, seriously thinking about relieving myself in other ways before Lucy arrives.

It scares me to wonder who I'll think about when I do it, though.

I immediately turn the water off and step out, wrapping a towel around my lower half. As I look in the mirror, I frown. My entire life I've wanted to look like Oliver—*be* like Oliver—and have the life that he has. I've never been satisfied with myself, even though I'm not exactly a disgusting troll. I work out, but no matter how much I try...I never match up to him.

I don't even know why I bother, really.

But Lucy doesn't even know Oliver, and that's an advantage I'm willing to take.

Before I get dressed, I do a few push-ups on my bedroom floor just for good measure. I know it won't make a difference right now, but it makes me feel good to know that I'm trying. Not knowing if Lucy is really showing up in pajamas, I decide to put on jeans and a t-shirt to make her more comfortable when she gets here.

There's a knock on my apartment door and I panic, looking at the time.

"Shit, she's here." I gather my laundry, putting it into the wicker basket in the corner of the room. She knocks again and I race to the front door, take a deep breath, and look through the peephole just to make sure.

Holy shit. She's really here.

"Hey," I say as I open the door. She eyes my clothes and blushes. I've made her uncomfortable within the first ten seconds—a new record for me. "I'm glad you could make it."

She smiles and steps through the open door, looking around. "I thought you said we were having a slumber party?" Her giggle bubbles around my skin. "Do you sleep in jeans?"

I blush. "No, I was changing when you knocked on the door. You can make yourself at home and I'll change now." I motion to the living room and smile at her. "The pizza should be here soon—you can pick out a movie if you want."

"Rom-com?" Her eyes grow wide. "I've always wanted to make a guy watch some cheesy, out-of-this-world romantic movie with me…"

My laugh makes her take a few steps toward me. "Whatever you want. I'm your slumber party slave."

"Slumber party slave, huh?" She tips her chin up and my stomach sinks.

She wants me to kiss her.

271

I'm still struggling with the Julie mess. I don't want to confuse her.

"I'll go change," I mutter and go back to my room, not bothering to shut the door behind me. I really don't want Lucy to act like Heather—slutty and cold-hearted—but I really think this is where she's headed. It's a major turn-off for me to be with a woman who acts like she's got so much self-esteem that it will explode on me at any given moment.

I like the kind of beauty and grace that creeps up on you.

Like, Nora and Julie…

"Hey, Casey?" Lucy's voice wafts through the open door, but she doesn't come into view. "I think the pizza is here."

I shove on some sweatpants and join her in the living room, where she gives me a look. It's the look I've been waiting for someone to give me: the look that says I'm the only person in the world they see. I try not to smile but I can't help it. It's nice being crushed on again. I honestly don't know how to navigate this, but I make a silent vow to myself to not ruin it.

I open the door, grab the pizza, tip the delivery guy, and shut the door before Lucy even gets up from the sofa. She feels so comfortable here and that makes me feel nice inside—even Nora didn't bother coming to my place no matter how many times I begged. We were always hanging out at her small, studio apartment in the Art District. Not that I can complain too much—we did get to watch some awesome street plays from her fire escape staircase.

The pizza smells delicious as I place it in front of her

on the coffee table and open the box. Keeping it casual, that's what I want from this. What's more casual than sharing pizza from a box without plates? She grabs a slice, snuggles into the corner of the sofa, and smiles. "Pepperoni pizza, food of the gods."

Okay. I can do this.

I grab a few blankets from the hallway closet, put them on the other end of the sofa, and sit down next to her. Her pink pajama pants have small kittens on them, and that makes me smile. The arm of her matching pink, long-sleeved t-shirt rubs the bare flesh on my arm, making me do something stupid.

I grab her arm and pull her closer to me, and she doesn't hesitate.

Before I know it, her legs are wrapped around mine and her body is flush against my side, pizza still in her hand and smile still on her face. "This is nice," she says, blushing. "It's nice to be close to someone without them wanting something in return."

I lean forward and grab a slice of the pizza. "All I want from you is your company, right now. Anything else can come when it comes."

She nods and hands me the remote. "You're not going to like the girly movies I choose, so you might as well pick one."

I shake my head. "No, lady's choice. You pick whatever you want."

She giggles and snuggles as deep into me as she can without sitting on my lap. Although, I wouldn't have pushed her off if she tried. Is this what it was like for Oliver and Julie? They were strangers until they just let themselves be and let the love grow between them?

I can love Lucy if I really try.

Halfway through the pizza and chick flick she chose, the sun starts to go down and the evening chill fills the apartment. It's early October, so I haven't turned on the heat yet, but I stand up and flick it on just for Lucy. When I sit back down, she nuzzles her head on my chest and the only thing I can do is put my arm around her shoulders.

Like a date.

"Are you cold?" I ask into her mess of red hair. "I have blankets." I find the blankets next to me and spread one across the both of us, feeling her smile move the fabric of my t-shirt. I slide my arm down her side and hold her against me, waiting for her to object, but she doesn't move an inch from my body. I make a grunting noise and take a deep breath. "I think we need dessert." I smile down at her and she raises herself from me.

Her olive-green eyes meet mine and it's the weirdest feeling I've ever felt before.

I need her.

Lucy is going to fix me.

She's going to make me forget all about Nora.

And hopefully Julie too.

"Oh, Dilaggio's delivers the best chocolate cake on the planet." She licks her lips. "It's literally to die for." She sees the stare I've fixed on her and lowers her eyes. "Oh, I'm sorry. I didn't mean to—"

Shit.

My body lurches toward her and I devour her lips. I know she's confused but I don't care; I want her so bad that it's hurting my insides.

I don't even remember what Julie looks like.

That's a lie. I'm thinking about Julie as my lips slide across Lucy's and she caresses my tongue with hers in small, circular motions. I grip the sides of her face and hold her in place, moving my lips from hers and trailing them down her neck and collarbone. My hands slide down her sides and grip her waist with force.

"Whoa," she says breathlessly. "Slow down."

I know I have to listen to her—I'm not that kind of guy to just keep going when a girl says otherwise. I press my lips back up the trail that I just went down and she moans as I reach her jawline. I know she wants more, but she told me to slow down. "I'm sorry...I don't know what the hell just came over me."

Lucy's smile reaches her eyes. "Let's just take a minute. You're a good guy, Casey."

Oh, no. I know where this is going.

I lower my eyes into my lap. "I understand."

Her long finger touches my chin and lifts my gaze back up to meet hers. "I've done some things lately I'm not proud of. I have secrets. Nothing illegal or really bad, but...I'm not a very lucky person in the love department..."

I scoff. "Join the club."

Lucy's lips taste like vanilla cupcake lip gloss when she sits on her knees to kiss me again. It's not a hungry kiss this time; it's more sensual and sexy. I wrap my arms around her and squeeze her small body against me. "You smell amazing," I say and tickle her neck with my nose. "I'm not the best person, either. I've done some fucked-up shit."

She giggles. "Like what?"

"I've cheated and I'm not proud of it. I don't know why I can't let someone be in love with me. I always fuck it up for myself."

The sadness that she has for me reaches my heart. "You're not alone in that."

I snort. "I'm sure you have men falling at your feet."

She laughs. "I most certainly do not."

Before I tear up, I clear my throat and find my phone on the table next to us. "I'll order some cake if you find the wine in the kitchen and bring it in here." She claps her hands together and jumps up from the sofa, disappearing into the kitchen. I call Dilaggio's and order a large cake. Who knows? We may need something for a midnight snack.

I plan on taking her to bed with me.

I just need to stop thinking about Julie first.

TWENTY-SIX
LUCY

I LOOK AT CASEY, and his short, sandy blond hair is matted to his forehead with sweat from worrying about saying the wrong thing to me. It's cute, the way he fusses over me and makes sure I'm comfortable and taken care of. Even though we just met, I can see myself with someone like him. Or maybe I just wish I could be with someone like him. If Casey ever found out that I went to a man's apartment just to sleep with him knowing he had girlfriend...I'm almost positive that would be a turn-off for him.

He likes good girls.

I'm not a good girl anymore.

That part of me is long, long gone.

He's a little skittish around women, but in a sweet way. He's so nervous that I want to just hold his hand to calm him down, but that probably wouldn't work. When we touch, even accidentally, his body tenses and he can't move.

I had to teach myself how to be with men. I didn't

have much experience with boyfriends or relationships when I was younger. Heather was the one who got all the guys. They were only "friends" with me to get to her, and it worked like a charm every single time. She would be so impressed by how they would treat me that she would steal them from right underneath my nose before we could even hold hands. Our parents grew up as friends, so it was only natural that *we* would be friends—except that she treated me like mud on her feet when we were alone.

I just want someone to hold my hand and never let go.

"Hey, you're quiet." Casey smiles at me around a big bite of chocolate cake. I melt a little inside, but I don't let it show on my face. We only met a few days ago and there's no way I should be feeling something for someone I don't even know. But, this isn't like the Oliver situation...I was only interested in him out of boredom. This time, it's for me.

Casey is for me.

I am a damsel in distress and he wants to save me.

I smile and my mind wanders to all the wonderful opportunities that I can daydream about. Far-fetched relationship milestones fill my brain when I hear him clear his throat and it knocks me back to our reality. "Are you okay? If you're nervous—"

"I'm not nervous." I laugh and wipe a small bit of chocolate cake from his lip. He smiles and welcomes my touch—the more time we spend together, the easier it is for him to just be himself. I don't want him to be anything else.

He leans down and presses his lips to mine while still in mid-bite, but I don't mind it. It's cute and fresh and all the things I want wrapped up into one little peck on the lips. "You can run a background check on me if you want. I'm not a bad guy."

Heartbreakers aren't in an online database.

A wide smile spreads across my face. "No, it's okay. I don't feel danger from you."

I thought this would make him happy to hear. Instead, he frowns as if I've offended him. "I guess I'm not the dangerous kind. Does that bother you? That I'm not a bad boy?"

I giggle, and I can't stop myself. "No one says the phrase 'bad boy' anymore, do they? Casey, nice guys are underrated and unappreciated. I've always wanted to be with a guy who opens doors for me and courts me."

He laughs. "Courts you? What, are we in the early nineteen hundreds?"

I know he's joking, so I stick my tongue out at him playfully. "You know what I mean. I've never been on a real date before. No one has ever taken the time to figure out what to do with me other than stick me on their arm and forget about me."

"Well, let's forget about our pasts and just focus on the future. Now let's finish this god-awful chick movie and watch some robots fighting or something."

I finish my cake and take our dishes to the kitchen, hoping he'll follow me. I'm not sure Casey has that intuition—the kind where you can read women so well that you keep doing things they secretly want and like without any effort. I'm sure it's a learned trait at best, so I don't dwell on the fact that he's still waiting for me to come back to him on the sofa.

He hands me a newly topped-off glass of wine and smiles as I snuggle back into the nook of his arm to watch the rest of the movie I wasn't even paying attention to in the first place. It's nice to be calm and happy with someone, no matter who it is.

The movie ends and we notice that the night sky is even darker now through the sliding glass doors that lead to his balcony outside. The crooked smile on his face warns me that he's got something up his sleeve, but I don't say anything as he pulls on socks and boots and disappears into his bedroom. When he emerges, he's carrying two sweatshirts and two more smaller blankets. "Put your shoes on, we're going outside," he demands, winking at me. There's nothing I can do but what he wants; I'm curious to see what he's planning.

I let him lead me outside and close the door behind us. The crisp October night air attacks my body and I shiver. He folds the blanket around me and tightens me into it, looking down at me for confirmation that I'm not freezing anymore.

"What are we doing out here?" My teeth chatter and I watch him pull a small bench away from the wall.

"We're going to do some stargazing. Have you ever taken the time out and just looked at them? It's remarkable; sometimes you can see things you wouldn't normally see."

I watch the child-like excitement in his eyes; he's really serious.

"Like what?" I join him on the bench and let him put his arm around me. "Like aliens or UFOs or something?"

His laugh is hearty and it's one I've never heard

from him before. It's almost like he's loosening up to feel something other than the pain he inflicts on himself by overthinking and trying to be someone he's not. "No, nothing like that. I don't think so, anyways." He laughs again and tightens his grip. "I come out here to think sometimes. It's nice to just be out here with nothing but the air and the night sky."

I want to kiss him, but my lips are a little too frozen for it to be pleasurable. This man—a man that picked me up from the side of a sketchy road wearing a too-short dress—is opening up to me, and it just feels so…real.

"And you're sharing this with me? I don't know what to say."

His blanket unfolds from around his body and he tucks me inside with one swoop of his large arm. Casey just wants someone to feel his pain—someone who understands what it's like to want something so bad but it's always out of reach. I can be that person for him if he really lets me try. I moved to Rockford to be close to Heather and feed off her infectious personality to try and get what I want out of life.

The problem is…I'm not even sure what I want anymore.

"There!" His voice electrifies me as he points to the sky. I immediately look at that section of the inky canvas above us and see it.

A shooting star.

"That means good luck is coming to us, right?" He smiles. "That something good is coming our way. I really hope that's true."

I can't take it anymore. I have to know something —*anything*—about him.

"Casey, can we talk?" My voice is almost a whisper because I'm not quite sure I want to open a conversation that can lead to him slamming the door in my face.

"Uh-oh, that doesn't sound good."

I make a point to lean up and kiss his lips before smearing a comforting smile on my face. "No, nothing bad. I just want to know more about you. You seem… reserved about something and I was just wondering—"

He sucks in air through his teeth, like pain is shooting through his chest. "There's nothing about me that you need to worry about. I'm just a guy who's looking for good things to happen to him, and you—" he tries to push the handsomest smile he can muster onto his face, "—just might be one of them."

My heart flutters and I have to clutch my chest for it to stop. "I've done some things in life that I'm not proud of, Casey."

"We all have, Lucy. I've been in love with people that I shouldn't be."

That doesn't sit with me well, maybe because I'm starting to like him. It's weird, being so close to someone you don't even know. He's a sad person but he tries to hide it so well that he loses himself in the process.

"Hey, I'm sorry. I don't mean to upset you." His voice drowns me in sadness. "I'm just really tired of messing things up for myself. I want a normal relationship where I'm not constantly worrying about losing it."

I nod my head because I know exactly what he

means. "I want that too." The tone of my voice surprises me. "So maybe we can get to know each other better before we go any further in finding what we both want."

"Okay, what do you want to know?"

I push myself out of his warm cocoon and he gets up, disappears into the apartment for a few minutes, and comes back with a new wine bottle and our glasses. He hands me my newly filled glass and bends down to light a fire in the pit a few feet from us. I like that he automatically puts his arm around me when he sits back down, and he makes sure that I'm comfortable before getting himself into a good position. "Okay, now I'm ready." He snorts and tips the red liquid to his lips. "Now, what is a good topic to start with?"

"We can start with…how did you end up in Rockford?" I say, hinting that I want to talk about how *I* actually ended up here. I vow to leave Heather out of it and sugarcoat some things, but for the most part I'm planning on being honest.

Unless he's not honest with me. But I have no way of knowing either way.

"I grew up here." He stretches his long legs out in front of us. "Born and raised. What about you? I know you didn't grow up here…I would remember someone like you."

I blush. "Someone like me? What does that mean?"

He laughs and it's like silk ribbons floating in the air. "I didn't mean any disrespect. I only meant I would remember someone as beautiful as you are."

I wasn't always this beautiful.

"I grew up in the south," I say and shake my head. I

know I'm being vague, but I just don't like people knowing things about my past self that will embarrass me. "I lived with my parents. I have two brothers and a pretty normal life."

"Vague." He scratches his chin. "Where in the south?"

I get nervous and he pulls his bottom lip in with his teeth. "I-I lived in a lot of places...we moved around a lot until we settled in a small town about thirty miles outside of Atlanta."

"Were your parents in the military?"

I start to sweat and swallow the lump that's gathering in my throat. "No, they're real estate agents. We just moved around a lot, nothing special."

He accepts that I don't want to talk about my family...and he seems okay with not talking about his too. The truth is inside of the lie; I *did* live with my parents and we *were* a normal family...right down to my very much older twin brothers, Max and Tyler. We lived a normal, boring life and at the time, I was okay with it. I didn't know of life outside of the lower-class outskirts of Atlanta. I lived the life my parents wanted me to live; I focused on school and more important things than parties and boys. I got good grades and I got my real estate license to make my parents proud while my brothers towered over me in everything else.

Max is a pediatrician who graduated medical school with no debt and top of his class.

Tyler is a lawyer, got loads of sports scholarships, and graduated from law school with no debt and money in the bank.

I'm the hopeless younger sister that they don't

expect much from. I didn't get a scholarship or any free money for school; I worked at a fast-food restaurant and took night classes.

I feel Casey's hand in mine and my body warms up from my fingertips touching his. He can feel my sadness, I'm sure. "Maybe we should focus more on the now instead of our pasts, yeah?" His deep chestnut eyes play with mine as he bends over to kiss the tip of my nose. "There's nothing more important to me than honesty, and once I can't trust that you're giving me honesty anymore…that's it. So just keep that in mind."

A small noise escapes my throat. "It goes both ways, you know. Maybe we should set some rules between us…judging that we both are in desperate need of something that we've been looking for."

He nods. "Okay, what are the rules?"

I shrug my shoulders. "I don't know, we can make them up as we go. Like…okay, our first rule can be something like—"

"Wait." He holds up his hands. "My best friend lives life by a set of rules and it's not working out too well for him. Maybe we should skip that."

I laugh and shake my head. "We're a mess."

His arm tightens around me and he makes a grunting noise. "You can say that again. Look, I don't know how to be with someone…like at all. I always ruin it, so look forward to that."

"Casey…" My voice trails off because I don't know what to tell him. I'm a mess just like he is. We both deserve better, but we don't know how to *get* better. It's even crazy to me that I'm sitting here with a man I hardly know, talking about intimate things that should be avoided on a first date altogether. "I think maybe we should just not try so hard."

He frowns. "That sounds promising, not trying so hard. I've always exhausted myself trying to get what I want, but you're saying we should let it be and come to us when it wants to?" The smile that spreads across his face is intoxicating. He's handsome, like really handsome, and that unsettles me. I'm no good around handsome men; I say and do the wrong things, but this time it's different. This time it feels...safe.

"I'm going to say or do something to make you run," he warns.

I sigh. "Likewise. Let's just promise to hold on for dear life."

He chuckles and unwraps himself from the blanket, pulling me up next to him and swooping down to pick me up in his thick arms. "Hold on, then." He laughs and we go back into the warmth of the apartment.

Casey is deep and has real feelings.

I don't want to hurt them, but I don't want him to know how painfully plain I was before I moved here.

I don't want him to know anything about me.

That is all shades of messed up.

TWENTY-SEVEN
BRANDON

MY HEART nearly explodes from my chest.

Julie is outside.

Julie. Is. Outside!

Wait, but she brought Oliver with her.

Look at his smug, annoying face.

For a guy who basically cheated death, he still looks better than me, and that pisses me off. There isn't any time for that right now, though. I have to warn Heather about who is walking up the driveway at this very moment. I should've told her when I got back home, but she was in the shower so I left it alone. I planned on telling her before now, but here they are, slowly walking up the grass to ring the doorbell.

Heather is humming to herself in her purple room when I knock on the door and open it before she has time to invite me inside. "Well, hello *boyfriend*." She puts a sweet tone in her voice and smothers me with it like honey. Her slippery, wet glossed lips dart toward mine and even though I'm totally grossed out by the sticky mess, I kiss her back anyway.

I fake a smile and grab her waist, pulling her away from me and getting a good grip on her so she can't run. "I have something to tell you, *girlfriend*." I look nervously behind me and see her glare at me in the process. "You probably aren't going to like it, either."

She pushes herself from me completely. "What is it?"

Okay, here we go.

I take a deep breath. "Oliver and Julie are here. She's picking up some of her stuff from that room upstairs." I blow out the rest of the air and watch her closely for a temper tantrum. She has about sixty seconds to throw one. She purses her lips together and squints at me, as if she's waiting for me to continue. I shrug my shoulders and turn to leave, but she gently grabs my arm and tugs me back to her, making me land a few inches from her lips.

"Is there anything I can do to help you get through this?" Her eyelashes touch her cheeks and I can feel excitement in my bones. I have to push her away and clear my throat to compose myself just as I hear the doorbell ring. Heather laughs because she knows I'm playing the fool. She knew that she would get me heated and that's why she did it, that little sneaky—

Bells ring around me.

"Okay, they're really here now." I breathe in deep for a few seconds longer than I should. Heather notices my nervousness and squints her golden-brown eyes at mine. I clear my throat to show her that I can shake it off, but we both know I'm not kidding either of us for a second. "Let's get this over with. You and I have a date with that bed." I playfully growl and point toward her ugly, purple-infested mess of a bed.

I know that once I'm able to be close to Julie and feel her warmth again, I'm going to be putty at her feet. She's my angel; she's saved me from everything without so much as me thanking her.

Heather gets to the door first and forces a perfect, welcoming smile on her lips. I snicker at her because I know how excruciating it is for her to play nice. For my sake, she will. I know she will. I just hope to hell she doesn't ruin my sudden interest in her. Most times she's dripping with so much desperation that it suffocates me; she's like a siren, calling you to her addicting song.

Not Julie.

Julie is sweet and pure—everything you can ever imagine a perfect life could or would be. I can feel Oliver's prestigious ego as the door opens and the four of us look at each other with such awkwardness that it actually hurts.

"Um…hello!" Heather's voice is even more fake than her smile. She moves her body to the side of the doorway with me, extending her arm out for the two of them to walk into the house without touching us. I can feel the confusion coming from Oliver and Julie and she helps him hobble into the hall. Julie looks around nervously, like she remembers only the bad times she's had here with me.

There were good times too.

A lot of good times.

Before I fucking ruined it.

I cringe when I think about how it must feel to come

back here for her. "Uh, hey it's nice to see you upright and walking again, man." I chuckle and look at Oliver, who doesn't even act like he heard me at all. I brush myself against Heather on purpose, so she can jolt me back into a normal person and help me through this. She takes my hand and squeezes gently; she under-stands how hard this is for me because she's feeling the same exact way.

Oliver and Julie are together.

Heather and I are...

Together.

Julie pokes Oliver's side and he groans. "I bet it is nice to see that I can't be erased." His eyes find mine and my blood starts to boil. Julie pokes his side again, giving him a look I know too well.

"I mean...*thanks*," he hisses. He takes a deep, calming breath. He doesn't want to be here any more than I fucking want him here.

Why didn't she just come alone?

She doesn't trust me.

I don't blame her. I don't trust myself with her, either.

My smile grows wicked and I let go of Heather's hand. "Are you going to be able to take those stairs and help Julie with her stuff?" I almost laugh, but Heather pinches my finger to make me calm down. I know that he would at least try to get up the stairs because he doesn't want me alone with Julie.

Heather picks up on my frustration. In her own twisted little way, she silently decides to help me get what I want. "I can get you something to drink or eat if you want while you wait, Ollie."

Oliver cringes. "Why can't you call me by my real fucking name?"

Julie holds up her hands. "Okay, calm down. Oliver, please…let Heather help you down here, okay? I'll only be a few minutes."

Oliver snorts. "Uh, no. I'll be okay. I'm coming up."

"No, please don't make me put my foot down." Her smile matches his and it makes me fucking sick to look at. I glance at Heather—from in between their little love bubble—and she frowns, looking at the floor. I instantly glide toward her and take her hand. We listen to the both of them while our eyes lock in matching pain.

"Oh, put your foot down, huh? I'm so scared."

Julie playfully slaps Oliver's shoulder. "You should be. I don't want anything more happening to you—I can't handle any more bad things right now."

He sighs. "Fine, only because I love you."

She giggles and Heather whimpers. "I love you too. Now, go sit down."

Oliver glares at me and does what she asks.

I am going to faint. That used to be me…I used to be the one who would do anything she asked of me. You just do that for someone like Julie, no questions asked.

"Actually, Heather…" Julie's voice breaks back into my head. "He really hasn't eaten anything decent in a few days. Would it be too much trouble—"

"No trouble!" Heather squeaks and lets go of my hand. I admit, it pisses me off that she's so quick to jump to Oliver's aid, but I understand so I let it go. Heather flitters over to the sofa and hands Oliver my remote.

My remote.

I almost explode when she looks at me. I clear my throat and open my arms to Julie, watching Heather's annoyed gaze. Okay, so now we are playing the jealousy game as well as the get-your-ex-back game.

This is going against all the rules of getting what you want.

I gesture an invite to Julie to walk up the stairs and I lock eyes with Oliver. I can feel his hate for me from twenty feet away. All I can do is smile at him without the girls seeing me and I follow Julie as closely as I can up the flight of stairs knowing that he's seething about it. When we enter the room with all the boxes, I shut the door behind us and she doesn't notice or act like she fears me anymore at all.

I never wanted her to fear me in the first place.

She starts rummaging through some boxes and places an empty one on a nearby table. She fills it with small knickknacks and other various objects. I wait for her to go through a few boxes before trying to fill the silence. "So…" I sit down next to where she stands. "He looks like shit." The look of horror on her face sends shivers down my body.

"He nearly *died*, Brandon." Her scoff sends me into a frenzy. "You'd look like shit too."

She opens another box and buries her thoughts into it. I have something that I need to tell her, but I don't know how she'll react, so I leave her to her walk down memory lane for a while, just watching her. The curves of her hips define more as she bends over, and I blush from wanting her so fucking bad.

I wish it would stop.

She's going to find my secret in these boxes.

There isn't much I can to do waste any more time, so I join her in opening boxes and sifting through them, holding up several things for her to approve or disapprove. We share photos with each other and talk about the past—the good past—and how many good times we shared.

"Oh, remember this? This is from that summer we stayed in that log cabin on the beach in Florida." She shows me a glossy photo and we laugh at the funny faces we're making in it. "Oh, and you got so sunburnt that we had to stay an extra few days for you to heal." She holds her hands over her mouth, laughing hysterically.

"Yeah, you weren't the one with a thousand fires on your ass." I smile and take the picture from her. Our fingers touch and she doesn't notice, making my good mood vanish quickly. "We had a lot of good times, Jules."

It's now or never.

I have to try before using my secret weapon.

"We can have an entire lifetime of good times if you come back."

Julie cocks her head, her gaze searching mine for an answer. "Wait, you wanted to get me up here without Oliver to do *this*?" Her voice shakes violently, vibrating the air around our bodies. "What is *wrong* with you? You have Heather downstairs, what about her?"

"Okay, okay," I growl at her. "Keep it down before Saint Jackson breaks his other leg trying to run up the stairs and save you from nothing." I stand up to walk across the room and sit back down far, far away from her to save a little face. "It's no secret I'm still in love with you, Julie. Heather can even see it, and that's why she offered to stay with Oliver downstairs—so I can do whatever it takes to get you back." Her face crumples when she thinks about Oliver alone with Heather downstairs, and her gaze goes to the closed door. "Don't worry, she won't touch him. I have her wrapped around my finger…remember what that's like?"

Julie makes a gagging sound, shaking her head. "You're as disgusting as the day I left. I'm going to just take these few boxes and go. I don't know what I was thinking coming up here alone with you. Everything you and I had was a lie." I see a white piece of paper sticking out of a box when she passes me. I quickly snatch it before she leaves the room and I wave it in the air as she turns to face me with disgust on her face.

Complete disgust.

"You and Heather deserve each other." She tries to handle the two boxes in her arms with grace. "You are both messed up, and you mess other people up in your self-pity process." Her eyes follow the document that I'm still waving in the air. "What is that? Why are you waving that around like a flag?" She puts her boxes down and grabs the paper from me. I watch the color drain from her face as she reads through it. "This isn't real…I would have remembered something this big." She continues to read, and her knees buckle enough for her to hold onto the now open doorframe. "When did this happen? Is this real?"

Panic.

There's panic in her voice.

This isn't going well.

And it doesn't make me feel good, either.

I know I can run downstairs with the paper and show it to Heather and Oliver, but Heather wouldn't even bat an eyelash. Oliver would be furious. I smile and see Julie's eyes scanning the paper with so much hope that it isn't real that it's upsetting.

She sees my smirk. "Oliver knows all of the things you forced me to do when we were together; he isn't going to like this." Her nose crinkles like she smells something sour and the darkness in her voice scares me a little. "If you think this means anything, you're wrong. I don't believe this is even real. It's a scare tactic to get me to stay."

I didn't even think of that.

I act offended, even though she's right. "Oh, please. You remember this and you know it. It's sad that I have to even show you this for you to remember."

"Why are you just now showing me this if it's real?"

I shrug. "I kept it hidden until I needed it."

"I didn't do this!" Her hiss fills the room and shakes my body. She snorts and pockets the paper for safe-keeping. "You can do what you want, but Oliver will never believe you over me. He loves me more than he hates you." She starts to bite her fingernails—she does this when she knows she's backed against a wall.

"Well, let's find out." I start to glide past her, but she stops me.

"Why are you doing this to me?" I hear the voice that I created for her: that certain mixture of fear and hopeless pain that she perfected years ago. "Haven't I had enough from you? What will it take for you to just stop torturing me? All I ever did was love you, and you threw me out like garbage…and I try to move on and be happy with someone who has healed every single burn you've given me, and for what? When will you just let me go so I can be happy? Why can't *you* just be happy with Heather?"

I want to wipe the tears away that are running down her cheeks.

But it's not my place anymore.

I can see that clearly now.

It took another round of me breaking her down to realize that.

"I won't tell him about it, Jules." I swallow the lump in my throat. "You can trust me, I won't tell him. You're right, I need to try and be happy with Heather. I've been obsessing over what we had for far too long...I'm only fooling myself."

She searches my eyes for the lie.

There's no lie.

She's right and there's nothing I can do about it.

I've lost her forever.

Nothing I do is going to make her love me more than Oliver now, after he's swooped in and saved her from her horrible life.

The life I created for her and then destroyed.

She shakes her head at me and then picks up the boxes again, but I take them from her arms. She lets me help her, but it's not without reluctance. "Hey, Julie?" She puts her fingers to her lips to let me know to lower my voice. "How do you know you didn't love me and that you do love him?"

"I *did* love you—don't think that I never did. There was a time when all I loved was you, but you ruined it.

We could have been happy forever if you didn't destroy everything. And here we are…strangers again."

Ouch.

My chest hurts.

She feels bad, but I don't bother calling her out on it. "There are lots of different ways that I know I'm in love with Oliver and not you anymore. Life with Oliver has its drama, of course, but nothing like *our* drama. I can see a healthy future with him, and I feel good about it, but with you I felt…trapped. I lived in a dark place for a long time. I'm not saying we didn't have good days, but you crushed me into a million pieces like it was a sport."

I let her come down on me because I deserve it. I'm pretty fucking much a piece of scum on her shoe.

"Just promise me you won't treat Heather like that. You two actually—in a messed-up sort of way—need each other."

She turns to lead me back down the stairs but looks at me once more, as if this is the last time she's ever going to see me.

"Don't get in the way of your own happiness. Set some rules for yourself and follow them. You're a good guy—you just need to find the right person that can handle you, and it wasn't me. Do everything the complete opposite and you should be okay." She gives me a small smile, but I know it doesn't belong to me anymore.

She belongs to Oliver.

She takes the boxes from me and I don't continue following her downstairs. I hear Oliver ask her a question and after a few long minutes, the front door opens and closes…I can feel her grace leave the house.

She's gone for good now.

Footsteps bleed into my ears and Heather peeks her head around the corner of the open doorway. She looks around the room and frowns. "She didn't take much."

I shake my head and try to hold back the tears. "Throw it all away."

She comes over and hugs me. My arms tighten around her thin waist. "I'm sorry you didn't get what you wanted," she whispers into my ear. "I didn't either, but I didn't even try." I smile and let her kiss my cheek. "But I'm still here, you know that, right? She's gone, but I'm still here."

My smile grows bigger. "Yes, you are."

Julie is so fucking right…like always.

Heather and I are going to be happy. Time to start making some rules for myself and actually following them.

"I think it's time you move into my bedroom and we act like we're in a real relationship." I feel her conviction but her arms ease when she pulls away and looks up into my eyes. "Unless you want to stay in that purple monstrosity of a room."

She giggles. "I hate the color purple."

I laugh loudly and pull her back into my body. "I hate the color purple too. But…" I breathe in her citrus perfume and hold her close. "But I think I might like you a little."

And this time…

I'm not lying.

TWENTY-EIGHT
OLIVER

"WELL THAT TOOK LONGER than I thought," I say as Julie comes down the stairs and glares at Heather as she passes her. I see the paleness of her face and my stomach drops. "Are you okay? What happened up there?"

She doesn't answer me as she takes my hand and helps me to my feet. She leads me out the front door while mumbling a "thank you" to Heather for feeding me. She shuts the door behind us, two boxes balanced awkwardly in her hands.

"That woman can't even boil water—she fed me a peanut butter sandwich and tried to give me a glass of whiskey. What is wrong with you? Why are we running away? I can still kick his ass like this, you know." I keep talking until we're buckled into the rental car and she pulls out of the driveway. "You better start talking or I'm going back there with Casey later to straighten it out."

The anger washes away from her, but her voice is

weak. "It was just too many memories, that's all. It took me on an emotional rollercoaster, and I realize that I don't need anything else from that place. Those memories aren't with you, so I don't want them." She smiles at me. The darkness settles in the sky around us, but there's still enough light for me to see the lies spread across her lips. But I don't want to press it and make her shut down on me.

We don't talk about Brandon for two full days after that.

Two glorious, love-filled days.

I know I stumbled upon my love for Julie; it definitely wasn't expected. I even tried to ignore it at first, but that destroyed me even more. I wait for her to return home with some of her things from Randy's house...he agreed to let her come over and pack her things before her classes start tomorrow. I offered to just replace it all, but she wouldn't hear it. She told me what her brother said to her when I was in the hospital and I wanted to go with her, but she didn't want me to cause a scene.

I would have caused a *huge* fucking scene. No one talks to her like that.

No one.

I pay the security guard to help her bring in her things, and once they bring the last of the load inside and he leaves, we laugh together at the lack of space. "Don't unpack anything just yet—we're moving into the new house after I get stronger."

Her eyebrows rise. "You've decided this without speaking to me?"

Oh, shit.

"We can move whenever you want. I just thought you'd want to settle in before your classes start."

Her chews on her lip. "I still have some thinking to do about that."

After organizing the boxes in the dining room so she can retrieve things as she needs them, I smell something delicious fill the apartment and my stomach growls at me.

"Have I ever told you how much I love when fall changes into winter?" I hear her come from the kitchen and open a window in the living room, breathing in the crisp October air. "It's hard to be in a bad mood from now until New Year's Eve."

I sit back on the sofa and take her in. Her small, curvy body leans out of the window, still breathing the cold air into her lungs. It's hard not to fall in love with her all over again every single day we spend together. There's something magical about her that makes you want to believe in yourself and believe in her; it makes all of life's little random moments make sense.

"Hey, stop bending over in front of me like that or I'm going to explode. You know we can't have sex for five more weeks." I smile and pat the sofa next to me. Her eyes lower in a sexy glare. "Actually, five weeks and four days, if you want to make it more depressing."

She sits next to me and pats my leg. "You'll make it, I promise."

"I'm going to literally want to have sex for like three days straight when this is all over," I joke, covering her hand with mine. "You drive me absolutely fucking crazy. You're sexy as hell and you expect me to actually wait?"

She kisses my cheek and I quickly turn my head to catch her lips with mine. She doesn't pull away—something she's been doing for a few days because she thinks she's going to hurt me or something—and I can only hope that she's starting to cave and give into her love for me too.

I can only hope.

She's hiding something, though, I can feel it.

"Hey, bring that last journal with you." I nod toward the kitchen. "We can eat and read some of it, if you want."

The fire in her eyes catches me. She knows that it's hard for me to listen to anything in these fucking journals, but for her, I'll try to face my fears. It's actually not as scary as I thought it would be with her next to me, reading the dirty—and harsh—truth of how I came about. If anything, it's giving me peace of mind that she sees my mother for the monster she is.

We go into the kitchen and settle onto the bar stools; I dig into the most delicious spaghetti I've ever tasted in my life. Everything Julie has ever made for me has been incredible; it comforts me to know that my life is going to finally consist of big, delicious Thanksgiving meals with a family scattered around the long dinner table.

I blush even though she can't possibly know that I'm thinking about.

"Let's read." I clear my throat. "While I eat more of this." She shakes her head, takes my plate, and refills it with a new steamy pile of food before sitting back down next to me like nothing just happened. After taking a few bites of her own food and smiling at me, she opens the book and starts to read to me.

January 11th, 1998

So much has happened. Veronica hasn't been back since she left Oliver alone. Although, I've been able to stay home with him these past few weeks...my father is chomping at the bit to get me back out there so I can help him make money. I've talked to Mrs. Atchley, and she's agreed to watch over Oliver whenever I'm gone. It didn't take much for her to say yes—she loves Oliver almost as much as I do.

He's growing so fast, it's incredible. He's tall and built like me, an "all-American boy," as my father would say. "Sports are in his future" is something else he would also say. I just want Oliver to be happy and do whatever he wants with his life. I want him to have a healthy outlook on love, despite what his mother has done. I know he'll remember her as a monster, and there's nothing I can do about that now.

If Veronica comes crawling back...I have to be strong and not let her in.

I shovel more food into my mouth and Julie giggles. "Are you even listening?"

I nod. "I'm listening; it's my story, after all."

"I'm just proud of you for sitting through these." My eyes fix on her tongue as it licks the corner of her mouth where a spot of stray sauce had stuck. "I'm almost jealous that my parents didn't keep journals of my life...maybe it would've made us closer or something."

I don't know what to say to her when she talks about her parents. I know they're sleazy people who used her instead of nurturing her—and at least I had my father and Mrs. Atchley to do that for me—but once she moved here to Rockford and left her old self behind...I hardly want to be the one to bring back those memories.

She takes another bite and continues to read.

February 14th, 1998

Veronica has sent Oliver a Valentine's Day card with nothing but her name etched on the inside and a hand-drawn heart beneath the word, "Mom." It angers me that she's signed this card from herself like that because she hasn't actually earned the right to be called a mother in my eyes. Maybe before she skipped town at Christmas, but now? No. Now she's just the person who helped me give life to my son.

I hate to be so cold toward her, but I can't help it.

She's broken all the rules of love.

All I can do now is rebuild my walls and make my own rules.

Starting with my first rule...

Never trust her again.

My eyes get so wide that it hurts. She doesn't dare look up at me; I know what she's thinking before she can even say it out loud.

"Rules." She breathes. "That's where you get that from."

I clear my throat and take the journal from her. "I think we've had enough of Colin Jackson for one day, don't you?"

She knows I don't want to talk about it, but it takes a few seconds for the questions to fade from her eyes. She tucks them into her mind somewhere where they'll sit until the most opportunistic time she can bring them up. We eat in silence for the next few minutes until I can muster up the nerve to ask her about what she's hiding.

"So, when are we going to talk about what happened at Brandon's house?" She starts to shut down; the air grows cold between us. "I know something happened, I just want you to tell me what it is."

"I told you, it was too many emotions. It wasn't a good idea to go there. I don't know what I was thinking. I'm sorry I dragged you with me." I reach over and grab her hand, squeezing it and hoping it's enough to reassure her that I never thought she did anything wrong.

"You deserve to have what's yours." I shake my head. "But I want to know. Did he do something to you upstairs? Is what why we rushed out of there?" I ask her as crystal clear as I can—there isn't any sugar-coating it anymore. "I just need to know, Julie."

She shifts her weight on her stool. It's not a good feeling, watching her struggle with whether to tell me the truth or a lie. "He had ulterior motives other than just me getting my things," she tells me, and I try not to crush her hand in anger as I listen. "But it's nothing to worry about now. I think he actually listened to me this time and knows it's really over."

I'm seething now. "You and I have been together for months—he hasn't been with you in almost a year. How is that *not* a clear indication of you not being together?" I don't want to see the amount of steam that might be billowing from my ears. I don't want to make it any more complicated for her, so I take a few deep breaths and blow them out slowly to calm myself down. "But if you say you handled it, then I believe you." I kiss her fingers and let go of her hand.

My phone dings and Julie jumps up to fetch it for me.

"I can still do things, baby…you don't have to be my waitress." I smile and take the phone from her outstretched hand. "Although…it is sexy when you take care of me."

She kisses me, letting go of the phone. "I like taking care of you—I love you." Her voice is like a dozen butterflies emerging from a light source—airy and free, just like how she makes me feel. Before I get too much of a hard-on, I look down at the phone screen and frown.

CASEY

Hey. Can we talk?

I excuse myself to the bathroom and call him.

"What?" I snap. "I'm busy."

"I want you to meet my new girlfriend. Can you meet us?"

I almost laugh, but I don't want Julie knowing I'm talking to someone. I don't want her associated with Casey at all, to be honest. "How the fuck did that already happen? Didn't Nora just leave your ass a few weeks ago?"

He walks away from someone and lowers his voice. "Okay, if you can refrain from talking about my past failed relationships, I would appreciate that very much."

I snort. "I don't want to meet some random chick that won't be around next week, Casey."

A small knock at the door freaks me out and Julie comes in, her eyes hooded and fierce. "You shouldn't be an ass to him—he's helped me a lot since you were in the hospital."

Yeah, I'm sure he did.

My jaw drops. "Little eavesdropper." I glare at her. "I don't want to meet some random chick he's dating. You two are too much alike."

I instantly regret saying this when I see the sick look on her face, and Casey clears his throat. "I really want you guys to meet her. I already told Julie about her. Come on, Ollie."

"Where?" Julie says as if she's on the phone too. "Where do you want to meet, Casey?"

It's so hard to resist her newfound assertiveness; I smile in spite of myself.

"Text me the place." I groan and hang up the phone, turning to meet her gaze. "Casey has a new girlfriend every few weeks. This one won't be around for long... why do you want to meet someone just to forget about them?"

She stands on her toes to kiss my lips, and there's so much magic wrapped up in her taste that I lose my train of thought for a few seconds. "I just want to be there for him like he's been there for me. Maybe this time—since someone is taking an interest in his relationship—it might last longer and be better for him. I know you love Casey. Don't act like you don't."

I watch her like she's not real.

She can't fucking be real.

"Julie, I can't believe you chose me." My voice starts small. "I can't believe that someone as kind and pure as you can love someone like me."

She smirks and I want to kiss the corners of her mouth. "I'm full of surprises."

"Yes, yes you are."

Her arms snake around my body and I forget that we're standing in the bathroom. "You need me, Oliver...that's part of why I'm so in love with you. You need me to be who you are destined to be, and that's all I can ever ask for."

Jesus.

What can I say to that?

I look at my phone, speechless. "Casey wants to meet at The Tavern."

She smiles and takes my hand. "Then let's get dressed and go be there for our friend."

I just want to tangle myself into you.

I feel like a kid in love the entire ride to The Tavern. I'm excited to be alive, for starters. I'm lucky to be anywhere near someone like Julie. Plus, I finally get to show her what life with me can be like for real. No smokescreens, no bad first impressions.

Just me and the love of my life.

I text Harley as we walk into the building. I want to buy him a few drinks to thank him for not saying anything to Julie about my bad decision to take another woman home with me. I still kick myself in the ass for not listening to him, and I don't intend for Julie to ever, ever find out.

Casey waves at us from a table on the far end of the bar. I nod back and we slowly make our way through the sea of people. Julie's hand is in mine and holding on so tight that I know she's uncomfortable and out of her element.

"Hey guys, thanks for coming out." Casey blushes and hugs Julie. The two of them look like stiff stick figures as they part ways. I notice their reservation and it pisses me off, but I'm not going to ruin this night for everyone by calling them out.

Julie is keeping secrets—she's following my third rule.

I don't know how I feel about that, exactly.

"Where's your girlfriend?" Julie's voice is raspy as we sit down at the table with him. "I'm excited to meet her."

He looks around the room and his eyes light up

when someone walks up to the table and puts four open beer bottles in the center.

"Guys, this is Lucy. Lucy, this is Oliver and Julie—two of my best friends."

Julie blushes and I don't bother to look up.

"Oh, uh...nice to meet you..."

Wait. That voice is familiar.

No. It can't be.

I raise my eyes and they meet hers. Her red hair taunts me as our fear connects and we quickly look away from each other.

Okay, she doesn't want to tell my secret.

Julie shakes Lucy's hand and my stomach melts all over my feet. This is a fucking nightmare—what is Casey doing with her? Does he know about Lucy and me? I start to feel sick, so I snatch one of the bottles and chug it down before I can start to think too much. Julie watches me carefully, but I swipe the amber bottle from in front of her and chug that one down too.

This is a fucking disaster.

"Are you okay?" she whispers, looking at my trembling hands. "Maybe you shouldn't drink when you're still taking those pain meds?"

I mumble that I'll be fine and feel her leg against mine underneath the table. I feel so fucking guilty that it's eating my insides away each second that Lucy sits here at this table with us. I don't fucking *dare* look at Lucy—in fear that someone will see through us and catch on—but I can only imagine that she's as uncomfortable as I am.

"Hey, Casey? Do you think we can cut out a little

early?" My ears focus on Lucy's voice as I smile at Julie. "I'm not feeling too well."

Julie's eyes leave mine and she looks at Lucy. "Are you okay? Sometimes when I drink beer it makes my stomach feel like a bowl of acid." Her giggle sets me on fire; I can't fucking lose her over this. I can't take losing her again.

"I'll be fine. I just want to lie down. It's nice of you to care." Lucy lets out a nervous, small chuckle. "Maybe we can do this again? When I'm better?"

No. What are you fucking doing?

I want to scream and rip my hair out.

What else in this fucking universe is going to try and take Julie from me?

My crazy ex.

My crazy mother.

A drunk old man who didn't stop in time.

Brandon.

Casey.

I can't breathe—the collar of my shirt is choking me. "I need some air." I pat Julie's leg and she nods her head, starting to stand up. "No, I'll be fine. You stay here with Casey."

Casey's eyes light up.

I know he would rather be there for Julie than for Lucy.

I half-expect him to smile, but he clears his throat and looks sheepishly toward me. "Ollie? Hey, man...let me walk you outside for some air. Lucy, can you hang in there for five more minutes? I want to make sure he's okay before we go."

I look directly at Lucy for the first time.

She blushes so hard that it could have lit up the entire room.

"S-Sure," she stutters and looks at Julie. "I think we'll manage."

Julie smiles and kisses my cheek. "Be nice to him. I love you," she whispers in my ear, and I want to grab her and run away. Anywhere, I don't care...she's going to fucking hate me when she finds out.

And then there's Casey.

She'll leave me and they'll be drawn together, magnetically bound by what I've done to both of them. They'll live happily ever after and I'll die alone.

Get a fucking grip, Oliver. Julie loves you. She doesn't even think twice about him.

The cold October air washes over me as Casey holds the door open for me to exit the building. He shivers and hands me my coat, watching carefully as I pull it on.

"I like this girl, Oliver," he says, and I look at his face.

He's serious.

"She makes me forget about how stupid I've been... she makes me forget things I shouldn't even be thinking about in the first place."

I lick my lips and the chilled air sticks to them. "Like what, exactly? Don't think I haven't fucking noticed you aren't over your little crush on my girlfriend."

He bites his cheek. "I'm just trying to be happy—can you say the same?"

Shit. He knows.

"Look, I don't know what you've been told—"

"Cut the shit, Oliver. You know that you aren't who people say you are."

My head spins with so much anger that if I weren't injured, I'd tackle his ass to the ground and swing a few punches. I know he likes Julie—he can't hide it well. How dare he pretend that he has no idea what I'm talking about?

"You have a lot of fucking nerve to act like she means nothing to you. Give her a little more respect than that," I snarl, watching his eyes grow darker by the second. His anger is at the same level as mine now, but he doesn't dare move an inch toward me.

He shakes his head and takes his first step toward me. "Leave Julie out of this."

"Leave her out of this? It's *about* her…what are you talking about?"

Casey takes another step. "No, this is about who you are and who I am."

He's fucking crazy.

"Dude, what are you talking about?" A few people that pass us give Casey hard looks to make sure he's not about to pounce before they head inside. "You're being fucking weird—get the hell away from me."

His laugh is startling. "You *really* don't know?"

"Know what?" My growl is so loud that he stops taking any more steps.

"We're *brothers*."

I take a deep breath and start to laugh. "Not anymore. That stopped the moment you started thinking about Julie as anything other than your friend."

He's inches from me now. I can feel his breath hit my face.

"We have the same mother."

I'm not sure who takes the first swing…

But I know that not even a broken leg—or the sound of Julie's scream—is stopping me now.

TWENTY-NINE
JULIE

I'VE NEVER HAD to force such a fake smile as I did when I watched Oliver and Casey walk away, leaving me alone with Lucy. I guess it could be worse—she could just be some random girl that he picked up in the bar. She looks nervous as the awkward air captures her and makes her realize that I know she's faking her sudden illness.

"Casey is a really nice guy." My voice hitches a little; I don't want her to get the wrong impression of my relationship with Casey…like Oliver does.

"Yeah, he is." Her voice is bursting with sadness. "Is it crazy that I like him this much after only knowing him a short time?"

A real smile replaces the fake smile on my lips. "No, it's not. Sometimes you can't control where your life takes you, you know? Don't discount what you two might have over time. Trust me, it's not worth the agony you put yourself through."

"How long have you and Oliver been together?"

I blush. "Just a few months." Her eyes glow with denial, like my advice is no longer valid enough to make her feel good. "But we loved each other from the moment we met."

"I'm a little jealous." Her lips twitch. "I wish I could find that kind of love."

There's a commotion coming from the front of the bar. People are making their way outside where it sounds like someone is fighting.

"You never know. You and Casey could have a love like ours someday. Everyone is different." My eyes go back to the door and my heart sinks a little because I know something is wrong. "And no matter how hard you try and believe it, there are no rules for love."

I stand up and feel my body drift toward everyone filtering outside, panic settling in my bones as I see Casey on top of Oliver, swinging on him. I start to scream and push my way through everyone standing around but not breaking them up.

"Stop it!" I find the power in my voice. "Casey, get off him!"

A sharp blow hits the side of my face and it's hard to breathe for a few seconds as I fall to my knees and try to focus my eyes.

"You're fucking dead!" I hear Oliver scream. "*Julie! Julie are you okay?*"

"Fuck, Julie, I'm so sorry." Casey's voice is soft. "I didn't know it was you…I didn't know it was her!"

Oliver pounces on him and tries his best to continue fighting, but he cares too much for me to let me writhe in pain next to him, so he lets go of Casey's bloody shirt and crawls the few feet over to me.

I swear I see Oliver's mother watching the scene and when our eyes meet, she takes a man's arm and pulls him out of view. It's probably just the ringing in my head that's making me hallucinate.

I can feel his warm hand on my arm. "Baby, talk to me…are you hurt?"

"Someone call an ambulance!" I hear someone in the crowd scream.

I shake my head. "No, I'm fine. He got me in the eye, but the worst that will happen is a black eye." My vision is still blurry, but I can see the tears running down Casey's cheek as Oliver tends to me.

"I didn't mean to hurt you." He winces as Oliver whips to face him. "Julie, please don't hate me."

I scoff. "I don't hate you. What is *wrong* with you two? Why can't you spend a few minutes alone without starting a bar brawl?" I scold the two of them like children, but I can't help it. They act like children when they're left to their own devices. Oliver resents Casey because he isn't stupid—he can see the crush Casey has for me. Even though I was late to realize it and would never tell Oliver that Casey had confessed a few days earlier.

"Let's go home. I'll tell you there." Oliver stands up the best he can, holding his hand out for me. His stability isn't exactly superhuman, but he manages to pull me up and wrap his arms around me. "I have to leave or I'm going to kill him for hurting you," he whispers into my hair.

I know that he's serious—I've seen the way he fights for me and I believe him when he says it will be hard for him to stop.

We hold onto each other as Casey keeps apologizing, following us toward the parking lot. I put Oliver into the front seat as he rubs his legs in pain. I try to focus on walking around to the other side when Casey comes up and places himself between me and the driver's side door. I try to walk around him without looking up, but I have such a headache that it's hard to concentrate on anything.

"Let me drive you guys home." His soothing voice meets me. "*Please*, Julie. You gotta believe me…I would never hurt you."

Lucy jogs up next to us and stays silent as Casey pleads for my forgiveness.

"Please, Julie, you know I would never hurt you intentionally. Are you okay? Can I see your eye?" He bows down a little and the car moves because Oliver has seen Casey talking to me. I shoot him a look through the back window for him to stay put and let me handle this. My fingers cover my forehead and I cringe in pain. "Let me drive you home, Julie."

"Casey—" Lucy starts to say, but he ignores her, so she closes her mouth.

I feel bad for her. I wish Casey would just focus his energy on chasing her instead of chasing me. I don't even want this—I don't want Casey, and how he hovers over me is starting to really piss me off. It makes me think of Brandon and his predatory stance whenever he wanted to remind me I was his property.

The paper in my pocket feels heavy.

A piece of paper is always dictating my damn life.

"Casey, move out of my way." The chill in my voice isn't from the cold air nipping at my skin; it's from the level of annoyance that he's pushing against me. "I don't want to even look at you right now."

"Julie, please—"

I lift my eyes to his and make sure he sees the disgust in my eyes. "Move out of my way. I don't want to talk to you. I don't want to be near you."

He sucks in air through his teeth. "You can't mean that. We're friends—"

"I can't be friends with you anymore. Oliver is waiting for me."

Lucy storms off with her arms crossed, but he doesn't care. "Oliver isn't a good guy—he doesn't deserve someone like you," he whispers. "You have to know that…he's hiding things from you and I would never do that…"

A loud slapping noise echoes in the air as my hand collides with his face. Oliver has gotten out of the car and stops in his tracks when he sees what I've done. Casey holds his face and tears form in the corners of his eyes. He's shocked and heartbroken.

"When is everyone going to understand that I'm with Oliver? I'm not free to be preyed upon by everyone who thinks I do something magical for them." I snap. "I'm not a fucking unicorn!" My voice rises and Lucy stops running away to see how it's going to play out.

My breath is so hot that I can see it in the air in front me. "I don't *ever* want to see you again. Oliver and I are better off without you."

The defeat on his face makes me a little uneasy. "Oliver started this. He swung on me first."

I look at Oliver, whose mouth is wide open in shock.

I move my body around Casey and he lets me pass—he doesn't dare reach out to try and touch me. "You two make me so exhausted, you act like children. Oliver has his faults, but yours are far worse. You tried to take advantage of the situation when he was incapacitated, and that's not fair to him. *Or* me."

I open the driver's side door and get into the car. Oliver follows me on the other side and I start the engine, waiting for Casey to move out of the way so I can back up and burn rubber out of here. So much craziness happens around me that it's hard not to get sucked into it sometimes. It's hard to calm down as Casey finally moves and I back the car up, his eyes bursting with sadness at the sight of me walking—or driving—away.

"Julie." Oliver's voice cuts through my anger. "Stop the car."

I shake my head. "No, we're going home."

His warm hand sits on my thigh and everything washes away. "Baby, stop the car."

I pull off the road into an empty parking lot and put the car in park. He takes my hand into his and holds it tightly. My body is still buzzing a little from the horrible instance we drove away from. "Casey is harmless." His voice is low enough to penetrate my thoughts without startling me. "We fight like that sometimes. There's no need to worry."

"He was on top of you, punching your lights out." I turn and look up at him. "You guys were outside for less than five minutes…when does this end? Why can't we have one freaking day without someone getting into a brawl or causing some sort of drama?"

He clears his throat. "I'm sorry, Julie. I'll try to be better. Just don't leave me, okay?"

A loud laugh escapes and it grows so fast that the car shakes. "*Leave* you? Oliver, in case you haven't noticed…there's literally nothing you can say or do to make me leave you again. I love you. I just wish things weren't so…*abrasive* sometimes."

"That's my fault. It's my temper…"

I put the car back into drive and leave the parking lot a lot calmer this time. "No, it's everyone. No one can just be there for each other—we have to scratch and claw and hate ourselves so much that we bring it on ourselves."

Oliver laughs. "That's pretty deep."

"Shut up." I snicker and poke his arm with my finger. "At least I never have to worry about *you* hurting me. You and your rules are probably the only thing that's consistent in my life right now."

His face looks sick but he changes the subject. "Maybe we can just move far, far away where no one else exists and be alone."

"You would miss civilization."

His longer, shaggier dark hair twirls around his head. "Not really. As long as I have you…what else do I need?"

A smile spreads across my lips before I can help it. "You'd miss chocolate chip pancakes too." He chuckles and I pull into the garage of his apartment. "And you'd miss your friends. I don't know what the hell Casey is thinking, acting like that. Has he done this before?"

Oliver violently shakes his head. "No, I didn't know he even slept with Heather until he told me a few weeks ago. He never openly tried to take her from me like he's done with you. Although…"

My eyebrows rise and I know what he's going to say.

"…I don't blame him."

I snort. "Well, I do."

"Julie…" His deep breath shakes me. "You have to understand what you do to people to be able to understand why they chase you. You radiate so much goodness that it's hard to resist wanting to even be near you sometimes."

I cross my arms. "Well, I don't mean to."

"I know that. It's just something that comes natural to you. You're an angel to a lot of people. You just don't realize."

I slam my hands on the steering wheel. "I don't want to be! I can hardly handle myself, let alone be that for other people!"

We don't speak for the rest of the ride home; even in the elevator, the air between us is so stale that it rips my lungs when I breathe.

I thought Casey was my friend.

Now, I've lost him because he can't figure out his own emotions.

Oliver has known him longer, but he doesn't seem to care that he's lost him, like this sort of thing happens all the time and they'll be back to being best friends.

Not me.

I don't ever want to see Casey again.

Oliver shuts the door of the apartment behind us and his rough hand grabs my arm, pulling me around to face him. "Let me see your eye." He smiles and touches the tender part below my eye. I wince in pain and he smacks his lips, trying not to show me his anger. "Casey is lucky I didn't kill him for hurting you… You're gonna have a black eye, baby." He lightly grazes the skin again and clicks his tongue. His lips find the side of my cheek and he gently kisses me, in fear that he'll hurt me.

I wrap my arms around his neck and sob into his chest. "Life is bullshit," I mumble against his warm skin, listening to his heartbeat grow faster with each second I cling to him. "At least I have you…I'm lucky to still have you."

"Hey, now…" He pulls my arms down and holds them at my sides. "I'm not going anywhere, you hear me? What else can happen to me?"

"Don't say that out loud. You never know what'll happen when you don't follow the rules." His lips turn into a smile. "Even though your rules aren't good for anything."

He playfully acts offended. "They mean something! How dare you say that."

I feel my eyelashes touch my cheeks as I lock my eyes on the floor. "You broke your first rule and it worked out for both of us. You broke your second rule and almost died. What do you think is going to happen if we keep trying to follow your rules, Oliver?"

The paper from Brandon's house burns a hole in my pocket.

I want to show Oliver what it is, but I don't want him to get homicidal for the second time today.

"Let's just calm down and think about something else." He holds my hand lightly. "We have a long time to think about all this other bad shit. But, I can tell you want to ask one more question. So, ask away, but then we're done with it for a long time."

"Okay..." I suck in air. "What were you and Casey fighting about?"

His tongue glides across his perfect teeth. "He was talking about my mother."

"Really? Like a 'yo mama' joke?"

The sick look on his face returns. "No, he said that we share a mother. Like, my mother is also his mother."

Holy crap.

"Is that true?" I squeak. "Wouldn't you have known before now?"

He caresses my cheek and kisses my forehead, walking around me to enter the living room so he can sit down and rest his legs. I follow him and make sure my thighs are touching his as I sit next to him. "Probably not. My mother wasn't exactly faithful to my father. It's weird, though...I knew Casey was adopted but no one ever told me we share a mother."

Well people don't always tell their loved ones the truth if it'll hurt them.

I swallow, and it hurts because my throat is dangerously dry. I carefully snake my leg around his and he smiles, like sunlight has finally broken through a long, cloudy day. I can't remember a time when I didn't love him. Even before I met him, I could feel him in my bones.

I felt him before I laid eyes on him.

Something would call to my heart when Brandon tormented me—something that told me that deep down, I knew that something better was waiting for me.

And that something better is Oliver Jackson.

All of Oliver Jackson.

His wide smile when I capture his bright eyes with mine.

The invisible, warm safety net he casts over my body when he's near.

The lies on the tip of his tongue as his mouth opens and closes tightly.

He has secrets.

We *all* have secrets.

Looks like we're finally obeying one of his rules: Rule number three.

We're keeping our secrets safe.

Or…at least *I* intend to.

BEFORE YOU GO...

If you enjoyed my book please take a second to leave a short review. These reviews help me as an author be found by other amazing readers like you.

Thank you so much! :)

ABOUT THE AUTHOR

I live in Kansas City with my husband and our son, Ryker. I have been writing for over a decade, I started out writing songs and music and then realized that those stories were too short for the tales I wanted to tell, so I switched to writing books and articles, which then blossomed into writing contemporary romance and fantasy novels. I am in indecisive person at heart, I love coffee more than a Gilmore girl and my most favorite time to write and create is during a rainstorm (with coffee!).

I love hearing from those who read my stories, I love to hear how much people relate to each character and how they are rooting for their favorites to succeed! I don't only create stories, I create entirely new worlds and people that come to life!

Wattpad
https://www.wattpad.com/user/NBenson